3/28/01

girl
Beside
Him

Girl Beside Him

CRIS MAZZA

FC2

Normal/Tallahassee

Published by FC2 with support provided by Florida State University,
the Unit for Contemporary Literature of the Department of English
at Illinois State University, the Illinois Arts Council, the Florida Arts
Council of the Florida Division of Cultural Affairs, and the National
Endowment for the Arts.

Address all inquiries to: Fiction Collective Two, Florida State
University, c/o English Department, Tallahassee, FL 32306-1580

ISBN: Paper, 1-57366-092-2

Library of Congress Cataloging-in Publications Data

Mazza, Cris.
  Girl beside him / Cris Mazza.-- 1st ed.   3 4873 00190 6197
     p. cm.
  ISBN 1-57366-092-2
  1. Wildlife relocation--Fiction. 2. Sex (Psychology)--Fiction. 3.
Zoologists--Fiction. 4. Wyoming--Fiction. 5. Puma--Fiction. I.
Title.

  PS3563.A988 G57 2000
  813'.54--dc21
                                        00-010680

Cover Design: Polly Kanevsky
Book Design: Tara Reeser
Cover Image: Ted Orland

Produced and printed in the
United States of America
Printed on recycled paper with soy ink

NATIONAL
ENDOWMENT
FOR THE ARTS

This program is
partially supported
by a grant from the
Illinois Arts Council

ACKNOWLEDGMENTS

Acknowledgments made to the following publications in which portions of this book first appeared:
Fiction International for "Girl Beside Him" (chapter one), "Protected by Nothing" (chapter nine), and an excerpt from chapter four; *High Plains Literary Review* for "Dim Beating Rhythm" (chapter three); *Other Voices* for "Her Behavioral Symptoms" (chapter five); *American Writing* for "In On Foot" (chapter four); *New American Writing* for an excerpt from chapter seven

This book contains references to lyrics from the following songs:
"Captain Jack" by William M. Joel © 1973 Impulsive Music (ASCAP), "Just Like a Woman" by Bob Dylan © 1966 Dwarf Music, "Like a Rolling Stone" by Bob Dylan © 1965 Warner Bros. Inc., "Mamas Don't Let Your Babies Grow Up to Be Cowboys" by E. Bruce and P. Bruce © 1975 SONY/ATV Songs LLC (BMI), "Someday Soon" by Ian Tyson and M. Witmark © 1964 Vanguard Recording Society Inc., "Train in the Distance" © Paul Simon Words, Music by Paul Simon © 1983 Warner Brothers Records, Warner Communications (BMI), "Worse Comes to Worst" by William M. Joel © 1973 Joelsongs (BMI)

CONTENTS

1
GIRL BESIDE HIM

Ski season continues — bunnies abound. Bouquets of grinning balloons. White teeth and sun-black skin. Pale raccoon masks tattooed by designer sunglasses. Tired muscles vigorously content, or endorphins still surging in hot bodies that breathe fog on alpine mountains in late spring. Fun recent enough to sustain a kick in those departing for L.A. or Dallas and beyond. Adrenaline-rush of anticipation fuels the shit-eating grins on those boarding for Vail, Snow Summit, Aspen, Jackson Hole. Nothing to you. You'll see none like them where you're going. But be careful, this time you're on your own, no one watching you but you. No one giving instructions and assignments to fill up every hour. Watch it — with a change like this, the cold clot may rupture, questions get answered, hypothesis proven.

 *A*RE *you a sex killer waiting to happen?*

The Denver airport sold cowboy hats in colors a cowboy — or girl — wouldn't be caught dead in. Brian fingered the hat bands made of anything from snakeskin to Indian beads to peacock feathers. He looked at baseball caps — one for every Colorado brewery, golf course, ski resort and sport team, plus some with pictures of fishermen, skiers or golfers. Then under a leaning stack of cloth fishing hats with *Denver* or *Colorado* stitched on the brim, he found an army green Robin Hood hat with a rooster feather. Airport white noise was Country. *Mamas don't let your babies grow up to be cowboys. —He's the—king of the road. —I wanna go home—oh Lord I wanna— Abilene, sweet Abilene. Unbreak my heart—* He crumpled the feather, dropped it, and paid for the hat along with his *USA Today.* Final boarding for the commuter flight to Cheyenne had already been announced. He held the hat on his legs, under the newspaper, which he opened, holding the left-hand pages perpendicular to the flat pages in his lap, making a newsprint wall between himself and the woman in the window seat.

The hair she still had was white blond, butch-cut, shaved up the back of her neck, little pixie points beside each ear, with a short soft cap of white hair like a toupee placed on the top of her head, the sides and back the exact same length as the bangs on her brow. Her neck was long and thin with skin like eggshell membrane, small throbbing veins under the surface. Earrings of clustered blade-shaped silver splinters tickled her throat when she tipped her chin down. Her nose small, upturned, pierced with a diamond. Her mouth full, as though swollen. Her teeth caught and released her lower lip over and over. Wrists cuffed with silver bracelets that looked like manacles for prison chains. Almost every finger sheathed in a silver ring.

Okay, enough, focus now, just take out the field report on the relocated cougars in south-central Wyoming, study the relief map, review the procedures for setting foot snares, preparing anesthesia, using a jab-stick, or testing blood for plague antibodies.

He remained carefully in place. His knees balancing the hat and newspaper as though they were fragile. And as though turning pages under water, to keep them from ripping or disintegrating, he found the section where a news item from each state is reported. It was one way he tried to get his first feel for the places he visited for months of fieldwork, but invariably had little to do with his interaction with the locale.

> **Wyoming.** Yellowstone National Park. AP   *A camper was arrested early yesterday after park officials caught him urinating into a pool of boiling mud just off the walkway in the sulfur pits area. Jerry Jersey, 32, of Toledo, OH, was booked on suspicion of public indecency, public nuisance, and fouling a national park. No one was hurt.*

Brian's arm, holding the left side of the newspaper upright, was starting to tremble, invisibly. Years of conditioning to be able to support a competition rifle with such sure steadiness that even a leveling sensor placed on the barrel couldn't detect any motion — suddenly it didn't seem to extend to any ability to hold a sheet of newsprint. *Okay, perverts go on vacation too. The cougar relocation area isn't anywhere near Yellowstone. No tourists. No skiers. And no one with you in charge of the fieldwork.*

It was Peter Gallway — someone Brian barely knew — who, about four years ago, had gotten a grant, along with the necessary permission and permits from Fish & Game and the states of Wyoming and California, lined up the participation or cooperation of whatever agencies or organizations would be helpful or mandatory; then, more than two years ago, trapped, tagged and sterilized a dozen lions in the back country of San Diego — where some had been starting too frequently to come into close proximity with human habitation — relocated them outside the most desolate ranch country in Wyoming, and stayed to observe their adjustment. Gallway's proposal had specifically stated its purpose was not to move the animals in an attempt to protect either the species or the human population of Southern California, but as a study to determine if such habitat relocations were a better option for wildlife management than killing.

But a month before Gallway's scheduled follow-up field work to assess the progress of the relocated cougars, he'd broken both legs and his pelvis skiing in Switzerland, and was still there, demanding frequent faxes — starting as soon as Brian arrived in Rawlins and then every time he observed anything, no matter how seemingly insignificant. Obviously it had been too late to find someone more experienced, in either the terrain or the particular study, or even someone who'd worked with mountain lions before. Likely anyone Gallway would've thought of calling before Brian had his own field work, his own book to write, his own on-going grants and proposals and lifelong study. Brian never finished, never even started his own PhD in wildlife biology. Never either regretted nor congratulated himself for the decision. Didn't remember that it *was* a decision. Instead, as though a long-standing appointment, the next step was flight school. An ability to fly both a small plane and a helicopter, combined with a degree in field biology, got him plenty of calls to work in the field for other people. And that was probably the real reason he had this job as well. *Maybe there'd been a recommendation from a friend of an acquaintance. Someone from the tortoise inventory in the California desert. Remember? You lodged in Independence, the county seat where they'd first held Manson after the murders. Sound traveled forever on the high desert, a shot lasted minutes when you did target practice at dawn, shooting at fenceposts — never cactus nor Joshua trees — the first shot still quaking against the Sierra by the time you were set for the next. Then at dusk, jeep races across the desert, once stumbling upon a long-abandoned dune*

buggy, you all circled it, went over every inch like archeolo-
gists, wondering if it had been one of the Family's stolen look-
out vehicles. You took your turn at the pranks and jokes. Once
you covered yourself shallowly with sand and jumped up at a
teammate like a sneak Indian attack.

The girl beside him sighed heavily. Afterwards he could hear every breath she took. The fuselage vibrating through turbulence was like a jeep on a dirt road, with softer seats but a closer ceiling. The pilot announced there'd be a spell of medium chop, so he was leaving the seatbelt light on. She was breathing hoarsely, through her mouth. Brian could feel the heavy metal buckle on his lap, under the hat. And then became aware of the entire oval brim of the hat, a warm circle on his thighs. He turned to the classifieds, the noise of the newspaper crackling like fire.

Help Wanted.
Year-long house-sitting position.
Sell Mary Kay in your own neighborhood.
Proofreaders needed.
Traveling companion for disabled elderly man.
Doctor wanted for small Texas town.
Address envelopes at home.
Female singer/bassist needed for steady gigging
     rock band in Tallahassee.

The first roommate? Maybe the second. One of your
college buddies played drums. Roadie for his rinky-dink top
40 band, your ears rang 'round the clock, a gig till midnight,
up for shooting practice at the indoor range at dawn. That
year it was difficult to hear a radio through the wall or pick
up whispered conversations in the library. A new roommate
every year as each abandoned the dorms for apartments,
every year a freshman roommate, but what better way to learn
to be the congenial college man? Spit and threw garbage out
the windows at your roommate's passing friends, three-day
old pizza under the bed, Olympic sliding contests across the
shower floor with a panel of judges lining the windowsill.

*Adopted by each roommate's circle and included. One year
you all played PacMan and had Rubic's cubes. One year beach
volleyball. Year by year you filled the dorm room with sharp-
shooting trophies. Illegal to keep rifles in the residence hall,
but you did anyway, locked in carrying cases. The rush of
triumph after each trophy dissipated by the next morning.
You had to start over, week by week.*

The girl gasped. Then the air came out of her with
a low moan. The plane had hit an air-pocket — the pilot
said *Whoopsie-Daisy*, and people laughed. Something
tugged gently, steadily on Brian's shirt sleeve. His
temples pounding, he looked around the edge of the
newspaper. There was a thin, curved scar on her forearm, seeming to originate from the inside of her wrist,
snaking up and around, mostly concealed under her
bracelet. She was gripping the arm rests on either side
of herself, digging her fingernails in, the tendons in her
hands straining under the skin. And she'd caught a little
of his shirt by accident.

He tried to move his arm off the armrest. There
may as well have been a knife jammed through his shirt
and up to the hilt into the upholstery. His head bobbed
with the turbulence, his eyes fixed on the newsprint.
The girl was making a little dog-whimper with each
breath. The seatbelt buckle under the hat under the
newspaper seemed heavier, hotter. His legs trembled.
He realized he was holding his heels off the floor, tensing his calves, holding his breath, as though necessary
to keep his lap level. As though someone were sitting
there. Releasing the air, slowly lowering his heels, his
chin dropped, his eyes cleared and continued reading.

Estate gardener, lives on premises, will move anywhere.
24-yr-old white male, educated, bright, works hard,
teacher, nanny, clerk, secretary, chauffeur, junior
executive, can learn.
Investment banker, stockbroker, looking to relocate.
SWF zoological animal trainer tired of the circus, looking for real work, from safari guide to vet assistant, can anyone hear me?

His body jolted but absorbed the silent impact without movement, as though still set for a next shot, ears insulated with noise protection headgear, but adrenaline flooding like oil spreading on water, waiting the hiss of a lit match. *You don't suffer from impaired memory. Hadn't big sister wanted to grow up to be a vet and go to Africa to work at a compound in an animal preserve, like on her favorite show, DAKTARI? Took you to the zoo on a bus when you were three or four. It must've been a howler monkey. Like an air-raid sounding off right beside you just as you, always the rogue, bent to scare some newborn chicks in the bushes. You screamed and ran, but she caught you and held you, and you were like a monkey yourself, watching over her shoulder as she carried you through the zoo's streets, watching the zoo unroll backwards, rows of primates and birds in cages. It was still an old-fashioned zoo, and she was just a skinny girl of maybe seven or eight. She kept having to re-hoist you, but didn't put you down until your distorted face relaxed and only the hiccup of fear remained. She said the howler monkey must've wanted you for her baby, but you were already hers — Diane's. Not your mother's. Hers. Taught you to tie your shoes. Played school and made a reading book with a picture that said "See Bob, Bob is a boy," the first thing you read. You and six or seven stuffed animals sat at upside-down cardboard boxes and learned to add. When they got in trouble for passing notes to you, they got the dunce hat, not you. You could throw spit-wads and make dirty noises and never sit in the corner. But mostly you played Daktari and all the stuffed animals were in the veterinary compound in Africa, hurt or sick. You were one of the animals too, and she gave you candy pills and bandaged one leg. Naturally you decided to also be the hungry leopard or cheetah that came prowling at night, and Daktari would come back to save the compound, pinning and tickling the cheetah.*

His arm snapped off the armrest as though it had been restrained there by elastic which suddenly broke. The girl's hands were at her face, clutching her own cheeks in each fist. Her mouth moving like a fish gasping. Under the roar of engines and rattle of carry-on luggage and mumble of other voices, Brian could hear her little voice saying "no, no, no, no, no . . ." until his pulse tapped the same rhythm in places all over his body—his gums, his fingertips, his stomach, his lap. And, throbbing in time with the practically imperceptible cadence, thready, ghostly, faraway —*now you don't talk so loud*— *now you don't seem so proud about having to be scrounging*

On your way for the first time to do field work alone. No other guys in a communal setting with a common time limit and single purpose, do your part and the whole project will wrap up, social needs crunched to an hour of cards around a Coleman before zipping the mosquito net of your tent behind you. Or go as a group to a tavern for a beer and discuss the project, discuss tomorrow's tasks, discuss the findings, discuss the problems, discuss solutions. Your input as crucial as anyone else's, so you can't allow yourself to be sidetracked. You don't stray.

The pilot said, "Now folks, if you can picture a water-skier bouncing across the wake of another boat, this isn't anything more than that. This little plane isn't concerned in the slightest—she's fat, dumb and happy, having the only fun she has all day. We'll just humor her for a little while and keep our seatbelts on until we get out of this choppy air."

The terrain, the scope of the project, the lack of a large team of field workers had made it almost necessary for Gallway to have a helicopter, unflown now for over a year, still hangared in Rawlins. Actually, a two-seater plane would've been cheaper, and in this case more appropriate, since homing was done without the need to buzz or hover close to the ground. Why Gallway owned a chopper instead of a Cessna was a guess Brian hadn't bothered to make. He'd told Gallway he hadn't flown a helicopter in a while and asked if Gallway's pilot would be returning to Rawlins to help gather data, but was told he was two-birds-in-the-hand, the *chopper* was his partner. Receivers mounted on elongated antennas on either side of the chopper sped up the ability to locate cougars, assess their general health, determine their individual territory and diet, pinpoint any problems. It reduced the amount of range to cover on foot looking for scat and scratch-mark territory markers, deer carcasses covered lightly with leaves and twigs, an occasional print in the mud beside a creek to tell him all was well. Cougars disappear when they're adjusted and thriving, and when they're dead. The chopper couldn't find remains of a skeleton scattered by coyotes—for that it would take an FBI crime task force to comb the area—but besides aerial homing, a view from above provided information on rugged or inaccessible areas, showed where the water was and where deer ranged, moved the biologist quickly through the square mile sections marked in a grid on his map.

Her flexed and rigid hands moved slowly down her face, pulling her eyelids down so the red showed like blood, leaving a trail of parallel white scratch marks on each cheek. Below her chin, her hands clumped into a single fist over her heart. The bracelet fell toward her elbow, leaving the scar alone to decorate her forearm. Then her fists dropped and dug into her lap, burying a deserted set of earphones and cassette player between her knees. The tracks of scratch marks filled in pink. Appearing from beneath her rubbed-away and melting make-up, fine etched lines, under her eyes, around her mouth. The whine in the girl's throat resumed, became louder every time the plane hit a bigger bump, sometimes *Oh* was jolted out of her mouth.

"Miss? You OK?" His voice. Then a faint, tinny verse from the abandoned headset *—on your own— with no direction home— a complete un*

Coming from behind your soon-to-be dead sister's bedroom door, after she started locking herself in there. You could hear the radio when you paused in passing. But you were getting older. Between nine and thirteen. Did a little surfing. Had a gang of friends. Threw rocks at the nude sunbathers from the cliffs at Torrey Pines. Tried to sneak down the bluff with binoculars to get better looks. Didn't — as most of your friends also didn't — talk to your mother much either. You never had, and it hadn't mattered, because you'd had Diane, until, apparently, you'd become grown enough to be on your own, given more and more independence, as nearing-adolescent offspring usually are. Your mother stayed in her room, often sick or tired, or was she praying or meditating? The radio softly playing, but you always had clean clothes, fresh sheets, new socks and underwear, paper and pencils for school, soda in the refrigerator. Cans of chili or spaghetti some nights, but other evenings gourmet meals with all three of you at the table. Your sister becoming lanky and gaunt, pimply. A sullen, ugly teenager with no use for her rude little brother. You tried to avoid looking at her. She smelled sour. Could be she no longer hoped to become a Daktari in Africa.

Going with the grain, the newsprint tore straight and even, but the other way ripped jagged like a row of pointed teeth. The *SWF* was in the middle of the piece he tore out, folded and put into his shirt pocket.

If the girl made a sound when the plane dropped like a stone for several full seconds, Brian wouldn't have been able to hear. A chorus of *whoa, oops, oh my god,* laughter, and the pilot's bland voice, "Sorry, folks, if I could see 'em comin' I'd sure avoid 'em," were too loud. His ears continued thundering, thudding, like the inside of a conch shell. Miniature speakers in her lap singing —*Everybody knows—baby's got new clothes—* The girl puked quietly into a bag. The smell of her sweat was freshly acidic. She came up for air murmuring *oh no, oh no.* A drop of perspiration hung on the point of hair beside her ear, then fell. The paper was folded on his lap now, on top of the hat, on top of the seatbelt buckle. Like the weight of a dentist's lead protection bib.

"We're starting our descent," the pilot said.

The girl was hyperventilating. An asshole in the back of the plane was doing a falsetto imitation of a crowd on a roller coaster, *wheeee, ohhh, ahhh.* The plane tipped sideways, banking in a turn. Brian's ankles, calves and knees squeezed toward each other to keep him upright. *Stay calm. Calm. Get in the zone. Remember target practice in a rowboat, shooting at buoys, using leg and back muscles to maintain vertical equilibrium. Or the other exercises: rifle in place, body positioned, eyes squeezed shut — tight, so colors swim — open the eyes and squeeze the trigger simultaneously . . . did you maintain the image of the target successfully in your mind? Did you maintain your body's steadiness, the aim, the focus? Or your slightly skanky shooting coach's favorite invention: two TVs on either side of you, each showing a different blue movie, volume up, move them gradually closer and closer to the target until they flank it. But your eyes must never see the bodies, your ears never hear the moans and whispers, the slushy sound effects, the cries. Your own voice counts silently,* STEADY, ONE TWO THREE *. . . your own breath is hypnotic . . . the target waits for the bullet without fear.*

He hadn't even started target shooting until he was in a foster home at seventeen. National championship and a money prize just in time to pay for flight school. Passed up the FBI, big-city SWAT units, ATF, Secret Service, US Marines. Shooting was a cool precision exercise, meant to soothe, not agitate. *You can't be stimulated and a sharpshooter at the same time.*

"There's one real quick way outta this mess, folks," the pilot said, and the plane continued the steep bank while it dropped in altitude. "There's our target right below, runway one-and-only at Cheyenne International, we'll just take a little shortcut while no one's looking." The girl moaned, *oh god, oh please.* If his ankle and knee bones had been eggshells, they would've crushed each other. *Try to count. See the target. You've never used a body outline target. Never competed at any level in any event that used one.*

His hands tucked under his thighs, pressed flat, knuckles against the seat fabric. —*your long-time curse hurts—what's worse—* He swallowed, and something the size of a light bulb moved down his throat, into his chest, sinking lower, heavier and brighter as it dropped. Until it reached the logjam where his body bent, where the seatbelt held him, where the hat and newspaper had become deadweight, the light bulb disappearing into a no-man's land, dwindling to a spark, a pinprick inside the rest of the numb, cold flab of his body.

At their tips, the plane's wings flexed like a bird flapping. The fuselage groaned and creaked and rattled. A plastic cup rolled down the aisle, and the girl drew in a long sputtering suck of air. *When we meet again —as friends— Please don't let on— knew me when—* the cassette player clattered to the floor, severing the headset's cord. The plane leveled for landing. Brian's buttocks started to slowly relax. But gusting ground wind made the plane sway, roll and pitch as it descended, and the air coming out of the girl was two whispered words, *please stop*.

His upper body bent forward then fell, dropping toward his knees, like an old skyscraper imploding, as the dying pinprick spark of light in his gut flared, a sudden gush of flame where there had only been the charred remains of a fire long extinguished, as though the last ember had finally worked its way to the undiscovered, hidden cache of gunpowder in the rubble.

Was it her perfume, or the sweat of her fear? Your self-surveillance on-going for over 23 years, but you've entered new territory this time. Why the sudden memories? What makes it different? Half a day into your first unaccompanied job, you prove how much you need to answer to someone daily, nightly, to adopt the quirks and jokes and recreations of your assigned buddies. A solitary life already proves too dangerous — you just verified an important presumption: that YOU need to be watched, in order to stay alert, to stay focused, to concentrate, to keep track of everything that's going on or even possibly going on. Plus you've just confirmed a hypothesis of much broader dimensions: that it's probably still alive SOMEwhere . . . the animal in you whose adrenaline gushes when it hears the deathcry, the scream. Can't just feed its hunger on the carcass, is driven by another need: to be there, to feel and hear the last gasp leave the throat. And after so many years — after you long ago stopped fearing you'd hear her familiar cries again, as though soaking through some thin apartment wall, through bathroom pipes or the ventilation, echoing and ghostly, your sister's thin wail followed by long minutes of muffled faraway whimpering, accompanied by a one-speaker radio. If it had ever found you, the sound would've most certainly thrown an image of your banished self — with your already sick fourteen-year-old dick in your fist — like a hologram into the air in front of you. And then you were fifteen. And sixteen. Getting better and better at timing, tim-ing, timing, and finishing with her scream . . . on the other side of the bathroom wall. Then, finally, not a scream but a gunshot. The biggest bang yet. The come you could've died from. Or died for. You never let go of that dick. But that was the last time you held it. The jump of adrenaline — head crash-ing back against the bathroom wall like a marksman who shoots before being set, kicked in the face with his own piece. Didn't YOUR shot put the hole in her? Now she never would become Daktari. Maybe you don't know why she lay bleeding from a mangled gap in her face, the smell of a pistol so close to your nose. Still not able to produce a conclusive explanation. But never ask yourself if she's better off nor mourn her. Ob-jectify your questions. Continue to observe and note behav-ior. Keep your own surroundings safe. And research similar animals. Know their patterns and M.O., know their warning signs, their mistakes. Study their past crimes and what's been learned about why they are who they are.

But, today, have answers already begun to form as twenty years of controlled environment and observation went down a stinking cesspool? Do you want to test it or hide from it? Either way, there's no cure, only prevention. Continue celibacy. And sustain the relentless scrutiny, re-establish the controlled environment. No women.

And for once, dig in and find some satisfaction in the assignment. Let it be as though it's YOUR project. Prove you can sink your complete involvement into something far more worthwhile than obsessing over what kind of tragedy you may be responsible for and how to keep yourself from repeating it. These abandoned lions should be all that matter to you — after all, you, if anyone, should understand their condition. In case their inappropriate behavior enlarges to new dimensions, they've been sent to a more desolate place where it won't matter or no one will notice.

FROM: BRIAN LEONARD
ADDRESS: TBA
PHONE: TBA
FAX: TBA

DATE: May 25

FAX TO: 031/45 33 31

ATTN: PETER GALLWAY

OF PAGES TO FOLLOW: 0

CONTENTS TO FOLLOW: NONE

COMMENTS: Have arrived in Cheyenne.
          Will my permit be ready when
          I arrive in Rawlins? Haven't
          settled on a home base yet.
          Will be hiring some help
          at my expense. More later.
             Take care.
             Leonard

———————●——•—————————
                  •

Hey Bri . . .? You awake?

"Huh . . . what? . . . who is it?"

Just me.

"Diane?"

The one and only.

"What's wrong? The house on fire? What time is it?"

Just out for my evening stroll, saw your window open, decided to drop by.

"Where are you?"

Like I just said, at the window.

"What's wrong with walking across the hall and knocking on the door?"

That's no fun. Besides, I go out every night. Almost every. **When I don't have a car, I hitch—I gotta thumb and she's a fine-ass bitch—** *Yeah, out the window and off I go, the world's my playground, a creature of the night . . . and all that.*

"Really? Before . . . or after . . .?"

Before or after what? **Highway 61 runs right by baby's—** *God that's hard to sing, it's not supposed to have a melody.*

"What the hell are you doing?"

Just lying across the foot of your bed. Like a dog. You don't want the first girl you sleep with to be me.

"What if Mom hears?"

God, that's all I need.

"Is there something wrong with Mom?"

She's just . . . sad, or disappointed, or . . . never mind, it doesn't have anything to do with you. She's probably proud of you, aren't you a good kid? You'd think I would know. I still live here, you know. You wouldn't think so, though, huh? Since it seems like we haven't talked for a long time.

"Yeah."

Someday we're gonna have kids and sit around a Thanksgiving table and talk like old old friends, like we never were the people we are now.

"What's gonna make us different?"

Than what?

"How we are now. What's gonna change us?"

Lots of stuff, stuff that happens from now on.

"This won't count?"

Yeah, they always call it the time you came-of-age, or your formative years, blah blah blah. Are you set in concrete by the time you're sixteen? So does that mean if you're a sweet simpering nothing as a teenager, you'll never have any blood and guts in your life, I mean never have something about you that kicks, you know what I mean, a fire in your gut about something, that you'll always be a simpering nothing? No.

What about college, suppose you're standing in line at the registrar when some radical group storms in and takes over the administration building. Some guy has hand grenades strapped around his waist. A bunch of chicks in tank tops with one black glove on and a black armband — that's a cool look if she's got some muscle. Anyway, you're scared shitless and pee your pants. That would make you scared pissless, I guess. Because if the cops or National Guard are called . . . well, not just because someone might get killed, but they might decide to search all the dorms and will find something in yours that's not supposed to be there. But one of the chicks lets you wear her pants and washes yours and goes in just her underwear until yours are dry. She's got long dark hair, parted in the middle, and someday you'll remember her when you read about how Bundy always went for those long dark-haired girls. But, you know, one thing and another, you know how these things go, she's in her underwear, and pretty soon you're at the window throwing books down at the cops, until the tear gas rips your throat raw, and you're just another body in the flood of coughing kids streaming out the front or back door and taken to the hospital for observation, and since your backpack is stuffed with biology books and notebook paper and a slide rule, they let you go, you're scott free, but . . . see? It's something that happened and now it's yours, you get to keep it, but maybe you don't have any choice. But see? Doesn't it help make high-school shit irrelevant?

"But it's not just high school that's—"

So how do you like high school, I guess I haven't asked you that yet.

"It's okay."

Any clubs? Teams? You a popular guy?

"About average, I guess. Gamekeepers and track, I run the mile. That's average too. And I'm average at it."

Want to know what I did, before and after school? Changed clothes.

"Fashion club?"

Yeah sure. Funny man. No, there was this girl, my friend who brought me clothes to wear at school, the kind of clothes Mom wouldn't let me wear — she was afraid of what it might mean. I had to wear dresses or skirts and flats or sandals from home, but this girl brought me her jeans and boots. She wore army pants and Mexican sandals. Sometimes we switched. The school had just ditched the dress code, and it pissed Mom off. She wears those pointy-toe wobbly heels every damn day, god, even Saturday, doesn't she, or am I exaggerating? Anyway I changed before school in the bathroom, then I had to change back during my last period 'cause I had to be back in my little skirt fast enough so I could get out to the front curb and be picked up by Mom as soon as the bell rang. No hanging out with anyone after school allowed. Maybe if I'd joined glee club or pep squad, maybe if I was the majorette for the band, that would've been different. She sort of flipped out when I wanted to join a Peace Corps preparation after-school class, she said it was a cover for Communists, then she nixed the Explorer Scout aviation troop, so I offered to join ROTC, and she really had a cow. So nothing after school for me, and the yearbook school-days pages didn't include MY little club or me cutting out early — luckily I was lab assistant for last-period chemistry and biology, and I could set up their lab work or correct their quizzes during the first half of the period, so then I could leave the back way through the biology lab — an off-limits room where the students don't go, except the lab assistant, where the fetal pigs were kept in their big crocks of brine, and shelves of microscopes and special lights and Bunsen burners — I took one of those — and flasks and beakers — I took me one of those too, 'cause it seemed kinda cool to drink coffee from it — anyway out that back door from the lab there's an interior hallway that runs between the biology classrooms and the back of the stage in the cafeteria. I'd change back there, and we'd smoke there too, hang there and talk. She was in last-period chemistry and just got up and split fifteen minutes before the bell so she could meet me. With something in her pocket, she's a rocket— da-da-da-da. No, she would've been a rocket even without the cash. A real pistol — that's a good one, huh? But she had a part-time job and her own spending money. I had to bring a thermos and sack lunch, which I accidentally-on-purpose forgot as often as I could. Anyway, that hallway opened, at the end, into an alley that ran along the side of the school, along the cafeteria and behind the gym, where the band used to form up before football games. I would leave through there and be at the front of the school when the bell rang, usually while it was still ringing, and Mom was already there waiting — can you believe it? She never even asked me how I got out of class so fast.

"She doesn't care what I wear."

Of course not, average man. You probably wear jeans and a plaid shirt, tucked in. Am I right or am I right? So, since you're an average guy, you'll probably have a thing for beer and cars— no, it'll be trucks, maybe a panel truck that you can lay a mattress behind the front seat. Or, I know, a big pick-up for getting around but maybe dune buggies will be your thing for fun. That's average guy stuff. Babes, beer, brawling.

"Maybe not that kind of average guy."

No? No suds 'n sluts? No guns? You won't work in construction or roofing or drive a truck like an average guy? No, you're the go-to-college average man, aren't you?

"Aren't you going to college?"

No, but don't worry, I've got it figured out. I'm going to Africa, get me a job as an assistant to a wildlife biologist, or even as a cook or someone to wash his clothes, learn on-the-job, you know? And get the hell away from here as far as I can, away from everyone telling me who I am and what I should be. I don't mean you, average man. But while you're doing your average thing, I'll be camped out on a steppe or savanna in the Serengeti or the Masai Mara or the Niger flood plain, in the Okavango Delta or in the Ngorongoro crater. With camp-fires banked right outside our mosquito-netting tents, we'll hear the soft, rich growls of a pride of lions padding through our camp at night, the chilling roars of the pride's patriarch — sounds like it's right on the other side of our jeep, his voice answered by the yi-yi-yips of the hyenas. In the morning before light, we wake to baboons and vervet monkeys in the trees screaming a warning, chasing those same hyenas who've gotten too close to a troop. With steaming coffee in tin cups, we watch morning mist rise from the grassland, the veld, and see the murky silhouettes of giraffe under the riverine trees start to take shape, then begin to move. All we see of rooting warthogs is their tails sticking straight up above the thick undergrowth. Vast flocks of white storks take off from the tundra — wetlands around the seasonal river — a tempest of white flashing wings, nearly blocking the red haze of the rising sun, as the grunting and splashing in the water means the hippos are wallowing, so many glistening gray bodies like boulders in the water, they expand the muddy squishy banks of the pool by three times its normal size, and big crocs lie there as though plastered in the mud, waiting to be able to squeeze past the hippos into the water, perhaps hoping for a wayward newborn to leave its mother. But the water dwindles a little more each day, and the hippos begin wallowing in mud, and soon only enough mud to slip like grease between their jostling bodies, the crocs dead or gone, the herds of impala and waterbuck, water buffalo and wildebeest, even the tiny dik dik — their skinny tails of little use against swarms of biting black flies — stop by to curl their lips in scummy liquid that gathers in the footprint hollows in the ooze.

"Very nice. Now will you please shut up and let me sleep."

You used to like me to read to you in bed, Old Yeller, The Yearling . . . you CRIED, *little brother . . . . This's just as good. It's better, 'cause I'll really be there. I'll have a wide streak of sweat down the back of my khaki shirt by ten in the morning, riding the jeep standing up, binoculars to my eyes, searching for white rhino, or counting the huge bald-headed maribu stork and measuring how much territory each seems to command, or following the migration of the herds of zebra, or tracking a family of elephants. We're tagging them, anesthetizing and taking vital data. A group of four females and three juveniles stand around a pile of bleached white bones, their trunks so slowly and gently caressing the ribs, the huge scapula, especially the skull with just stumps where the tusks were — not a new discovery, we knew poachers got this cow over a year ago, but the herd pauses here to stroke her bones each time they pass by, and we do nothing to disturb the tomb. They bring their new babies, and even the young ones pass their sensitive pointed-tipped trunks over the smooth, creamy bones.*

"Where'll you get the money to go to Africa?"

You could fly me to Africa. C'mon, Bri, get a pilot's license and let's go. Maybe Daktari needs someone who can fly a bush plane.

"Why don't *you* get a pilot's license? And if you were really planning to go to Africa, wouldn't you at least have a job and start saving?"

My, aren't you practical. Maybe I've got an inheritance. Ha ha.

"From our father? Do you know who he is? Is he dead?"

What I inherited from him was Mom.

## 2

FUN WITH COWBOYS

The map was tacked to the outside of the bathroom door at the Wrangler Inn just off the interstate at Rawlins. With push pins of colored flags from Alco — red, blue, green, yellow, white, black, cutting and taping together extras to make red/blue, red/green, red/yellow, blue/green, yellow/black, black/white — he had enough flags to match all of the ear-tag colors listed in Gallway's field reports. A posted list, taped to the wall beside the door, told him the age, gender, radio frequency and ear-tag color of each animal.

In a taxidermy/hunting shop in downtown Rawlins, he laughed quietly as he picked out bumper stickers — *Protected By Smith & Wesson, My Colt Kicks Harder, I Trust My Gun Not My Senator, My Heritage / My Right* — to go with the gun rack from Alco, designed for the back window of a little pick-up, but which he'd already installed with ropes and bungies behind the chopper's two tiny seats. The rifles were visible through the clear bubble. There were no doors to lock, but the rack had a security mechanism so without a key the rifles couldn't be removed unless the ropes were untied and the whole unit taken out. The helicopter was equipped with collapsible antennas mounted on either side with a hinged bracket so, from inside the chopper while in the air, he could flip the antennas down from their upright inactive location to a horizontal position, then extend them to full length for use in aerial homing, giving the chopper as much directional sensing as a small airplane with antennas mounted on the tips of each wing.

The taxidermy shop also had ammunition and targets. And again, hats — camouflage baseball caps; cowhide cowboy hats with the short, stiff black-and-white hair still in place; neon winter hunting caps with ear flaps. Brian wore the Robin Hood hat.

He picked up a sleeveless hunting vest with fleece lining and filled the loops with shells for his competition rifle. But before taking his purchases to the counter, he stopped to study the bulletin board which he'd spotted through the window from the sidewalk. Mostly faded Polaroids, faces where noses all but disappear as the skin becomes the same watery yellow as the background. And mostly elk, pronghorn, mule deer, a few bighorn sheep. One cougar, stretched flat on its side, the hunter behind on one knee, rifle like a walking staff held upright, cowboy hat low over the brow, no eyes visible, the rest of the face bleached featureless by cheap instant-photo chemicals.

The man behind the counter was on the phone. "Be sure to bring in whatever lure you want in the lip . . . . No, a fish that size we can't save any meat."

Brian flipped the cougar Polaroid up, noted the date on the back, then moved up to the counter.

"You fly a chopper, don'cha?" the taxidermist said, as he counted the shells in the hunting vest.

"How'd you know?"

"Hunting season's over . . . and don't no tourists come in here, 'specially not and buy anything much . . . ." He squinted at the price tag on the vest. "Besides, my buddy happened to see you looking it over. Figured you'd bought it. It's near his plane."

"So?"

"Well, hey, pardon the questions, but he wondered, is all, who y'were, and . . . . What're ya huntin' anyway?"

"Bulls-eyes." Brian pulled the targets out from underneath the vest so the man could ring them up.

"With 300 mags? Guys shoot at cans and fenceposts to stay sharp for a rack come fall. Clay pigeons for birds. But . . . ." The man looked at Brian's hat which he'd placed on the counter.

"That's already mine," Brian said.

"Yeah, I never carried them kind."

Brian paid, picked up his things, then smiled and said, "Don't you worry, I'm not the FBI nor a drug agent. Just a competition shooter looking for a quiet friendly place to prepare for the next competition season . . . maybe even the Olympics next year."

"That so? Hey, mind if I tell my buddy?"

"Go ahead. By the way, is there a good tavern around here? You know, where a guy can nurse his beer for a good hour without pressure, slow and easy, big TV, jukebox that works good, where your ranchers would go but truckers or bikers passing through wouldn't — that kind of place?"

"Lincoln Lodge . . . down about two blocks."

It was a two-mile walk down Cedar Street back to the Wrangler Inn. He filled the pockets of the vest with the bumper stickers and targets, and wore it over his white golf shirt.

```
FROM:        BRIAN LEONARD
ADDRESS:     WRANGLER INN, RAWLINS, WY
PHONE:       (307) 678-0990
FAX:         (307) 998-0550

DATE:        May 27

FAX TO:      031/45 33 31

ATTN:        PETER GALLWAY

# OF PAGES TO FOLLOW:   0

CONTENTS TO FOLLOW:      NONE

COMMENTS:    Okay, I won't bring in an
             assistant. You're right.
             Wasn't thinking. Yes, my
             permit came through. It
             might be your original study
             was mistaken in determining
             few indigenous animals range
             here. Or maybe I'm wrong and
             this freak loner just wan-
             dered in and was killed on
             a depredation permit. If a
             hunter takes down one of
             yours, is there information
             on the radio collar in-
             structing him to inform you?
             Chopper's all set for hom-
             ing. Don't know how I'll
             manage the controls and get
             a reading on the map at the
             same time, but I'll figure
             it out. Don't worry.
                  Best,
                  Leonard
```

```
FROM:        BRIAN LEONARD
ADDRESS:     WRANGLER INN, RAWLINS, WY
PHONE:       (307) 678-0990
FAX:         (307) 998-0550


DATE:        May 27


FAX TO:      (619) 993-3572


ATTN:        LEYA KARNEY


# OF PAGES TO FOLLOW:   0


CONTENTS TO FOLLOW:      NONE


COMMENTS: Lincoln Lodge, downtown
          Rawlins, May 30, 4 p.m. Look
          for the only guy in Robin
          Hood hat, table in right rear
          as you enter.
```

The tavern — decompression chamber or fun house? Are you
LOOKING *to be noticed and watched, to be thought of as a mis-*
fit weirdo, to have some rube silent type say, WHAT THE HELL'S
WRONG WITH YOU, BUDDY? *Have you already gone too far?*
You call this a controlled environment? A double-dare stare-
down with yourself, game of chicken, experimenting to see
when you'll back down and call it quits? Or make a public
display as some kind of warning? What are you up to, invit-
ing that girl here?

Just testing. A scientific, regulated evaluation. That's
okay, isn't it?

Right now, take time to review the profile: a loner, be-
trayed by society, low esteem but craving control and power,
acting in defiance of a society he feels is not paying him due
attention. These psycho-babble generalities still seem to mean

little or nothing. Seeks a victim's vulnerability, shows lack of remorse — the victim is not human. The carnal aspect of his violent nature can be divided into categories: does the assault happen before, during or after the homicide? Is the murder accompanied by torture — creating fear in the victim? Those who fall in the during-killing and with-torture categories are the ones exhilarated — to a fevered pitch — by fear. Is the killing itself the sexual experience? Does he masturbate later while thinking about what he's done, or before, while planning it? Either way, you already know auto-eroticism is a poor choice for someone with any of the other key characteristics, and should still and always be avoided, even if overall diagnosis remains in doubt.

Yes, you're tired of all this. But don't let that weaken your guard. You don't have a gang of guys provided for you this time, so put together your own. Don't worry about what to talk about, it'll come — probably women and hunting, you can handle that.

At 3 the bar was predictably empty. Summer travelers only got off the interstate to line up at Burger King or get a 32-oz. cup of cola while filling their 30-gallon gas tanks. In the spring, ranchers were too busy to be drinking in the afternoon. It wouldn't be dark until after 7:30. But the tavern was already dark, and the two guys at the bar, with big-buckled belts, pearl-buttoned cowboy shirts, and hats without sweat marks, turned in unison to watch Brian take his beer to a table in the back.

"Dude ranch closed for the day?" Brian asked quietly. "Why ain't'cha out roundin' up stray heifers?"

One of the guys turned to the other. "If a guy was gonna go crazy and start shootin' people from a rooftop, it wouldn't be *too* crazy for him to sit in public with a fairy hat and vest full'a shells without even a *shirt* on underneath."

Brian watched the bartender selecting tunes from the jukebox, then when the first song started — a wild down-hill tumbling good-time cowboy tune — he said, "What makes guys in a sweet little Western town think about snipers?"

Red and blue lights on the jukebox bounced with the song. —*best to brave the wind and rain*— The other guy turned around on his stool, gestured with his beer, the handle turned toward Brian as though his hand was too big to be expected to hold the mug with the loop of glass. "Our way'a sayin' hello. What's yours?"

Brian stretched his legs out and crossed his feet at the ankle. His new hiking boots came up to his calf. It was too warm for the vest *and* a shirt. "I guess something *is* wrong with my manners. But the new kid in school might be eaten alive if he says, first thing, *wanna share my lunch?* Trade insults — that's the way to break the ice. Am I right? Two bull elk meet in the woods, they don't play footsie, they lock antlers."

"Ain't elk season."

"What season *is* it?"

"None. Fishin'. Rabbits always OK, but who cares."

"You mean I'm too late for the annual jackalope roundup and tournament?"

"Isn't this the guy Pete wanted to talk to?"

The other shrugged.

"Hey, call Andy," the guy said to the bartender.

"I should've asked, is it against the law to wear a hunting vest indoors? Or maybe just inappropriate for it to be so *new*. I'll sweat it up as fast as I can, but blood stains'll be tricky if nothin's in season."

"Pete won't care how you dress if you can shoot."

"Who's Pete?" Brian sipped. "Why'd you call Andy?"

"Pete's place is too big — can only leave a message at the machine at the house, he wouldn't hear of it till dark, unless he's wearin' his beeper which he don't too often. Andy's his buddy — gun store down the street."

"And who're you?" Brian asked.

"I sell Fords. This here's my sales manager. We're closed Mondays."

"You can make a living selling cars out here?"

The jukebox song ended. In the kitchen, a TV ran an ad for a livestock auction. A woman was walking past outside with a crying baby, the sound mingling with the next song starting in the jukebox, a twangy girl lamenting her life.

When the man from the taxidermy shop came in the bar, he stood still, squinting, took off his camouflage baseball cap, wiped his brow and replaced the hat. "I ran into Jimmy at the gas station. He'll be right down too." He approached Brian's table, turned an empty chair around and straddled it. "Andy Lefferts, we met the other day. I tol' my buddy Pete about you. He has an offer, if yer in'erested."

"I'll listen."

"He don't care why yer here, what'cher doin', but . . . when yer not practicing with targets, maybe you could be interested in cash on the side. Five bucks for every tail."

Brian looked down at his finger making slow circles on his kneecap. "Well . . . I know you can't mean escaped convicts . . . or gorillas . . . or baboons, or—"

"Huh?"

"What kind of tails are you interested in collecting?"

"Coyote. They kill newborns. Range cattle drop their calves wherever they are. But sometimes the coyote get 'em as fast as they drop. One pack even surrounded a yearling, tore her up pretty good, ate parts of her without botherin' to finish her off and *kill* her. We know hunting from a chopper is more efficient—"

"*Five* bucks?" *No! Don't tell them you haven't gone there — have yet to use the practiced accuracy, the years of hours of focus and repetitive drills, to kill with a rifle.* Brian scratched his shoulder, looked at the skin on his upper arm. "God, I'm white. And soft as a *girl*. Hope to start getting a tan soon."

"Any girl I'm with better be a hell of a lot softer than *you*." The taxidermist grinned. "You want more? He'll talk. Hey, Jimmy, over here."

Another guy in a baseball cap was squinting in the doorway. Lean, with long arms. Clumsily kicked a few chairs and almost tripped on his way over. The cap had a feed company insignia, an ear of corn with wings. "Jimmy," the taxidermist said, "this's him, the chopper pilot, the sharpshooter."

"Glad t'meet'cha." Jimmy's hand felt like he was wearing old crusty leather work gloves. "Well?"

"You a cattle rancher?" Brian asked.

"Mostly oil, but the cattle keep me humble." Jimmy put one boot on a chair, leaned forward on his knee. "I mess a little comparing growth rates on the range versus confined with various feed mixtures. Also like to dabble in genetics, for fun. But coyotes're running a population control program, cattle and sheep both."

"I guess raising cattle's pretty difficult if you can't have babies. Tell me . . . breeding cattle, or any livestock for that matter . . . um . . . it's always consensual, right?"

The car dealer snorted into his beer mug. The phone rang and the bartender turned the TV in the kitchen off. The taxidermist stared, breathing through his mouth.

"Never asked," Jimmy smiled, raising creases like cracks on his cowhide face. "He's heavy and dangerous, she's hollering — but in the end, *she* decides yes or no. If she says no, she may get hurt — maybe killed if no one gets her outta there — but she don't get no cock." Everyone laughed. Jimmy pushed his cap back. "An A-I is sure as hell easier. Safer too. What with all the STD's in livestock these days. We use a lot of invitro implants too. Some breeds are just plain better incubators. And cheaper to bring in cold-stored sperm or an embryo than ship a whole bull!" One of the creases on his brow was actually a scar.

"Well . . . ." Brian looked around at the four men facing him from various angles and distances. "Sorry, forget I asked."

The car dealer and his manager each reached for some peanuts at the same time. Their hands crashed over the bowl. Peanuts spilled on the bar. Jimmy put his foot back on the floor. A shell crunched under his boot. His face made a scratchy sound as he wiped his mouth with one hand. Rap music blared from a car outside, then passed by.

"I heard when you reduce the adult coyote population, they'll have bigger litters."

"Where'd you hear that?" Jimmy asked.

"Dunno. I forget."

The taxidermist's chair screeched as he stood up. "I left the shop open."

"Five bucks, huh?" Brian said, his thumb polishing the end of a shell in his hunting vest. "You know how much fuel for that thing costs?"

"Ten."

"Well . . . fifteen. And I also need a car. I can't be taking a helicopter to the grocery store and laundromat, can't take a girl to the movies in a *chopper*." He leaned backwards over the chair so he could see the guys at the bar. "You gotta Jeep you could loan me?"

"Ford don't make no Jeeps."

"Okay, a Bronco. That's perfect. Make me into a real Wyoming man." Ignoring the rockabilly song on the jukebox, he sang off-key and out of rhythm, "*Cowboys ain't easy to love— la-la-la-la-la-laaaa . . . .*"

Jimmy turned and reached an empty hand toward the bar. The bartender handed him a mug.

"*Da-da-da da-da-da —poolrooms and clear mountain mornings— La-la-laa la-la —and children and girls of the night,*" Brian sang softer, smiling.

"You may think yer puttin' us down, mister," Jimmy said in a low voice that cut underneath both the record and Brian's song, "but . . . people that haven't lived here tryin' to slam *us* for doing what *they* can't? *Hell* . . . ."

"*Them that don't know him won't like him, and them that do— la-la-la —know how to take him—* Hey, don't misunderstand. I admire you, you're the real thing."

"You got quite an attitude," the manager said.

"Shut up, Hal." The dealer paid, eased his big butt off the stool, hitched up his new jeans and moved to the door, the sound of his thighs rubbing together like a knife sharpener. After a quick glare, the manager followed.

"Bring the Bronco out tomorrow, boys," Brian said. "Wrangler Inn. Great name for a motel."

Someone came in as they went out. The last of the jukebox choices ended, the machine went cold and dark.

Jimmy sat on a table and once again put one boot in an empty chair. "Take the tails to Andy's shop, he'll pay you, we'll feed the cash through him. Getting contributions from everyone in the county's for me and Pete to deal with. We kin handle as many as you bring in, there're enough coyotes out there t'keep you in movie money."

The girl in the doorway began threading her way through empty tables. Brian finished his beer. "'Scuse me, Jimmy, I've got another appointment. But I'd like to talk to you about your stock again — why d'you think nature made it more like a kill than a caress? We're actually in similar lines of work. But my animals have longer, sharper nails and higher voices. You'll likely find me here, when I'm not out in the field."

"Brian Leonard?" The girl had wound around several tables, but was not making the most direct approach. Two empty tables were still in the way. By the time she navigated around one, Brian was opposite her, the remaining table between them.

"Howdy," he said, extending a hand. Immediately his arm ached as though holding it out in front of himself was too much of a job for his muscles. The girl shifted a small backpack to her other shoulder to free up her right hand, but as she began to reach to meet his handshake, Brian dropped his own hand, picked up an ashtray from the table. "Leya Karney," he said softly. "You came."

"Certainly. This's a wonderful opportunity."

"Wait before you decide that." Then he looked up and grinned, still clutching the ashtray.

She was a freckle-faced girl, about 28, maybe 30. Small sharp nose, small almond-shaped obliquely placed brown eyes, small high cheekbones, thin brown lips, thick straight brown hair in a single French braid hanging down her back, stretched off her brow so tightly it appeared her eyebrows were being pulled up at the ends.

Brian sat abruptly, turned and retrieved his empty beer mug from the table behind him. "You came just in time — rescued me from the locals." He laughed. "But I was having fun with the cowboys."

"These people have probably lived generations here. They know more about the wilderness areas and natural wildlife populations than books can tell us." She hooked her backpack on a chair and sat down across from him.

"Whoa, young lady, first rule, no ethereal idealism." He held the ashtray with both hands circling the rim. "This's a simple wildlife observation study, not even high profile enough for an article in National Geographic. Whatever you've imagined about the higher plane of field work, forget it all right now." Looking down at the table through the ashtray, "The money just wasn't there to do this job the right way — the *regular* way. So it's just me out here instead of the team I should have. But, technically, I'm here to make a report to the guy who started this project so he can be ready to come back and continue his work himself. If I went out there first thing and found every animal had established a home territory and steady diet, no fighting, no accidents, no attempt to go back to where they came from, the job would be all but done." Looking up, raising the ashtray and looking at her through it like a single lens, "I don't think it'll be that easy, but I hope so."

She reached across the table and took the ashtray from him. "Fidgeting makes me nervous."

"You get nervous?" He swept his beer mug close, held onto it with both hands. "Then maybe this isn't a good idea for you."

"I didn't say anything about the work would make me nervous."

"Let me tell you about the work." One finger traced the rim of the glass. "I'm supposed to locate as many of the animals as I can, see if I can estimate their range, their home territory, their diet, their general health . . . potential problems or set-backs . . . without snaring or drugging, if possible." Glancing up for a second showed him the eager flying wings of her eyebrows, the shine in her eyes. "But . . .," his voice thickened, "these locals you've romanticized . . . it's important for us to be included in their circle, that means bullshit with them *their* way."

"What are you getting at?" She was still smiling.

Brian lay both hands on top of the mug, rested his chin on his knuckles. "Okay, say you're out with me all day in the field. We've been miles following the thin beep on the receiver that never seems to get any louder. Several times we've separated and each of us climbs a different hill to try to triangulate and get a point on a grid where we can reasonably look for the animal, but every time we get there, hours later, the beep is no louder. The dust is making mud with our sweat. Rashes and chafing everywhere skin touches skin . . . . So . . . it's been a shit of a day, right? So I'm about the *last* thing you'd want to share dinner with." He used one finger to gather foam clinging to the inside of the mug, then put the finger in his mouth. "So you come into town, and, to your surprise, it's Saturday night. The gang's all here. But there aren't enough girls to go around. The two-step's blaring. The tables're cleared. They start dancing. Cutting in. Dancing. Cutting in. They're passing you around. And they never miss a step. They can rotate in and out, catch their breath, gulp their beer, when it's their turn again, there they are." The last words had become soft and hoarse, as though he was out of breath. But he wasn't panting. Took in air and went on, "I have no idea how to do a cowboy dance — I don't dance at all. But you already passed up dinner with me, remember?

Good idea, I'm bad company after . . . work." His eyes rose, following her hand. She was gesturing toward the bar. "Doesn't sound like such a grand job anymore, does it?" he said.

The bartender came with two fresh beers and took away the empty mug.

"If you're testing my mettle," she said, "believe me, I've worked where men are a vast majority. Zoos were a totally male world until not too long ago." She held her beer mug with a fist on the handle. Between sips, she didn't touch it at all, folded her hands on the table in front of herself.

"You're a pretty steady girl, aren't you?"

"Woman." She laughed slightly.

"Oh . . . ." He sat up then leaned back in his chair. " . . . *but she breaks just like a little girl.*"

"Not me," she laughed again, delicately. "I'm not squeamish, but I have enough healthy caution, so don't worry about me being rash and careless."

He chuckled, focusing his eyes on the edge of the table in front of her body. "But . . . ." At arm's length, he held his beer like a crystal ball. "Will I have to be taking care of you?"

"Mr. Leonard—"

"Brian."

"Okay, Brian . . .," she ran her fingers lightly over the sides of her hair, touched the small gold studs in each earlobe before folding her hands in place again. "I'm not sure what you're trying to say."

He balled his hands into a single fist and pushed it into his lap, then, in the same instant, jerked his hands back up and lay them flat on the table top, fingers spread. Like a suspect spread-eagle on a squad car. "I think you're probably the right temperament for a job like this, but . . . maybe you ought to re-consider." His voice suddenly softer, "But maybe you always wanted to be Daktari."

"Be what?"

"Never mind. Why do you want to do this?"

"I've wanted an opportunity like this for years. I never even expected anything to come of that ad. Placing it was like a rite of passage, a gesture I had to make . . . after my divorce. So when you called, I couldn't pass it up. I understand you're just trying to find out how focused I am, how well I can keep my mind on the job 24-hours-a-day without getting bogged down by a personal agenda. I can assure you . . . . I wasn't even going to mention my divorce, believe me, it's in the past, and I'm ready to start over and really stay focused on important work with wildlife."

"You sound like a kid writing an essay to get into forest-service training."

She laughed, still tentatively. "I guess I do."

Brian looked down at his hands on the tabletop. He had to concentrate to find his heartbeat — it was normal, low and steady. "Okay, let me start over. I just want you to be aware of the hardships. Miles and miles and miles on foot. Snakes and mosquitoes and more granola bars than you'll ever want. Kneeling beside a creek in the stinking mud made by herds of cattle — you have to try to drink from the little clear riffle two feet out from the edge. And days and days and days without seeing a cougar . . . you'll be ecstatic just to see their poop."

"It all sounds wonderful to me." After a sip of beer, she licked her lips with a kitten tongue.

He squeezed his eyes shut, went on talking, "But . . . maybe the other hardships can be real too. Our new friends . . . the kind of guy who works for these big ranchers . . . transients . . . disillusioned dreamers . . . ." Speaking even more gently, "Who says cowboys can't want the same thing as everyone else? Someone to be closer to him than his own heart. Would that make a good verse in a cowboy song?"

"It probably would."

He opened his eyes a crack. Her hands were still folded, but tighter, knuckles squeezing each other. He didn't raise his eyes. A semi coming into town stopped and idled in the street outside. It caused vibrations in the floor he could feel through his boots. "Is this crazy?" He heard his words between his ears as though they'd come over a headset, but wasn't sure if he'd spoken out loud. He cleared his throat. "So you're not afraid to come here by yourself and work with and among people you've never met and don't know anything about?"

"Well, I'll be honest, this line of questioning concerns me somewhat."

"I'm sorry, I really am." He turned his chair sideways and stretched his legs, leaned back with his hands behind his head. "It's meant to reassure *me*."

She stood and lifted her backpack to her shoulder. "How about if I find a motel room, call and give you the number, and you can let me know your decision later."

Heavy footsteps approached the door outside, boots stomped in the foyer, then a large man came in followed by the clomping boots of two others. The truck outside released its air brakes and moved on. The big man was wearing a western suit, complete with string tie and lizard-skin boots with silver toe-guards. The suit coat was leather, with a darker color over the shoulders and on the elbow patches. His shirt was neon yellow. His hat's brim was curled tightly on the sides and jutted sharply down over his brow in front. The other two were in requisite jeans, T-shirts, baseball caps and boots. Their jeans had faded places in the back pockets where their wallets had sat for too long. The two in jeans sat at the bar, but the fat man put his hands on his hips and stared at Leya. "Even without the standing order for my broncs, you kin always tell rodeo season." His loud voice was directed to his pals. "The most unlikely wanna-bes just *askin'* t'get their skulls mashed."

Leya looked at Brian, but he shrugged and gazed toward the ceiling. She quickly sat back down, the backpack requiring her to perch on the outer two inches of the seat. The three men lit cigarettes and settled onto the creaking vinyl stools. Their voices, still loud, seemed muffled by the smoke streaming from their nostrils.

Bull-sessions . . . guy-talk . . . when you don't partake, they think you're different . . . TOO different. Homosexuals learned this years ago. So did you.

Suddenly Brian spoke toward the lazy ceiling fan, "Maybe we'd like to see what'cha got — a sneak preview, t'see if it's worth our time t'get in the saddle."

Leya kicked him under the table while she said, "I'm morally opposed to—"

"Hey," the big guy slid from his stool and approached, grinning, "not a bad idea. Be glad t'show you what I've got. I provide broncs for rodeos all over the West. Y'may change yer mind, but y'may say *let's have at 'em!*"

The two guys in jeans were turned and watching. Leya muttered, "Let's *go.*"

Brian didn't take his eyes off the ceiling, just shook his head which was still cradled in his hands and tipped over the back of the chair. His body flowed in front of him down to the floor where his boots seemed like two hunks of cement. He was suddenly cold. Or maybe hot. His skin prickled. A current snaked through him.

"Is she sorta shy?" the guy said, looking at Brian. "That's a treat, compared to — Hell, *you're* no rider, fella. Looks like your tour bus made one stop too many at Chief Yellowhorse's Trading Post." He turned to accept snorts of appreciation from his sidekicks.

"What makes us your business?" Leya snapped.

Brian blinked slowly like a dozing animal. But below his nonchalant face, inside his languid long legs, a buzz became a tremble. Sweat breaking felt like rubber bands snapping against him.

"But if you must know," she continued, "we're here because of your wildlife, not your barbaric sports. A biologist would be appalled at your involvement with animals. Only an abnormal-behavioral psychologist would be interested in studying what you do."

Brian winced, shutting his eyes for a second. It felt as though steam might be rising from his skin. *Hey, you're hot. Churning. Relax. Easy, easy. Ease off.*

"Let me prove you wrong, sugar, you come on out and see how I treat my stock."

The two other guys belched out laughs made of smoke.

"Hey, it's my duty, ain't it?" the big guy grinned back to his buddies, "t'open her eyes to some *real* wildlife. It's an honest invitation to tour the ranch."

"Yer wife'll sure be happy 'bout that," one of the guys in jeans said. The other smirked, lighting another cigarette.

Leya had both hands on one of the shoulder straps of her backpack, standing where she had been sitting. The man approached the table, so the two of them plus Brian made a triangle. Then, as he spoke, the guy moved around so he was between Brian and Leya. "Honey, most people round here get mad at the things yer sayin'. I think yer just uninformed. To me, it's *art*, what I do. People don't realize it's art to make rodeo broncs. And that's not all I do. Barrel ponies and cow ponies too. But, you know, a man can't stay content doing the same things all his life. I went into thoroughbreds a couple years ago. Lookin' t'breed me a derby winner someday. You'd love t'see em, I gottum from two-week-old to two years, cavorting on the green pasture with their mamas, kickin' up them heels and squealin' like girls. There's no prettier sight."

The guy was leaning back, half sitting on the table between where Brian was stretched out and Leya was standing. His weight held the table up off two legs. Facing Leya, he was close enough to reach out and put a hand on her upper arm. She flinched, but didn't back off, and he wasn't gripping her. He moved his hand quietly up and down her arm. Breathing through his parted lips, Brian was numbly surprised no smoke came out of him as well. *What's wrong with you? Put a stop to it. Going too far. End it.*

"Spooky little thing, ain't'cha? But scared fillies quiet right down under my hands, darlin'. I got the touch. And I don't show my foals to just anyone. You look like you could 'preciate well-bred horses."

"I don't know anything about horses."

"Oh, darlin', they're warm and firm and alive and full of surprises, silky to the touch, and a smell sends you to heaven."

A sound like an electric saw splitting logs was just a beer glass on the table starting to slide. When the horse rancher stood up, a sound like a shot was the table banging back down on all four legs. *Wait— who took the first shot?*

"What kinda horseshit you slingin', Harry?" one of the guys at the bar laughed, snuffing his cigarette.

"Go on, Harry," the other said, as though calling out jeers at a boxing match. "Get to the *good* parts."

Brian opened his mouth wider and breathed slower. *It's okay. Steady. Like an exercise. Put your target on the doorknob across the room. Feel the pull of the trigger between breaths, between heartbeats. If you can get in the zone, you won't hear or see or feel any distractions.*

The horse man's hand closed on her arm. "You don't mind, d'you pardner, if I take her out t'my place, show her around?"

"No . . . thanks anyway," she sputtered. The three men were laughing and talking at the same time, stools and boots scraping the floor.

Brian rolled his neck around, one hand holding the Robin Hood hat on the back of his head. Her dark eyes looked like holes cut in a paper doll — by mistake, too high and at an angle. Her eyebrows flying off her face. Her freckles scattering. Her nostrils flaring. Her mouth shaping words or sounds still lost in the din of male voices. Alone, she seemed surrounded.

His chair screamed then clattered to the floor as his body lurched forward. Barely steady on his feet, he stammered, "That's enough for now," as he grabbed her arm then shot himself toward the door, dragging her along with him. Stood panting on the sidewalk, leaning with one hand against a pole holding up the awning. The fleece lining of the vest was damp in the armholes. A breeze cooled his neck. His legs still buzzed as though waking up from a numbing sleep.

"Hey!" she said. He was still gripping her arm. "Why did you start all that?" A sparkle of spit flew from her mouth, but he couldn't tell where it went or if it hit him. He stood up, released her and put both hands in the pockets of the vest. She threw her backpack onto the sidewalk between them. Her feet braced, hands on hips, chin slightly forward.

He took a step back. "Everything's okay now."

"That's not my point!"

"I'm sorry. I thought . . . ." He took a deep, slightly shaky breath. "You know what?" he said. "You check the parking lot at the local Safeway — there's just as many station wagons and mini vans there as in Omaha or Boise or the San Fernando Valley." He looked over her head at a banner stretched across the street announcing the county fair and rodeo. When he lowered his eyes, she still hadn't moved or changed expression. "He was just playing around. Nothing was going to happen, I promise." Brian picked up the backpack.

"But what did happen amounts to a pretty clear example of sexual harassment."

"Only if you were employed by him." His eyes flicked back out to the street, up to the banners, sideways toward a rusty truck pulling away from the curb, then came back and settled slowly on hers. "I . . . I'm sorry I didn't leave sooner. But I do think it's important for us to . . . fit in. Maybe this time I miscalculated . . . ." He wiped one hand down the front of the vest, leaving a damp sweat smear. "Remember, I asked if I was going to have to save you?"

"You said take care of me . . . so what was this, a test?"

"No, nothing planned, I assure you." The shopkeeper of the closest storefront came outside to water petunias in a window box. Brian waited for her to finish, then said, "This is a stupid time to ask, but . . . why'd your ad in the newspaper say you were single and female? Not that I . . . ."

She blinked. "I . . . don't know. Just kidding. I guess that was dumb."

"People kid in dumb ways, don't they?" He smiled, still looking at her.

"Maybe that's why I'm best working with animals."

"Does this mean you've weighed the positives and negatives, considered the minimal rewards and tremendous hardships, and accepted the job?" He extended the pack toward her.

She stared, then took her pack, holding it like a bag of groceries to her chest. "I might not get another opportunity for years. But is this what women have to put up with in order to get what we've already worked and studied for?"

"Let's don't philosophize or lecture on social issues. It makes me as nervous as fidgeting does you. It makes *everyone* nervous, okay? And we don't want to make these ranchers nervous. They're *not* going to like what we're doing here."

The tight line of her mouth eased. Blood flowed back into her lips. A light changed at the end of the block and held traffic off the street. A flag snapped in the breeze and the fringe of the awning made a purring rattle. Kids on bicycles rode by, one with a boombox radio strapped behind the seat playing something with a heartbeat bass and shimmering harmony. "I'm sorry, I never much liked the pop-psychology easy-answers either," she sighed. "I must've picked up the habit in my women's . . . group."

"Group?" He grinned. "Is that like a pack? A pride? A herd? A flock?"

"A divorce therapy group. But, I told you, it's all behind me now. I promise."

She sighed, looked up and down the sidewalk. "I guess I need to find a place to stay."

"Try the Interstate 80 Motel, an easy walk."

"Is that where you are?"

"No." He pulled his hat lower onto his brow. "We'll have a vehicle tomorrow. I'll pick you up at 5 a.m." Hands returned to his vest pockets, Brian moved on down the sidewalk, then stopped and turned back. Leya was crossing the street. "Hey," he shouted. "They were just kidding. I mean . . . don't worry about it."

She ran the last few steps to the other side, turned when she was on the curb. "I'm not. And I'll lighten up, I promise!" Then the light changed and cars filled the street between them.

What have you gotten yourself into, is it going too far? You think it's a good idea to be putting yourself in a chopper, with a girl beside you, then shoot at things running on the ground? You know shooting is something you do with a paper target and a gallery of people watching, keeping score. And it takes a tranquil, cool head to be any good at it. Cool heads and blood don't equate. Or is this even true? Assassins, SWAT sharpshooters, Marine marksmen . . . dispassion with deadly result. But that's not what a sex killer is about. You've stayed away from blood for almost three decades. Or is it your hope that if it takes calm control to shoot accurately, then shooting will KEEP you rational, composed, and in control, even with her along for the ride, even when it's for blood? Admit it. You're setting up to test yourself. Is it dangerous to feel strong like this? You call this strong? Don't start thinking that flooding is the best technique to bring about successful behavior modification, or that slowly raising the level of endurance will stretch endurance farther and farther. You can creep to the breaking point as slowly and carefully as you want, but the breaking point, if it's there, hasn't moved farther away. Okay — test to see if you can stay in the zone. Test to see what it takes for you to stay in the zone . . . and what can take you out.

Dear Sal,

May 30

Hooray, I got the job! If they can't hold my
position at the zoo more than six weeks,
and if I'm not back by then, oh well. By
then I may have a future in field work. And,
no, I'm not necessarily just running away
from bad memories. A clean break from
everything and starting over--new job, new
location, new friends, new life, new
personality(???)--is probably every post-
divorcee's fantasy, but that's all it really
is. (Nothing ever turns out as great as you
fantasize, anyway!) I know I still have
you, silly. Not all my memories are
wretched. You and all the "kids" in the
Kritters Show were my salvation last year.
We should go on Oprah as the newest style
alternative family: two straight women as
"husband" and "wife," a bunch of orphaned zoo
babies as the children! They'd call it
"Women Who React Weirdly to Rejection." You
guys are my family and we'll always have
that connection, okay?

     Of course you'll be interested in my new
boss. If we had a boss like this at the
zoo, Sal, there'd never be a dull day, but
we might end up acting like two bitches
competing to be the one who gets to lick
the ears of the sole Alpha male, who would
rather spend his nights alone howling. You
know, the type of man who isn't Mr. Charm/
Personality/Could've-been-a-movie-star, not
even close, but it seems like women might
claw each other's eyes out over him. A guy
whose take on things seems so alien, but
all of a sudden he's smiling and your
greatest desire at that moment is that he'll

remember your name tomorrow. God, aren't
women _dumb_?

Really, though, he's about 40, I guess.
Maybe 45. You can't tell with these career
field biologists because they've been
outdoors all their lives. With so many sun-
streaked colors in his hair, impossible to
tell if there's any gray. The most gorgeous
set of crow's feet setting off his cloudy
green eyes, which one minute might sparkle
like a devilish imp, the next are overcast
with some sort of unhappiness. God, listen
to me. Anyway, the usual ruddy, nearly
leathery skin you'd expect, but these
amazingly beautiful hands, _little_ hands for
a man, slightly pinkish knuckles like he
just finished doing the dishes for his June
Cleaver wife who's off to the PTA. No, really,
he's not married. He _couldn't_ be, he's too
. . . . I can't even describe it. Like a shy
gawky 6th-grader who hits or trips or snaps
your bra strap to show he likes you, but he's
trapped in a grown man's body. You're
supposed to smile with nostalgic warmth at
the little boy, but glare with hatred at the
man. Only I can't. Or I can't mean it for
long if I do. He'll probably make me furious
a thousand times, but I think there's
something soft in him that he's afraid to
show. I know _that_ sounds clichéd, but it
makes this gauche, tactless, oddball guy
linger afterwards like someone exotically
attractive. (Another post-divorce symptom?)

Anyway take good care of our kids, don't
let my (blond?) replacement smile too
dazzlingly during the show (convince the kids
to mess up for her!), and I'll be in touch soon.

Love, Leya

3

DIM BEATING RHYTHM

```
FROM:        BRIAN LEONARD
ADDRESS:     WRANGLER INN, RAWLINS, WY
PHONE:       (307) 678-0990
FAX:         (307) 998-0550

DATE:        June 1

FAX TO:      031/45 33 31

ATTN:        PETER GALLWAY

# OF PAGES TO FOLLOW:   0

CONTENTS TO FOLLOW:      NONE
```

COMMENTS: First survey, aerial hom-
                 ing, located 2 maybe 3
                 animals (one signal very
                 weak), all female.
                 Roughly 1250 square miles
                 covered—Shirley & Seminoe
                 Mtns., around Seminoe
                 Reservoir on grid #1.
                 Just trying to plot some
                 preliminary possible
                 ranges for certain indi-
                 viduals, then each
                 animal's potential home
                 territory will be
                 searched until the cat is
                 located. Sources of food
                 appear to be no problem—
                 some elk, deer, pronghorn
                 easy to find. Sport-
                 photographer's paradise
                 this time of year.
                 Shooting's easy, no com-
                 petition (except the cou-
                 gars themselves, but
                 plenty to go around). Not
                 hunting season and no
                 tourists in on these dirt
                 roads.
                        Leonard

Within an oblique oblong area in the south-central part
of the state — an area that stops short of including the
three splotches of Medicine Bow National Forest on the
east, skirts the edges of the Shoshone and Bridger-Teton
National Forests and Flaming Gorge to the west, contains Rawlins but avoids anything else that passes for a

metropolitan center — dirt roads outnumber paved by a wide ratio, cattle outnumber people by a wider one, and deer and pronghorn might outnumber cattle. In the whole oval there're only two, maybe four, establishments that could be termed *Ranch Recreation* or get themselves listed in a Bed & Breakfast guide. Just west of Rawlins, the wasteland Great Divide Basin surrounded by the Continental Divide takes up about four thousand square miles in the middle of the oblong. The rest contains wild uninhabited hills and mountain ranges, some inaccessible wetlands, uranium and oil mining districts, empty badlands, and — for lack of any other gratifying term — rangeland.

It's prairie but not flat — the varicose veins of the Rocky Mountains. Where once the rangeland itself may've been jaggedly dramatic with towering vertical bluffs and deep gorges cut by an ancient flash flood, millions of wet or freezing or dusty storms have melted and softened everything except the horizontal cap in some cases, in others the whole bluff. Then while the flood plain became hairy with semiarid shrub, or even dense with cottonwood and willow where the creeks manage to trickle year round, the former bluffs remain sparsely grassy or nearly bare, sandstone or hard-packed dirt and rocks, eroded still more with every scanty rainfall, etched with foot-wide gullies running downhill, miniature replicas of what the soft bluffs themselves used to be. Here and there a butte or mesa may pose — mimicking the more colorful landscape of the Southwest, or mocking the wide, clean, spacious desolation here.

On a level grassy area between two of the rounded scrubby bluffs — which reach like fingers but don't come near touching the four-inch deep creek, miles away, buried in small dusty trees — coyote, three or four, maybe five, will gather to fight over, tear apart, gorge themselves on, and display dominance over the carcass of a young pronghorn chained to the ground. Their voices clamoring, the unmistakable chorus of laughing yips will carry sharply a mile in every direction, and if it were midnight or the small hours instead of 7 a.m., might seem a creepy, eerie echo of a war-dance, conjuring sensations of glowing campfires behind the hills, and beating drums. At very least, cause for a small rancher to lift his ear from his pillow and wonder. But just after dawn in clear light that's still mostly watery blue, their growls and yelps will simply signal an orgy over a cache of food discovered and won without a struggle. The raised, wailing muzzles will be bloody, likewise chins and chests matted and sticky. Even those individuals who must slink around on the outskirts, heads down, tails tucked, backs arched in the wounded dance of submission, will have blood on their cheeks and whiskers. Their world at this moment will be only as large as the circle of grass flattened around the cache, where they display, advance and retreat, yanking the tortured carcass back and forth on its tether. How many generations since any of their ancestors heard the drumbeat? Not that they would be unaware of other sounds — the snap or rustle of twigs that warn of joiners, or the impatient cry of buzzards and crows — but their caterwaul is as important as the raw greasy food, so the dim beating rhythm will mean no more to them than distant thunder, no greater than the harsh rush of wind over rocks and through grass or the pattering of rain advancing across the rolling prairie as a storm approaches. From some other, higher viewpoint, the animals moving back and forth and around the mangled meat will seem distinct and significant despite the wide-angle backdrop of shadowy, endless unfocused land and huge colorless pale sky. But, if the scene lasted long enough, it might also appear that the slowly increasing light, which makes the chaparral more specific and tints the sky blue, will seem to push their noise into the distance. And the thudding beat will grow stronger, seem faster, wind whips the grass, but they won't turn their heads to look behind themselves with the first twinges of alarm until it's eminently obvious this isn't the patter

of pronghorn hoofbeats nor the roar of an unseason-
able June blizzard. The chopper will rise like an enormous sun from behind the next hill, early rays glinting
then suddenly flaring off the clear bubble, and the crack
of shots begins.

Had she been screaming since he first started accelerat-
ing and skimming close over the hills and bluffs? If so,
there hadn't been sentences, maybe not even words, just
frenetic static, like a radio turned on too loud but not
tuned, until you suddenly find a clear station and a female voice that shatters glass: *"What the hell are you
doing?"*

The helicopter seemed balanced on the verge of
uncontrollable agitation. A canvas strap kept him attached inside the doorless chopper. Unused to shooting
in any position but the most stable — but now firing with
only his right hand, his left hand still on the collective
pitch lever, the main cyclic control stick held between his
knees, his feet working the directional pedals — he was
unable to maintain a peak level of precision.

"Take the lever."

"What!? Why're you *killing things*?" It was more
shrill than the characteristic shouting always necessary
for conversation in a helicopter. *And don't you feel like
screaming the same thing? Feel it, not fun, good sign.*

"Take it!"

"Which one! I don't know how!"

"Just *take it*. The one between us. Keep it *exactly* in
the same position. I'll take care of following them."

"Wait—" But her hand closed around the grip.

"Hold it steady." He was then able to momentarily
release the main control and use both hands for each
shot, afterwards his left hand could return to the stick
to steady the agitated chopper. Every time he shot he
leaned as far he as could to his right, his head out in the
thudding wind.

Her voice tore back and forth before it reached him.
"I don't know what I'm doing!"

"Just keep doing it!" He needed to reload but could
barely move his arm — it had somehow gotten wrapped
in the harness and his shooting sling. The telescopic
sight banged into his chin as the chopper rolled, churned
like an unbalanced washing machine, dropped suddenly then rose. But his eyes stayed cool on the blue
steel barrel, his fingers feeling for new shells from his
vest. She was beside him, but almost behind him as he
shot to his right out the door. He couldn't see if her
mouth was an open grimace, if tears streamed from feral eyes, if ropes were tight in her neck, if her face either
blanched or went red and what happened to the freckles in either case. The coyote seemed to be running in
slow motion across the prairie below — suddenly fixed
in his imperturbed radar no matter how the chopper
jolted and swayed. He couldn't see the bullets pop
through their hides, the little spray of blood at the en-
try point, the bigger one at the exit. They just crumpled,
motionless, one down six to go, two down four still running, three down, three getting out of range, four down,
the last two a parallel blur heading into higher brush.

"Help!" she shrieked.

"You're doing fine." The harness was twisted,
pulled tight, like firing in a strait-jacket. Yet the rifle was
fluid in his hands. When his eye went through the sights,
the rest of him followed. Everything was working prop-
erly: His heart counting the rhythm, his lungs filling
slow and low, his muscles loosening to accept the kick
of each shot, one hand engaging the bolt, setting again
instantly without disturbing the position of the rifle.
Each shot came off in sequence, even though the targets were fewer and farther away.

"Jesus-fucking-christ, you're fucking insane, I can't—"

He cut her off with a final volley of shots. Like an
extension of his arm: *when you're in the zone, like you can
reach out and touch the target gently with one finger; all the
body control and precision, the concentration, the calm focus*

may as well be drugged serenity. A milky warm cocoon, both mind and body, difficult to have to leave it.

He tried to turn one way or the other. "The damn thing's all twisted. Unhook me, okay?"

"Are you crazy—you'll fall out!"

"Dammit, do what I say!"

When she unsnapped the harness, the release of pressure was almost a pop. "I think I got five. Pretty shitty." Both hands back on the controls, he took the chopper higher, made a U-turn, returned to land and retrieve the tails.

A major indication? The initial test just to see if you could stay in the zone with her beside you, ended up testing more than her mere proximity. Scared out of her fucking mind, but you were NOT MOVED by her hysterics, had yourself in hand like a precise oiled pistol, every impassive spring and pin in perfect position, every indifferent crumb of powder accounted for, doing the job, letting her scream, you stayed sharp, stayed focused, stayed unimpassioned. And she's fine.

Okay, she's out of her visionary-wildlife-conservationist mind spitting-mad at you, arms folded, her chin jammed forward, her chisel-point eyes aimed dead ahead. Sorry, but, in retrospect, it WAS necessary. The horrified, panicked girl flailing at images of her own violent death, three feet away, and you STAYED IN THE ZONE. What could be a better experiment or a more legitimate result? Proving again that the shooting keeps you sane. Knowing that, now maybe you can become that biologist she reveres so mightily. Daktari, keep the rifle with you.

But wait, this test isn't over.

The rotors left in motion, even on the slowest speed, he still had to shout. "Go get them, okay?" Two fingers over each eyeball, rubbing gently, didn't look at her.

"What?"

Took a knife from a sheath attached to his belt, passed it from right hand to left, then, holding the blade, still not looking at her, extended the handle toward her. "Go get the tails."

"What for?"

"Proof."

"What the hell— *You* killed them, *you* go get the tails." She actually pushed at the knife handle and he felt the blade in his palm.

"Careful."

"Sorry, but unless you explain to me just how this is part of a wildlife study, I'm not going to follow blind instructions, especially concerning a bunch of animals you just slaughtered for no reason."

"Okay, okay, okay, Jesus *Christ*."

Pretend they've been drugged, and you're going out for data. Chopper noise blasting, its wind blustering, always makes for the ingredients of melodrama, like a rescue mission or evacuation. The whole way walking to the first carcass, he stares down at his palm where he can feel but not see a thin pressure-line caused by the blade when she batted the knife away. *Say all the old things: vermin, pestilence, their-life-or-yours. Take it easy, it's already done. Stayed in the zone, before, that's all that matters.* The thumping chopper fainter and fainter, its gusts now mere puffs of air. The coyote are scattered literally hundreds of yards apart. *You've seen dead things, you've touched dead things, but they weren't your own creation.* The same each time he approaches. Musky gray fur blows quietly in a breeze. Fixed eyes, dark but still clear. Mouths half open, glistening, gums pale. Lips pulled back from essential teeth, some worn, some youthful. Tongues lolling into the dust. Occasionally blood seeping out like drool, soaking into the sand. Buzz of flies already seeking to deposit gluey eggs in still-moist mucus membranes. *Easy easy easy easy easy. Breathe deep, not shallow.* The neat hole, sometimes two, nearly undetectable in matted fur, back of the head, temple, chest, spine. Limbs limp, crumpled beneath or splayed. Body covering the leak of blood. At times no blood at all. *They call it a clean kill, but you can smell it.* Waxy, hot, greasy, fetid, muggy. The base of the tail heavy, thick, the knife cracks bones, a sound like collapsing, each time, each one. But he stays on his feet.

Easy easy easy easy, get your mind back on paper, back in the fieldbook, take note: maybe it's okay you lost the zone this way, strayed momentarily from the calm eye-of-the-storm, killing shouldn't be comfortable, can't be therapeutic. You're fairly sure this agitation isn't tinged with thrill or deranged desire. It could be another response that you needed to discover, a second indicator the test wasn't even designed to produce, a subsidiary result the scientist hadn't the foresight to realize would be linked to his primary question.

He reached to open the door for her, but she knocked his arm away and went into the tavern ahead of him. An older man was sitting on a stool, a waitress singing softly while she poured orange juice for him. *Okay, the grin you want is devil-may-care. Turn away. Practice.* Brian stopped at the counter for two beers before joining Leya at the table she'd chosen. Arms folded, foot tapping, eyes averted, lips pressed, a tiny crease above her nose, her eyebrows wings in flight. As if mounting a horse, he swung a leg over the back of the chair before sitting. "Okay, young lady, let's talk lions."

"No," she turned on him. "Why are you shooting coyote. You're *some* biologist, killing—"

"Did you know a pack of as few as three coyote can usurp a lion's kill?"

"Is that why you're shooting them?" Like the sound of a big bird landing slowly, her voice seemed to flutter and soften.

"Just an auxiliary benefit."

"Well," she bristled again, "I don't know how I can work with a biologist who—"

"I have to earn your salary somehow." He noisily sucked foam from the top of his beer. "Let's negotiate. Fifty bucks a day? Make it sixty. That'll cover room and board, right?"

"Just. That motel is like forty."

"It's over minimum wage, and tax free." He sipped again, watching her over the rim. She finally loosened her shoulders and reached to touch the mug he'd filled for her. "So far you're not doing too much," he smiled. "When you start to *do* more, you'll earn more."

"I flew the helicopter today." Her voice a defiance, a challenge. But then her lips relaxed, color returning. She looked down into the beer, looked up, smiling. "I did, didn't I? Sort of."

"You did." He slid his mug over and touched it gently to hers. "Sort of. And you'll get better. So maybe $75 a day, that more like it? When I can get it. Got rent to pay back home?"

"No. I was living with a girlfriend. You know . . . didn't want anything around me that was left over from . . . the holocaust." With both hands she swept some loose strands of hair back toward the French braid, a deep breath and a sigh. "Here we go again, too dramatic, I know, and I promised I wouldn't talk about it, didn't I?"

"People just aren't as territorial as cougars, that's all. Nor as solitary. Maybe they should be." He looked at the jukebox, cold and dark. It was just after 10 a.m. "'Lord of stealthy murder, facing his doom with a heart both craven and cruel.' Teddy Roosevelt's take on cougars . . . . I did my homework." The guy at the bar was eating pancakes and eggs, the waitress changing channels on the TV. "When cougars fight, it's a sign of something — not always something *wrong*. Isn't that true of people?"

"I don't know." He could barely hear her. She used a cocktail napkin to dab at a spot on her jeans.

"With cougars, the reasons could be anything from territorial instability to . . . natural selection, the young taking over. You want me to play something?"

he gestured toward the jukebox. Leya shook her head without looking up. Brian glanced around at the unlit neon beer signs. A crisp oily fried-egg smell arrived, as though on a breeze, and feathered out. "Sometimes the loser's skull is literally crushed. There's hardly ever a good time for them to be at the same place at the same time."

"Except how would they reproduce?" She turned her head away from him, bent for a second to touch the napkin to one eye.

"Even then. I understand you can hear it for miles. And it goes on for days." With one finger, he twirled an ashtray in circles on the hard tabletop. "The male cougar has to do his copulating with the female's vicious, violent screaming in his ears the whole time." The ashtray went faster, making a faint overtone like a loon's call. "It must drive him *on* somehow, otherwise why wouldn't he just leave her alone. So, I guess sometimes he just snaps and lets her have it." Abruptly the ashtray escaped his finger, skidded off the table and landed with a clanging fanfare on the floor. Leya jerked upright. "Luckily," Brian bent to pick up the unbroken ashtray, "in a field study, you can tell who's doing all the killing, and, if it starts to be a habit . . . I don't know, remove the trouble-maker? I haven't been asked for my opinion."

"How . . .," she flexed her shoulders like a slow shrug — like just waking up — then relaxed, turned and looked at him, her eyes red-rimmed but dry, "how do you know which one . . . ." The words didn't waiver or wobble.

"The radio collars." He surveyed the ceiling fans which were not yet moving. "We can locate an animal's transmitter from up to sixty miles away. So we would know when two lions come together. If it's two males, they'll be fighting. When one doesn't move for six hours, the collar changes to the mortality signal — you know who lost, so you know who won. He'll probably hole-up somewhere to recoup. But he'll at least move — lick himself, flick his tail, change position." His lower teeth bit his upper lip, then let the lip escape. His teeth snapped softly together, his jaw popped out of joint then back in. At the same time the pungent warm scent of maple syrup hit a nerve right there. "We won't have to worry about this, but if it's a male and female together . . . well, there's no other reason for them to *be* together. So, if reproduction was part of your study, you would know when the litter was conceived and who the father was."

"Without ever seeing anything."

"Welcome to the field." He saluted her with his beer, then drank several gulps, suppressing a wince. "Every time you catch a cat, they get harder to catch the next time. So unless we have to snare and drug an animal to change the battery in its collar, we may do this whole job without seeing *any* of them." His jaw ached. He put his hands, the fingertips, at the joint on either side of his face. The guy at the counter asked for another stack of pancakes. "Gallway just wants the data: where they are, at least one point on the map for each lion each week—preferably every other day—so he can shoot the sightings into his computer and get a reading on probable ranges, home territories and how the population is handling the relocation, how far they've established themselves, or if they've disappeared altogether."

"What about the young?" She sounded hollow.

"Like I said, we don't have to worry about that. Our relocated lions are a different sub-species from the indigenous population, so reproduction could be a disaster. They've all been sterilized." He glanced at the jukebox again. "We should be drinking coffee and listening to *Stand By Your Man*. Beer tastes like sour mouthwash this early."

She flipped an invisible wisp of hair out of her eyes. "What's the point then?"

He laughed out loud, but it didn't sound right. "Good question, since no one will ever actually attempt to re-populate a region with animals from a different part of the country — there're over twenty sub-species if you count South America. Mixing genes and destroying a sub-species . . . no one would risk it." The second stack of pancakes were sizzling in butter, the thick cakey scent making the beer in his stomach feel like a wound. "So this study is just to see what happens if you *did* transplant a population of animals to a completely new region. Will they settle in and establish the same size home territories, or will they just remain like adolescent transients until they're eventually killed off by each other, or indigenous cougars, or hunters, or unfamiliarity with the terrain, or . . . ."

"So we just fly around and make dots on maps?"

"Basically. Dots with dates."

"Great, even when I make a huge step, go somewhere and try to *be* something more stimulating, I'm just . . . ."

"Out flying a chopper while a crazy man shoots at things running on the ground!"

She smiled, shallow and faint, her eyes glazed, staring at nothing. "Yeah, if *that's* not *stimulating* . . . he may have Elvira, but *I've* got Indiana Jones."

"Excuse me, but, what're you talking about?" Brian got up to take his half-empty beer mug to the bar. The TV was playing a talk show where several people were speaking at once, each trying to be louder and faster than the other. He nodded at the old guy wiping up yoke with a fork, lifted the coffee carafe from its hot plate, hooked his finger into two mugs from the stack on a tray, and returned to his chair.

"Sorry." Leya slid both hands across the table and cupped them around a mug while he poured coffee. "I thought I left all that back home, but . . . ." Another sigh. "Apparently not. But I don't want to sound like I'm blaming *you* for not being . . . the answer."

Brian leaned back, holding his coffee under his chin, forcing the steam to rise and separate around his jaw. "I'm *no* one's answer." His words quiet. He could feel the cold tails in the hunting vest's pouch, a congealing lump between his spine and the back of the chair. "But, strictly speaking, Leya, answers aren't part of this job. Not for us. I'm not here to determine *why* the animals attack each other or wander around without killing prey or decide to live in downtown Rawlins instead of the seven-thousand-plus square miles of habitat they were given. Whatever they do, it's got to mean *some*thing. Gallway didn't hire me to do any analysis, but I guess he can't *stop* me, either. Maybe it would do us both good to not think about — not even talk about — anything else, just give every calorie of energy to the cougars who've been dumped in these scrubby, empty hills." He leaned forward and shifted the lump of tails away from his spine.

The guy at the bar put some money down and left. A fly walked in the egg yolk and syrup left in the plate.

"I think I know you a little better now," she said, her lids half lowered, sipping her coffee.

"Shit, are we doing *that*?" he grinned. But his gut made an inaudible moan. He slipped one hand under the table to press against his abdomen. Nausea rose. *Easy easy easy.* He shut his eyes and it subsided.

"Have you ever been married, Brian?"

"Me?" He opened his eyes, put a hand over his mouth, tried to laugh, but it sounded like a stuttered groan. "What a horrible idea." He bit his knuckle. The waitress brought a black plastic tub to the bar and loaded the slimy dishes into it. His teeth found a sliver of loose skin, then peeled part of his cuticle away.

"It *is* a horrible idea, for *any*one." Leya raised her voice over the clatter. "It teaches you to trust somebody . . . above everyone else on earth . . . and then *that's* the person who decides you're a contradiction to his *growth* as a full human being . . . ." She grimaced after another swallow of coffee. "A fucking *accountant*, Brian, but he was discovering new *areas* of his mind that *I* couldn't help *fertilize* . . . or whatever crap . . . . That's what marriage does, tells you you're not stimulating enough, you don't *enrich*, you don't *enhance*, you're basically just a hundred-twenty pounds of *cells*, taking in fuel, putting out waste."

Brian took a little packet of sugar in both hands, bent it in the middle, back and forth. He was breathing shallowly, stopping each breath before it was deep enough to touch what felt like a bright spot in his stomach. A tenderness, or queasiness. Or deformed hunger. There was a granola bar in his vest, but it had been there over 24 hours now, it might smell of his own sweat . . . or dead coyote. *Easy . . . easy.*

She snorted a short laugh. "It's actually funny. One of his clients was an art supply store. So there's a cashier he meets there who convinces him she's an *artiste*. She gives him her frumpy works-de-art — made from faded school construction paper, paste, and dried navy beans — wears long black dresses and crystals on chains and pointy-toed black boots, weighs in at 240, 250, brings him to lectures on herbal healing, meditation for mind expansion, concerts for hand-made wooden flutes accompanied by finger-bells and tambourines, and tells him it was a contradiction of his newfound inner self to be married to *me*. He needs to *recreate his personal space*, she says . . . so her kindergarten art is on our walls, our bed sent to the Goodwill to make room for the futon they put down on the floor, my books and records mysteriously disappearing one by one, electric appliances turn up missing when I go to use one — all this before I even know she's *in*, I'm *out*; before I'm even *informed* what a contradiction I am, what *deadweight*, what *inertia* I create." Her voice a tight, suppressed scream, directed at the tabletop in front of her. "And I'm going along, *moronically* oblivious, until the day *she moves in!* He's says that's just proof of the basic fallacy of our relationship in the first place, how we're *spiritually* out of sync, and that *I didn't belong there anymore!*" She was panting, her fists balled on the edge of the table, leaning forward, staring into the oily glaze on the surface of her coffee.

The sweetener packet broke in half in his hands, creating a little explosion of sugar up toward his face.

He swept it into one palm. Looked down at it. Thought of touching it with his tongue, but it might feed the bright hotspot in his guts. "I'm sorry that happened to you." His voice surprisingly rich since his heartbeat felt like it took several jerky breaths. He looked at her glossy eyes, still staring at her coffee; her hands now open, the small soft-looking fingertips slowly touching each other; a spot of hushed color marking the point of each tiny cheekbone; her very white earlobe, barely bigger than a drop of water; her lips dark and swollen. Then she touched her lower lip with one finger.

"But it's not happening to you *still*," he said.

She closed her eyes. The lids were engorged, reddish, the color on her cheeks deepening, the skin around her nostrils almost transparent like a baby.

He crossed his legs, thought he smelled the feral musk of the coyote tails behind him. And the nausea buzzed again, rose like bile, cramped his gut, everything in his ribcage closed like a fist. "Okay," his suddenly high voice surprised him, "so *now* do you want me to play *Stand By Your Man*?"

She laughed through glinting tears, put her hand on his arm. When he jerked, the sugar in his hand flew as though he'd tossed confetti. The waistband of his baggy canvas pants felt like a thin-roped noose around his middle which someone was yanking tighter and tighter. A spasm in his stomach, he almost retched. His boot kicked one of the table legs, jarring the mugs so the coffee sloshed over the rims. His chair skidded backwards, then tipped and fell as he jumped to his feet, grabbing a napkin to catch the rivulet of coffee heading for the edge of the table.

Leya was also standing, mopping coffee.

"Good thing I didn't have the map out yet," he said breathlessly, backing away from the coffee dripping from the table to a spattered spot on the floor. "I'll let you take mine back to your room, to familiarize yourself with the three areas where the cougars were released, you can't miss them, in neon highlighter, twenty-five hundred square miles each. And just to ease your mind, the places we'll hunt the coyote are highlighted in pink. No overlap." *Visualize, visualize: see yourself holding the rifle, cradled in your arms across your body, the way hunters do when they meet in the woods.*

"If it's because of the money, Brian, I really wish you wouldn't do it. We can figure out something else."

The waitress held up a mop and raised her eyebrows. Brian shook his head. It made him dizzy for several seconds. He stuffed his wet napkin into the coffee left in his mug. "If it bothers you, you don't have to come along for the coyote. I can do it alone."

"That's too dangerous." She glanced at the coffee-soaked napkin she held in her fingertips. "I can't really understand why you're doing it. It's *not* the money, is it?" It seemed to take forever for her to place the wet napkin gently on the table and draw her hand away.

Perhaps serendipitous, your impromptu plan for how to make the locals trust you, now you're pretty sure it's a test that has to be repeated, not only to be sure shooting keeps you in the zone, but to see if there's adjustment, how easy it gets, and does ease turn to pleasure?

He wiped his palms slowly down the front of the hunting vest, needed to sit but his chair was still lying on its back. The nausea was something else . . . like a toothache in his groin — like too much maple syrup on a cracked molar.

"What would happen," she asked, "if people found out a wildlife biologist was shooting coyote while on a field study?"

"I'd never be Daktari."

"What's this Daktari thing? Some sort of wildlife-biologist ranking?" She was chuckling, more like a giggle, her fingers once again pushing tendrils of hair off her brow, then her hand stayed on her face as though feeling for a fever.

He tried to share her smile, but, his own face hot, could only right the chair and let his suddenly feeble knees buckle.

Review: (Forget for a minute your swoon over the deaths you created, it doesn't change this.) After mastering neutral tranquillity this morning with her four feet away believing she was fighting for her life . . . next a stock orientation briefing . . . okay, slightly more than that, a harmless conversation in a bar . . . and you can't maintain or reestablish the previous calm. Any other time you might've leapt for joy to be with her that close, that long, and only show that much inappropriate unease. But now it's a contradiction. It means your short-lived euphoria before she put the chopper down was way too early, the brief sense of freedom a MISTAKE.

Every field scientist at one time makes this immature error: to let yourself actually believe it's over and the triumphant verdict attained so easily. But in every bit of data gathered, even the inconsistent, SOME*thing's got to be gained. Go back over it slowly, step by step. Was there too much going on at once? Were you still overwhelmed by the neat accuracy of your bullets finding their prey? What did she do, what did you do? Objectify. Where were your hands, where were your eyes? Is this an account of a predatory psycho seething under the surface, or just a pleasantly affable, but socially inept guy . . . or is there a difference?*

Prescription: no more patter, no more personal exchanges, not even amicable small talk. Tell her again and mean it this time. Test the physical proximity only. Simplify the experiment to limit the number of variables affecting the outcome. And use your analytic mind, look at the data, the details . . . there's almost always an explanation somewhere, a reason, a hypothesis, something present when you were beside her in the chopper that was missing later on in the bar . . . . OF COURSE, *you already noted it:* THE RIFLE. *Did you forget already? But do you have to* BE *shooting? How long can you maintain the quiet afterwards?*

They say each serial predator's victim is his own mental suicide, each killing a suicide gesture. Why not just shoot your own balls off? A bloody apocalypse, if this study leads to

an indisputable conclusion. But that's a promise made by a
subject whose balance, while always tentative, is still intact.
Just keep the rifle with you, with a pre-assigned target avail-
able. And remember the secondary test: Can you kill dispas-
sionately? Perhaps both questions can be put to use with
simple psychology: Redirect the impulse.

After a shower, he changed into cut-off jeans, sandals, and a T-shirt. His towel-rubbed, finger-combed hair rose and lightened as it dried, shaggy around his ears and neck. The coyote tails were transferred from the vest to a white plastic shopping bag.

At first the taxidermist just glanced up and nod-ded, then went back to dusting the nostrils of an elk head mounted over the cash register. Brian put the shop-ping bag on the counter. "Help you?" the taxidermist said, stuffing the rag in his back pocket. "Oh, barely recognized you. The hat really set you apart."

"Sometimes you feel more like blending in."

"I gotcha. How many here?" He fingered the lump in the bag.

"Five."

"That all?"

"There'll be more."

"Well, here, I got the money in back."

While the taxidermist was gone, Brian took a box of shells, placed it on the counter. There wasn't much available space for anything new between all the deer, elk and pronghorn heads, flying game birds and jump-ing fish mounted on the walls. Tacked all over the ceil-ing were mass-produced wildlife posters, a wolf pow-dered with snow gazing from a thicket, whitetails with their flags erect, fox kits peering from a den, a sky full of wild swan. Then the taxidermist was back, paused in the doorway to the back room, said something to someone working in there before shutting the door and handing Brian four twenties. "You're five bucks ahead."

Brian put one of the twenties on top of the box of shells, pushed it a few more inches toward the register.

The taxidermist grinned, fingering some long hairs growing from his earlobe. "Hey, if you got time, Harry Hathaway wanted t'meet you. Lotta times he visits his mother in the afternoon. I can see if he's there."

Brian tapped the box of shells, so the taxidermist finally rang up the sale. "Who's Harry Hathaway?"

"Only rancher around exclusively in horses."

"The big guy?" Brian turned away, leaned back against the counter, looking at the ceiling poster nearest the front door, a white rabbit being pursued through the snow by a bobcat. "Met him already."

"Well, he don't know that," the taxidermist dropped the box of shells into a tiny brown paper bag. "Yeah, big man, mustang's strong as a mule, but the thoroughbreds, you know, those little ankles, no bigger'n your wrist, he knows he'd break 'em down too fast . . . that's a frustration t'him, 'cause he just started in thoroughbreds about five, six years ago." The taxidermist picked up the phone. "I'll try over to his mother's."

Brian wandered down an aisle, picked up each style of bird-call whistle, read the instructions on a boxed electronic dog-training collar. Strange that the shop was without a mounted jackrabbit head with pronghorns added, like the ones Brian had seen in the motel lobby, in the convenience store, in a barbershop he'd passed, and in the gas station. He still hadn't eaten and had promised himself an unencumbered lunch of steak and all-you-can-eat salad bar. When she got out of the Bronco at her motel, Leya had mentioned something about dinner, but he hadn't given a coherent answer.

"Hey, he says come on over," the taxidermist called from the counter. "Two-twelve Walnut, just round the corner, past the old prison."

Brian let the screen door bang shut behind him without answering.

The big guy came out onto the porch. *"You're* the hunter?" He was wearing a short-sleeve Hawaiian shirt and held onto the screen door until it softly sighed shut.

"Yeah, and I'm no rider." Brian felt his eyes crease — squinting, not grinning. Then he added the smile. "But look," gestured toward his feet. "No polish on my nails."

Hathaway laughed. "Y'looked more like a hunter *then*, but, hey, I was a little blitzed."

"Before you came into the bar?"

"There's more'n one bar in this town — y'may've noticed." Hathaway sat on the porch bench, painted green but peeling, showing gray underneath. "I guess I don't hafta introduce myself, then. You're hunting coyote . . . ." He leaned back, hands behind his head, legs stretched and separated, boot heels caught on a slight crack between porch boards, brown denim jeans as tight as sausage skin. "But y'know what else kills stock?"

Brian tipped himself backwards against the porch rail, crossed his bare ankles. The sun, although he was squinting into it, was drowsy — as though *it* was what made the long sweet melancholy sound of the train whistle.

"I wanna show you something, but it's out at my place. Tell you what, I'll bring it in and put it in Andy's freezer at the taxidermy."

A wind chime hanging above Brian's head tinkled. "Can you just tell me so I know what we're getting at here?" The wind chime was pieces of pottery in the shapes of roadrunners and cactus. Another chime was made of rusty horseshoes. There wasn't enough breeze on the porch to move it much, but each horseshoe slowly rotated.

"Well, as long as you're out hunting . . . I may want to hire me a hunter too. But it won't be as easy. I need a special kinda hunter. Y'gotta know wha'cher doing."

Brian laughed mildly and looked down the street. The same banners for the rodeo and state fair bowed in the breeze. "Does *any*one know what they're doing?" His voice soft and sonorous.

"About two years ago, someone brought more cougar in the area." Hathaway sniffed and cleared his throat. "Know anything about that?"

"Government thing?" Brian continued gazing into the street although the hair on his legs prickled slightly. He smiled lazily.

"Hell, I don't know. But I lost a newborn, a thoroughbred — know what it costs to breed a mare and bring her through gestation? Then she drops a perfect foal, a colt, the next triple crown for all I know, know what I mean? But I find him torn to ribbons in a near paddock. Close's you can get to my house. Brood mare didn't even have time to scream. Stupid bitch could've kicked his head in, but instead nearly broke her leg trying to jump *out*."

"She was afraid, poor girl." Brian slowly turned back to face Hathaway. The sun glinted, but he didn't raise his hand to shield his eyes. The train's whistle sounded again, farther away.

No wildlife poster goes so far as to show the yellow-eyed feline with blood caked on its whiskers, steam rising from a mangled twitching corpse as the cat tears away fresh muscle engorged with the last gush of adrenaline-laced blood, the fear that was supposed to keep the prey alive. Warning labels attached to nature films that have the audacity to include the unpardonable stalking and slaying of a doe. Loathed for being a beautiful and perfect predator. Amoral drifters, too close to society, tracked with dogs, snared and drugged and caged and shipped in the dark until — their own bodies aflame with fear — released, in lieu of incarceration, 2000 miles from home in wickedly barren, impassable places like the Haystack Mountains and Rattlesnake Hills.

"If that's not enough," Hathaway dropped his hands to his knees and sat up, then leaned forward, "a six-month-old ripped up so badly, had to be destroyed. Like the deranged cat took *bites* outta him while he's still *alive*."

Brian took a deep breath. *"Everybody loves the sound of a train in the—* What's the name of that song?"

"You hearing me, buddy?"

Brian smiled gently and reached to touch the road-runner wind chime. "I was working in New Mexico, trains right outside my window all night, got so I had to go to a record store and sing it to the clerks. *—the sound of a train in the distance—everybody thinks it's—"* He hummed the tune softly for a moment. "Not the same feel as Chopper in the Distance, though. That's a song *I'll* have to write."

"What were you doing in New Mexico?"

The wind chime moved for a minute without making a sound. "Same as here. Looking for an uncomplicated place to train for competition."

"You know anything about cougars?" Hathaway lit a cigarette. "I doubt you'd hunt 'em from a chopper."

"Yeah . . . probably not." *Visualize the slow undulation of tawny shoulders — the only thing visible moving through dawn-tinted chaparral. Beautiful.* Brian turned to prop his back against the support beam, put one foot up on the rail. *You can see yourself looking into the quiet remorseless amber eyes for a long motionless moment, admiring each other, then the blur of fawn-colored strength, a slow-motion graceful leap, and you'd each be alone again.* "A hunter might need dogs if he had to track them into alpine terrain." Laced his fingers together around his bent knee.

"This could eventually pay off handsomely." Hathaway's words and a shot of smoke came out together.

"Eventually? What's that mean?"

"Eventually it's . . . . It's not *just* hunting. I usually try to accomplish more than one thing at a time."

Singing again, his voice airy, *"Negotiations and love songs— da-daaaa dee-dee daaa dee-dee —one and the same.* Sorry, same song, it just goes round and round."

"But, rough estimate, wouldn't be any less than five hundred." One foot up on his other thigh, Hathaway gingerly trimmed ashes against his boot heel.

"Tracking's tough work." He massaged the back of his head against the post.

"What about snares?"

"What about 'em?"

"Ever use 'em?"

"Doesn't seem a fair fight that way, does it?"

"Wasn't fair to my foal either."

"How long ago that happen?"

"'Bout six months. Less."

"What about a depredation permit? There doesn't have to be a hunting season to legally shoot a threat to livestock."

"Not interested in waiting and watching, can't spare the time, and I never was much'uva hunter." Hathaway shot smoke from his nostrils. "B'sides, I can get a bigger return. I can tell you more, if you're interested."

Brian moved his folded hands to the top of his head where the sun made his hair warm. His lids half closed, he blinked slowly. "Damn song's putting me to sleep," he smiled. *The thought that life could be better— la-laaa la-la laaa da-da —into our hearts—and our brains.* Wasn't this one of the ones I heard through my sister's— Maybe . . . maybe not." He smiled at two dogs trotting purposefully down the sidewalk as though they had an important meeting to attend.

"I can guarantee it'll be more than five hundred."

You need to see where this goes. For the sake of the study, but more for those fugitive cats roaming the hills and badlands, preoccupied simply with finding enough to eat. It's as though they were put in the face of temptation to see just how fallible — or instinctively carnivorous — they are. And by virtue of their innate natures, they've failed their test. If you could give them back Wyoming, or their native California, as it was 500 years ago, in a heartbeat you would. Now you sound as romantically innocent as your pure-of-heart Leya. Should you make it your task to protect her vision — Daktari — and live up to it?

Brian swung his foot back down to the porch and sat up just after the dogs passed by on the sidewalk below him. "Let me think about it."

"That's all I want for now. We'll talk again." Hathaway stood and they shook hands. "Hey, Friday nights, come on down to the bar, bunch of us get t'gether, have a few, watch *Jeopardy*."

"Maybe I will."

FROM: BRIAN LEONARD
ADDRESS: WRANGLER INN, RAWLINS, WY
PHONE: (307) 678-0990
FAX: (307) 998-0550

DATE: June 3

FAX TO: 031/45 33 31

ATTN: PETER GALLWAY

OF PAGES TO FOLLOW: 0

CONTENTS TO FOLLOW: NONE

COMMENTS: Am looking into something which may mean bad news. Will update you as soon as I have any information. ʜere's my plan: will cover ▯rid from the chopper ▯y. That means each ▯every 3rd day. ▯ time between ▯ill remain uni- ▯alysis of indi- ▯ovement less vari- ▯ou'll start receiv- ▯pinpointed sightings ▯ a few days.

        Leonard

TVM6A
GOOD FOR ONE RIDE IN EITHER DIRECTION WITHIN 3 MONTHS FROM DATE OF SALE.
Not refundable after one year from date of sale.

SENIOR CITIZEN/ HANDICAPPED TICKETS
THESE TICKETS ARE VALID ON ALL TRAINS EXCEPT WESTBOUND PEAK TRAINS. PROPER IDENTIFICATION REQUIRED.

CHILD FARES
CHILD FARES APPLY ONLY TO CHILDREN AGES 5 THROUGH 11. SUBJECT TO REGULATIONS

Dear Sal,

                                    June 5

I'm sorry (not!) that Lil Sheba made
Safari-Barbie cry (and quit). Who'll they
bring in next? Careful, it'll probably be a
male-model surfer type who looks marvelous
in the khaki shorts but can't tell a sea
lion from a harbor seal. Give Sheba an
extra biscuit for me.
      Well, I think some of what I'm doing
here is sort of classified, but I'll
describe what I can. Guess what--I'm flying
a helicopter! Talk about learning new
skills. Can you imagine a man just _giving_
you the controls on your first day? He even
had to talk me into it. (Wouldn't take no
for an answer.) Now I'll fly the helicopter
at least half the time so he can shoot
videotape of general wildlife and landscape.
If there's a documentary of his mountain
lion study someday, at some later date he'll
have to bring in a film crew to take the
actual stuff he's doing with the lions.
(We'll see if I'm still here when that time
comes. Keep your fingers crossed!) Anyway,
it's absolutely breathtaking. The cleanest
pale-green prairie suddenly gives way to
one-sided bluffs strung along one behind
the next (like a line of dogs humping each
other), then on the other side maybe a flat
sand wash that goes forever, or a treeless
hard-packed desert (maybe a huge prehistoric
sea), or various groups of mountains that
range from low scrub hills to steep, bare
and sharp (rock-climber heaven). When we
find wildlife, that's when things get tricky
(and fun) because I have to keep the
chopper steady enough for him to get clear

shots, but the animals are running, so I
have to follow them. Mostly we've found
pronghorn, deer, and some coyote. But let
old what's-'is-name call my life limited and
unexplored _now_. That's the other thing,
Brian really helps me put things in
perspective and see _my_ value beyond just
what I couldn't do or be for Mitch. Sometimes
he says just the _right_ thing, Sal, and you
never know when it'll be, but waiting for it
becomes almost, I don't know, _ecstasy_. Okay,
I'll calm down. Don't worry, I didn't tell
him _everything_--I left out the part about
being no good in bed. And no, I'm not losing
my head or doing anything dumb like, as you
put it, rebounding. Really, we only work
together. We've had a few beers, no big
deal. He's pretty much, obviously, a loner.
Maybe that just makes him more intriguing.
I don't know what he's doing when we're not
working. I don't ask, he doesn't tell me,
but I'm sure curious. He has told me a few
stories about previous field work he's done.
I think he might've worked in Africa once,
but he seemed hesitant to admit it. His
nervousness is so pathetic, it's poignant,
and his strange sense of propriety is as
much a fragile vulnerability as it is an
irritant. Yes, he gets me mad and flustered
and confused, but then he says something
only _he_ could say, or smiles, or else
suddenly the light in his eyes dissolves,
and I want to touch his hand as much as I
was just wishing he would touch mine. Get
this: One time we landed to look at an
animal that was down, turned out to be a
coyote--a single carcass like that, I think
he needs to know why--but he wouldn't let me
go with him, thought it might get to me,

but when he came back, he was holding one
hand real weird and stiff in front of
himself, he'd gotten a little blood on
himself and he was acting like, I don't
know, he'd never touched blood before? That
can't be. It was weird, but touching. Don't
worry, I won't do anything rash. I admit, I
probably think about him more than I
should, but I distract myself by going on
walks and visiting some of the local
museums (a big old state prison with
electric chair!). I don't have a vehicle (he
does) so I can't go many places by myself,
and I'm not sure about asking him. But we go
to plenty of great places in the helicopter,
and soon we'll probably be going in to find
the cougars, up close and personal. So far
we just hear their radio signals and mark
their positions on the maps.

Well, I'd better go, but just for good
measure I'll turn the warning around to you:
if they hire a Ken-doll next, keep your
distance and your guard up. You know how
susceptible you are to youth and beauty.
And remind Lil Sheba, she only does her
high-wire walk for _me_!

Love, Leya

"No, I mean do you remember him?"

Who, dear-old dad? No. How do I even know if we have the same one? Except I would've seen yours buzzing around Mom. Unless of course she was out somewhere when she got knocked-up with you. Guess anything's possible, but who'd she leave me with? Did either of us ever have a babysitter? There's probably no one she would trust. No, we better face it, it's the same dude. So why don't I remember him hanging around much before she popped you out?

"Aren't there any pictures?"

Yeah, I think there's a glossy 8x10 of a test tube. Maybe she was artificially inseminated, she went and chose a dude from a list of statistics, leave it to her to find a perfect genetic subject to make sure she'd get herself some perfect children. And I'm sure she's thrilllllled with the results. **Mother, you had me, I never had you. Laaaa—la-la-laaaa—la-la-la-la-laaaa.**

"What's that from?"

Lennon. He gets real folksy-bluesy sometimes. Lennon meets B.B King and Leadbelly.

"Is that all you do all day, listen to records?"

I don't have any records, little bro. Contraband. Just a little radio — stuck with what they play on the stations I can get.

"No records at all?"

My friend, Paula — you know, the one with the clothes — she gave me a few tapes she made. Laura Nero, Billy Joel,

Dylan, Moody Blues, a weird mixture. **Nights in white satin—Goin' down the stoney end—Your sister's gone out, she's on a date—Lay lady lay—You just sit and home and masturbate—Nights in white satin— La-dee-da-da-da-daaa.** *Not bad, huh?*

"Hey, what're you doing down there, *growing*? Why'd you need so much room? I'm gonna need t'get some sleep, you know."

Oh I forgot, still a schoolboy.

"So, what do *you* do all day? Sit in your room and memorize songs, or maybe plan your trip to Africa and study biology?"

Sure, I dissect frogs. Ha ha. Mom'll never miss that steak knife, right?

"Mom can't *like* it that you just stay in your room all day."

Hey, didn't you know, I'm still grounded from when I got caught shoplifting in high school. Did I tell you about that?

"You can tell me tomorrow morning."

No, now's better. Well, we decided, Paula and me, to go somewhere besides school. You know, to the movies, to the beach, get something to eat, you would know, average-boy: average THINGS, things people do together. And you know what? You can do all of it in one place, Ocean Beach, so I told Mom I needed to go to the library downtown, and, miracle-of-miracles, she dropped me there without coming with me, I think 'cause you were sick at home, little bro, I think you being sick is what decided us on what night to try it. Anyway, Paula picked me up at the library, and we had three hours for an adventure in OB.

The movie alone would've eaten a big chunk of our time, but luckily we hated Deep Throat and left after 15 minutes.

*The first scene was pretty good, but the rest . . . not exactly
our dream thrill, you know? So we had tacos at this cool
Mexican place, then went down the street which dead-ended
at the beach. It was dark, of course, being that it was nighttime, but it's kind of eerie how the foam of the waves, the
white of the breakers, seems to be like dim lights, like anything we could see was because of the dim breaker lights,
slowly going on and off. We walked on the sand, trying to get
as close to people making out on blankets as we could, to see
how close would make them stop. I suppose we wouldn't've
looked away if we got a peek of anything either. Paula had a
flask but I knew well enough that Mom would've smelled it
from ten miles, so I didn't, but I pretended — I left the cap on
when I pretended to drink. Paula must've wondered how she
got so drunk so fast, but she did the whole flask herself. She
started to ask, real quietly, "how about a threesome?" or "want
to try a foursome?" whenever we passed a blanket in the dark,
I was laughing so hard, I was the one who threw up instead of
her. Lost my tacos on the beach. Mom would've smelled that
too, so we went back up to the street to get some gum, but went
into a head shop instead, or maybe by accident, I don't remember. All the good stuff was under a glass counter, unisex earrings and ear cuffs, roach clips and water pipes, knives, hand-
cuffs. Who would've thought a guy with hair and a nose like
the Wicked Witch of the North would care if we bagged some
Zig-Zags and one of those palm-held thingies that measure
your body-heat with bubbles in colored oil. You shoulda heard
Mom's heels clicking down that police corridor to where they
had me and Paula sitting on a bench waiting to be picked up
and screamed at. Luckily Paula's came first, so I was alone,
and I swore up and down — innocent hand on my heart, teary
eyes, the whole gamut — that I'd done the whole thing alone,
that I didn't know the other girl the police picked up with me.*

"You're not really still grounded for that. You could
leave if you wanted."

*Like I said, I got plans, don't you worry. What about you?
What're you gonna be when you grow up?*

"I don't know."

Haven't you been to that genius guidance counselor yet? They have this nifty test, questions like, What would you rather do, drive a taxi or arrange flowers? Play professional sports or bake pastries? Run a cattle ranch or serve cocktails? The choice is always so clear, separating the men from the pansies. She sure didn't like my answers.

"Didn't you tell her about going to Africa to work at a field research compound?"

Hell no. I just fucked with her silly statistics. Told her I really wanted to be a cement contractor or drive a bull- dozer or do auto wrecking — maybe even drive demoli- tion derby on the side. I think she tattled to Mom, which I knew would happen anyway, and Mom flipped out all over again.

"Why would you want to antagonize her like that?"

Yeah, she might've put me down a manhole or tied me to a backhoe until I promised to never work any job that wears a hardhat.

"Really, Di, doesn't she—"

Oh, Brian . . . . Never mind, it doesn't change anything. So how about you, what careers did you choose?

"We didn't have that test."

Maybe they only gave it to borderliners, those showing dan- gerous lurking characteristics.

"Of what?"

You know . . . hippies, radicals, feminists . . . all the other immoral rabble. C'mon, let's talk about you. What're your interests. Oh, we covered that. No career direction, huh?

"My legs are kinked up, I need to stretch out, could you move?"

How's that?

"Great, another inch, thanks."

Okay, I'll be your career counselor. Without a handy little test, I'll just have to figure out what kind of average guy you'll be. Don't have much to base my findings on, do I? I mean, little moon-faced melon-head who panted with your tongue hanging out the side of your mouth, crawling on hands and knees on a leash door-to-door and did puppy tricks for cookies and gave me the bigger half of every one, and believed me when I told you the reason Mom wouldn't let us have hamburgers was that ground beef was a cow's brains, and did every reckless stunt I invented for you on the tire swing 'cause I was too chicken to let fly myself. God, even AVERAGE *boys are a different breed from girls. So, will you be average job-man or average family-man, or average type-A hobby-man?*

"What's that?"

You know, the kind of guy who turns a sport or hobby into a career, or tries to or acts like it's one, maybe punches a cash register at 7-11 on the side, but every minute other than that he's on his surfboard or making a ship model or rebuilding a car or playing softball. So for a guy with such boring interests in high school, I mean, running in a circle and, what was it, future farmers—?

"Gamekeepers. It's just a group that plays games once a month. Used to be the chess club."

Don't tell me, your favorite is checkers.

"No, I—"

An average guy with such boring interests, he'll be the kind no one will ever believe had one glass of wine one night in his freshman dorm and ordered a monkey from a mail-order catalogue. But by the time the little shit is delivered, of course in a wooden crate, you've forgotten all about it, don't even have a cage, and the damn thing isn't even tame, will bite the shit out of your hand and arm if you try to touch it. And maybe this has nothing whatsoever to do with anything, but when you finally find someone to buy the crazy mean thing, it's the same guy who sells you a service rifle, your first one. But did the guy decide to buy the monkey and you found out he had guns, or did you decide to buy a gun and he found out you had a monkey? Was it a trade? The mysteries of Planet Brian. But what a beautiful piece of equipment, this M1 bolt-action Garand with .520 diameter hooded rear aperture. A blue brushed-steel barrel and extra fine-grained extra-light mahogany stock and forearm. A delicate pistol grip, thin as a girl's wrist, flaring smoothly but quickly into the heavy, but smooth-as-silk stock and thin black butt plate, a satisfying weight that balances itself easily in one hand hanging down at your side, or two hands across your body, and that cool, sleek barrel passing through a ring made of your thumb and index fingers, how beautifully unemotional.

And you want to be good. This is a new drive, to be good, to be really good, to be so good you'll be almost perfect. What a weird thing for average-man.

"Are you on something?"

What a straight little average man you are.

"Shut up."

Okay, but this is for your own good . . . 'cause all the other shooters at your first match are going to be lugging in a lot of equipment, scopes and stands and slings and mats and stools,

*and they have special jackets and gloves. And yet you, cool-
headed little bro, in the first stage, unsupported offhand position at 200 yards, time limit twenty minutes, you blow them
all away with 175 points out of 200. Twenty shots, sixteen of
them in the center ten-ring. Who is this guy, they're whispering. Second stage, you're a solid, unflappable Buddha in
the sitting position, two ten-shot strings, another 180 points,
you don't even feel the recoil, don't even hear the barrage, like
a war, like news clips of Vietnam with the TV turned real
loud — no, it's louder than that, but you don't hear it. Third
stage, rapid-fire prone, this time at 300 yards. Your toes and
elbows barely dent the ground, you barely feel the sights at
your eye, your hands so light on the forearm and trigger, you
could be flying instead of shooting, except when you dream of
flying, you're always flapping and flapping your arms and
barely skimming over the surface of the ground, you can't get
really, clearly, freely airborne. THIS is as close as you've come.*

*But you don't win, do you? No. Before the fourth stage,
600 yards, twenty shots in twenty minutes, you see a girl.
Someone's wife or girlfriend or daughter. Not all shooters are
men, but this girl isn't wearing one of the heavy leather shooting jackets, not gloved and no military-style sling. So what,
so it's a girl. Is she cute? Does she have long, dark hair? Is
she wearing a big T-shirt and a bathing suit bottom? At a
highpower rifle competition? Are you kidding? Why would
you think so? It's okay to like girls, little bro, you aren't the
only one who does. She doesn't do anything, doesn't even say
anything to you, maybe walks past with a cup of coffee —
decaf if it's for a shooter. And you blow your last stage. Not
really blow it, but only score 145 and come in third overall.
All because you were no longer a single-cell brain, know what
I mean? No longer the soaring but motionless Buddha, the
thoroughly fixed-focused picture of fluid concentration. It
wasn't as though you attended an all-male college, hadn't sat
beside girls in class or paid them for razor blades and candy
at the drug store. But it'll seem a wrong thing to be thinking
about a girl while you're shooting a gun.*

"Rifle."

What are you, some kind of wise-ass? Maybe there's hope for you yet. Yeah, your trainer saw hope in you, that's why he snatched you up even though you didn't win, even though after it was over, you'd started shaking a little, a tiny invisible vibration. It's okay, little bro. Nerves, you tell your coach. You want nerves of cold concrete — no, nerves of cold clouds. You want nothing less than sublime, ethereal, rarefied, aloof dead-on precision. Zen and the art of putting holes in a target from a thousand yards. Except he'll never use zen techniques, more like weight training, body building, sculpting your brain to fit in a tiny blue steel tube with no room for looking around.

It'll help, I guess, with school, studying and all, and with photography when you first start going into the wilderness and decide a rifle probably shouldn't be strapped across your back, and with flying lessons — like the time you have to fly under a bridge to miss a collision with a coming-out-of-nowhere crop duster, and your flight teacher loses his lunch. But you're the cool melon-head. That blue tube. A lot of guys have tunnel vision, but yours will be not only closely tended but secretly clutched like your blankie, and most of the time successfully concealed . . . you wise-ass.

4
IN ON FOOT

There aren't many spots in Wyoming where you can stand on the plains, prairie, or badlands and be without a mountain range in view. One of those few sites is on the floor in the center of the Great Divide Basin. The only place along the Continental Divide where the divide splits, circling the Red Desert, and takes two routes, just a slightly higher rim around this high shallow bowl where lakes are acres wide and inches deep all the way across. Where oil field workers need no roads to drive their pick-ups from one natural gas instillation to the next and wear hard hats to guard their heads only against the amount of unobstructed sky that's available in a four-thousand square mile-high desert basin. Cattle and pronghorn stand around a wind pump or beside the illusory lakes, staring stupidly at each other, but the wild mustang run and have roughly a hundred miles in any straight line to exercise their privilege. In the sky, the chopper restores a view of mountains in the distance. No better place to practice flying, to learn to keep at a steady altitude of about 75 feet and a steady speed of as fast as a wild horse can run, to rehearse turning gently and naturally when the animals veer and to follow their course without jolting the shooter, who's already going to waste enough shots in these imperfect conditions.

For several days in a row, several hours in the middle of the day — as she practiced landing and lifting, turning a circle to land again, lifting and turning around, lifting to circle wider, hovering, looping again, landing — all afternoon he would keep a rifle in both hands diagonally across his chest, muzzle toward the open door space beside him.

Then in a few days she was probably minimally skilled enough, finally understood how the collective pitch lever was different from the throttle, so he said, "Let's go find the horses."

"How? Where?" She hadn't yelled loud enough over the chopper noise, so he could only read her lips.

"Just like homing," he yelled. "Start with a big circle around the rim, then make each lap a slightly smaller circumference. If we don't find 'em they ain't here."

"You're not going to shoot *them* are you?" That time she screamed loud enough to hear.

And this time he spoke softly under the engine roar and beating blades. "Now why would I do that?"

"What?!"

"Let's go." He used the rifle to gesture upward.

Six or eight mustangs were clumped beside a trickle of water that the map called, appropriately enough, Sand Creek. They broke together, without seeming to be startled, just a smooth shift from standing and dozing into a rolling gallop. They'd seen choppers before. As they turned gradually south, then east,

Brian again used the gun to point, this time toward where the sky was plum-purple far beyond Rawlins. A needle of lightning danced for a second. Nearly invisible lines of water slanted out of a cloud but disappeared, vaporized before reaching the earth.

"We'll run them to death!" Leya shouted.

From above, the horses moved like cursors across a grid. "See how steady you can keep me."

"Huh?"

He pointed to the leveling device attached to the barrel of the rifle. "Keep me stable, I'll let'cha know how much the bubble moves." He stayed in his seat and aimed out the door space.

"No!" She grabbed the back of his shirt. The chopper veered, churned.

His body convulsed then quelled, hardened into position; kept his eye on the sights, trained on the ground where there were no longer any horses in sight, just the wheat-colored floor of the Red Desert. "Get both hands back on the controls," he said between his teeth. Long after she'd let go of his shirt, he was still aiming, and later, outside the Great Divide Basin, east of the divide and about fifteen miles northwest of Rawlins, he bagged four more coyote. *Easy easy easy . . . each one, just a target, just paper torn to shreds where your trained bullets, after being discharged from the barrel one by one, passed through the same four tattered square inches, as though seeking reunion. The target isn't your score, your victory. The target isn't your impassive precision.* They were just shy of the official border of grid #1, the most southerly of the three grids — the one that included two big reservoirs and which they'd homed that morning for the second time, looking for signals from the five cougars that had been released there.

```
FROM:          BRIAN LEONARD
ADDRESS:       WRANGLER INN, RAWLINS, WY
PHONE:         (307) 678-0990
FAX:           (307) 998-0550

DATE:          June 7

ATTN:          PETER GALLWAY

# OF PAGES TO FOLLOW:    4

CONTENTS TO FOLLOW:        Maps and sight-
                           ing locations
                           for June 4, 5,
                           6, and 7

COMMENTS:      Not every individual
               present and accounted for
               yet. A more pressing
               worry is female #4 (grid
               #1, maps from June 4 &
               7). As you can see, she
               hasn't moved in 4 days,
               but not picking up the
               mortality signal either.
               She's border-line juve-
               nile. Going in on foot
               to locate her and find
               out what's up. No news
               on the other development
               yet. Will update you when
               I know something.
                         Leonard
```

Returning two days later with five more tails and three
new dots for the map from grid #3, Brian dropped Leya
at her motel as usual, handed her a hundred dollars

and said, "Here, you worked hard, Friday's payday, go live it up tonight."

"Yeah, sure, with a *People Magazine* and carry-out chicken." She polished her watch crystal with the tip of a finger. "Have you tried that bar-b-cue place in town?"

He ran his hands from the top of the steering wheel down around each side, a motion like a circus strong man bending an iron bar. Repeated the motion with thumbs on the inside curve rigidly extended toward each other, his eyes trained on both thumbs, wagering which thumb he would choose to stay fixed on as his fists separated toward the sides of the steering wheel. Then realized his stalling for an answer *was*, to her, an answer. She sighed and got out of the Bronco. By the time he looked, he could only see the back of her white T-shirt and her daypack slung over one shoulder.

The taxidermist had a kid working the store. "They're all down to the Lincoln," he said, one fist in the other, popping each knuckle one at a time.

Brian left the Bronco in front of the hunting store, considered taking the rifle with him down to the tavern, then covered it with a blanket and locked the truck's doors. He entered the Lincoln Lodge during a burst of simultaneously shouted words or statements, followed by cheers mixed with groans. None of the eight or nine different butts and backs lining the stools at the bar noticed that he'd come in. Hathaway was closest to the TV, Jimmy at the other end, a hardhat beside his beer. The game show host presented another riddle, "Notorious for her appetites, this Russian queen has become a subject of folklore." Fewer shouted responses, and even less reaction to the answer given by a contestant. Stumped, four of them called out orders for another beer.

"She the one who fucked horses?" Brian said gently.

Almost every head turned. "Someone say somethin' about horses?" Hathaway shouted from the end. The game show played a rhythmic count-down music-box tune as the contestants wrote their final answer for the big prize.

"Everyone's heard of *farmboys* fucking horses," someone else said, "but how would a *broad* . . .?"

Jimmy raised his beer mug in silent greeting. The taxidermist swiveled all the way around and reached for the plastic bag of tails.

"I heard she had a stallion lowered onto her with a rigged-up scaffold." Brian moved in closer, accepted a beer from the bartender. "Story goes it broke. That's how she died."

"Well, if that didn't do her, his cock *woulda*," Hathaway boomed. Everyone smirked or grunted a low laugh or made a comment buried in the shuffle of three or four other comments.

"Oh, trail mix, never get enough'a *this*." Brian left his beer on a table and reached between two guys to dig into a bowl on the bar, then stepped back, holding a fistful of mix in one hand, using the other to lift a pretzel, nut or cracker to his mouth one at a time. "Hey this's quality stuff, you even got these puffed Japanese thingies."

"I don't have the kitty on me," the taxidermist said. "We can go back to the shop when the show's over and get you paid. How many here?"

"Five." Brian returned Hathaway's hand gesture of a pistol being aimed and fired.

"Don't have enough collected right now, we need another ante-up. Can you wait a few days?"

"For seventy-five dollars? Why not do a collection right now?" Brian was standing directly opposite the TV on the other side of the line of guys on bar stools. All of them remained turned in his direction now. He was the only one still facing the TV. He grinned, finished off the last of the party mix in his cupped hand, then did a thudding tap-dance step with his hiking boots, pirouetted, and bowed.

"That's quite a *babe* I seen you with. Your wife?"

He didn't know who'd said it, but answered anyway, "No, but she's thinking of starting a divorce-therapy group if anyone's interested."

"I'll give her therapy for a divorce!"

Amid some light flustered laughter, a guy asked, "So this's our hunter?" A scowling curmudgeon face right in front of Brian, hadn't spoken till now, could've been thirty or fifty.

"We're having a little . . . debate," Jimmy said to Brian as Brian drank from his beer and winked over the rim at the guy he didn't know.

"He likes you, Roger," Hathaway laughed. "So tell 'im your complaint."

"Hey, it's simple free-market logic," the guy returned to Hathaway. His boots were dusty, his Levi's acid-washed, his T-shirt had a faded football helmet printed on the front, his hands gnarled with calluses, a few places the skin had even broken open into dry cracks. Probably closer to thirty. "We could get a better price. With an open hunt, we easily get hundreds of carcasses for five hundred. And they covered over ten-thousand acres."

"We're more subtle," Jimmy said quietly. "And we've made a deal."

"They got bad press for that hunt," the taxidermist added.

"So the tree-huggers threw a tantrum. Big fucking deal."

"What, is there a home-on-the-range P.C. we're not adhering to?" Brian asked. Still no one had turned back to the television. Closing credits were rolling over the contestants and host having a friendly pow-wow on stage while the audience clapped and the theme music blared. The bartender turned it off. "Sorry, I keep forgetting my humor isn't P.C. either. Go on, you can take a shot at my soft skin if you want." He thrust one knee forward, pulled up the baggy pant leg, a pointed toe touching the floor, he flexed his muscle, the defined ridges stood up. "Look good to you, Sweetheart?"

The grumbler glared. One guy who hadn't said anything yet slid off his stool, adjusted his jeans, making ready to leave, but then retrieved his half-full beer from the bar and said, "I like our way better, but we could renegotiate. I'll agree to five bucks."

"We made a deal," Jimmy repeated, still quietly.

After a moment, the taxidermist said, "End of last winter around Gillette, they had an open coyote hunt with prizes for most and biggest carcasses. Drew about 200 hunters. Got national attention—the wrong kind— and the governor and state officials were bent outta shape about it."

"They thought the tree-huggers were gonna come after the whole state with scud missiles," the grouch said without smiling, although several others grinned.

Hathaway, sitting sideways to the bar, leaning forward, hands on thighs, arms braced, watching Brian steadily as though through binoculars, said, "If he'd still been here, our Dr. Wildlife-Professor woulda had a fuckin *cow*."

Brian glanced at Hathaway, showing him a brief silent laugh, but noticed that Hathaway didn't stop his staid observation. Now unusually silent. The two guys closest to him were the same two he'd been with before. They weren't doing anything in particular, but as though on cue when they saw Brian's awareness of them, they got up together and went to the jukebox. Then it was like the driving beat and rough-voiced lyric roped the others off into private two- or three-man conversations farther away to the sides, and at the same time put a brighter spotlight on Brian. —*went by your house the other*— *mother said you went away*— *wish I coulda been there*— He smiled, sat on a table, put his feet in a chair, without aiming his words at anyone in particular, said, "Sorry I missed *Jeopardy*. I could be good at it, if the right category came up."

As expected, Hathaway was the one who answered, "What's your specialty?"

"Oh, what you'd expect," he fingered the shells in his vest. "Firearms, shooting . . . and . . . stuff like that."

"What're you using for the coyote? Automatic?"

"Bolt action. Make it a fair fight."

Hathaway wiped his mouth with a cocktail napkin. "Let's go on down t'the shop with Andy."

"He said he didn't have the money yet."

"I got somethin' t'show you." Hathaway was off his stool, making his way past the other guys, tapped the taxidermist on the shoulder, motioned toward the door. Brian went out first and waited on the sidewalk.

A long gentle dusk was stretching across the sky. But thunderheads gathered in the west as though waiting for the lovely purple light to finish creating a serenity, a weakness in mood, before moving in. Normally the time of day of least intensity, by far, on this project or any of the ones before, as a member of a team. *Working with a team in the field, you do your job, your part, you don't do anything more than that; you don't veer off independently or you'll screw everyone else up. The normal threats in field work are time and money, either running out. Gathering raw data, poring over maps, making sightings and taking notes, trailing, photographing, categorizing, waiting, listening, waiting . . . but it's never been an investigation into* ANOTHER *guy's agenda. You never stopped to think about it, didn't worry about anyone else and didn't mind if they worried about you. Just like shooting, you never wonder about the guy shooting next to you — ten guys with high-power rifles to your right and left, coaches or kids or wives in the gallery, you weren't in solitude but always just took custody of* YOUR *immediate task: the target, the fffthup of the slug hitting the center. But now as though the threat of piling thunderheads could actually thwart your usual cool-of-the-evening aplomb or composure . . . .*

Their feet walked in unison.

Without any pretense that he was aware of it being another man's property, Hathaway led Brian into the gun store's back room. The taxidermist came in last with the sack of tails. "Excuse us, Andy?" Hathaway said politely.

"Sure. I'll give you what we got in the kitty for now, fifty."

"If we're changing the price, we'll just call this even."

"I don't know if that's what we're doing." The taxidermist shut the door to the back room behind himself as he went out.

There was one long table down the center of the room, divided lengthwise by a stainless steel trough. Hathaway went into the walk-in freezer which occupied one whole wall at the end of the room. Around the other walls, cabinets and drawers for tools, one set of shelves stacked with pre-stained wooden plaques for mounting anything from horns to heads to flying fowl or jumping fish. Another bookcase of nearly empty shelves held a few finished pieces with name tags taped to the plaques. Most sat on the shelves propped against the wall behind. There weren't any deer, pronghorn or elk heads, none were in season. A whole bobcat was stuffed, frozen, stalking prey with one front foot raised, poised in mid-step, glass eyes resolutely aimed. Between his fingers Brian twisted the fringe of fur flying from the tip of one ear.

Hathaway came from the freezer with a large bundle enclosed in a black garbage bag. Brian flinched when the bag hit the table like a rock. Then Hathaway untied the end and peeled back the plastic, exposing the small foreface of a newborn foal. "Ready t'see the rest? Got the stomach for it?"

"I don't *need* to see it."

The foal's nose was pinkish-white, the upper lip and nostrils raked by a cougar's claw, probably as the cat reached from atop the foal's back to sever the throat. One eye huge and staring, almost all white, the other a hardened deflated withered bag seeping from its socket, frozen solid to the cheek. Hathaway ceremoniously rolled the plastic further down, like a coroner unzipping a body bag. One ear was gone, and the foal's neck was indeed ripped open, the flesh bloodless, flaps laid open, shredded but barely eaten at; the two front legs broken, splintered bone piercing the hide. The back and sides repeatedly sliced by parallel talons, exposing ribs, hips, even the spine. The body cavity looked like it had been surgically opened. A loop of intestine protruded. One hind leg was missing.

"What my heart wants," Hathaway said, "is to do to that wildlife-guy what this cat did to my foal." He gently circled one formerly-velvet nostril with a fingertip. "But my head says, let's just get ridda the cougars again, and let's stop scientists from fuckin with rangeland, let's let ranchers do their business and vermin learn to stay outta the way." Abruptly he snapped the plastic back up over the dead foal. "I don't mind cougars living in the mountains. Hell, I love nature as much as the next guy. But they should just stay up there where they belong."

"Their territory . . . ." Brian took his fingers away from the stuffed bobcat and pushed his hands into his vest pockets. "I mean, *isn't* their territory . . . don't they live almost anywhere, in anything from alpine country to badlands?"

Hathaway shifted his weight, kept one foot on the floor, leaned on the table, one big hand open and flat on the covered body of the foal. "You tell me."

Adrenaline made a quick fist in his stomach. "Well, I've been reading . . . since we spoke." His fingers in his pockets were pinching tufts of fleece, ripping it loose. He also leaned back, but as though suddenly debilitated or exhausted, as though catching himself mid-fall against the shelves behind him. "Interestingly enough, it seems the alpine cougars tend to be more docile, less unpredictable, possibly . . . I've read . . . because food is more plentiful up there . . . and . . . maybe that's an explanation for what happened to your horse. A simple need to eat. You know, the food chain and all."

"Who's the asshole who wrote that theory?" Hathaway twisted the end of the plastic bag and tightened a wire around it, then lifted the bundle into his arms again. "Thousands and thousands of pronghorn out there. And he took *one* bite of this baby. One leg. Guess again."

Brian shrugged. A pair of flying quail mounted to a board and propped against the wall slid and clattered flat on its shelf, and in chain reaction — as Brian jerked his body away from the bookcase and the whole unit rocked — a huge lake trout also flopped flat and a jackrabbit seemed to come flying off the top shelf. It hadn't been fastened yet to a base board.

"Easy," Hathaway smiled. "But I know it makes you feel jumpy . . . to see violence like this done so senselessly. Complete *loss*, know what I mean? Neither this one nor the half-grown one the vet destroyed were insured. Talk about jumpy, I went out the next day after the second attack and insured *everything*. Down to the last broken-down nag."

"You can do that?"

"You can insure anything you're willing to pay enough for. And, believe me, I *paid*. Strapped myself, I admit. Way overboard. Can't even make up the loss by selling the ones that aren't worth it — sale price would be a fraction of how much I paid to insure them. Hold on." He turned and carried the plastic-sheathed bundle back into the freezer.

Brian was half-surprised to feel himself sigh and his muscles sag in a release of something similar to competitive tension. But without the pleasant satisfaction, the lazy ache of accomplishment or success.

"So, whadda you think," Hathaway returned. "I'm keeping my foals protected, but I do have some horses ranging. Am I going to have to go through this again? With an adult mare or gelding?"

"Why have you decided I'm the only person who can help you with this problem?" Brian picked up the stuffed jackrabbit and put it onto a shelf. "I haven't figured out if I can do it, if I have the . . . skills or tools . . . if I'm capable."

Hathaway brushed past and opened the door leading to the store. "Stop out at my place sometime next week, I'll show you around, on horseback. Bring your girlfriend, if she's not too afraid of me. You like to ride?" He didn't wait for an answer.

Rather than approaching the location of the cougar's signal by driving into the state park and recreation area near the reservoir, he circled the target spot, going north to where the highway met the Oregon Trail through Muddy Gap, then northeast toward Devil's Gate but turning south on a dirt road before seeing any of the trail's historical landmarks. It would've been too dark anyway, but dawn seeped in by the time the tires started crunching and hopping over rocks and pebbles off the paved highways. The dirt road seemed a division between a wildlife bird refuge — life-rich and green — and, to the west, the Ferris Mountains, steep peaks of saw-toothed rock, like the top third of the Alps or Himalayas sliced off and set down on the Wyoming plateau, ten-thousand vertical feet of beyond-the-timberline terrain where it didn't seem to belong. "I wish she was in there," Leya said, almost reaching across him to point out his window toward the bird refuge.

"If she was in there, there probably wouldn't be a problem."

They would be hiking together for a while, in a rugged area that didn't seem to have any maps readily available with marked or known trails. After a while they would likely have to separate, in order to home in on the cougar's signal from two different locations; then with compasses determine the exact direction they were pointing their receivers, plot the two lines on a map and find the exact point where the axes crossed. They were each equipped with receivers, binoculars and walkie-talkie, daypack with snakebite kit, food and water — enough for 24 hours — and Brian had a .22 rifle.

He'd only looked sideways at her boots as she climbed into the Bronco in front of her motel, still lit at pre-dawn with a red neon sign. Then, looking over his left shoulder to pull out onto the deserted frontage road beside the interstate, said, "I hope hiking's not a problem for you."

"I was a Girl Scout for ten years."

"You mean you never went to Africa on scouting expeditions for the zoo to bring-em-back-alive?"

"Someday I'll tell you all about my duties at the zoo." Her voice had been placid, fluid, dreamy. "But . . . didn't *you* work in Africa? What was the study?"

"Oh . . . I was just an intern. A flunky. A team guarding the preserve from poachers."

"Did you catch any?"

"It was . . . I just followed along. I flew the chopper, but went where I was told."

"What was it like? Breathtaking, I'll bet."

"Hot. And flat. Dusty."

"Those are your only impressions? Isn't it more teeming with wildlife than any place on earth except a rainforest?"

"That's what they say."

"How could you ever leave?"

"I don't know . . . maybe I wanted to be the one doing the shooting, so here I am."

"Well, a new record, you stayed on one subject three minutes before getting snide." She'd leaned forward to turn the radio on. "What kind of music do you like? As if they have anything besides Country."

"None."

"Fine," she'd snapped, but she must've softened in the silence that lasted until they were near the bird refuge. Then when he pulled off the dirt road, she said, "Wow," looking at the destitute, arduous, hard-as-rock region that would have to be covered on foot before they could even try to get a signal.

"I'm gonna make a man of you today," he said, grinning, looking at the serrated peaks.

"You mean someone who can't go anywhere without a *gun*?" she retorted.

"I don't have a gun."

"So what's that long thing you're always aiming at everything? The thing you left Africa for."

"Oh that," he said blandly. Then, in a moment, "It's a rifle."

They pulled their equipment from the back of the truck in silence. The faint voices of calling geese carried from the reservoir. She drained a small can of orange juice, then stomped the can flat under her boot. As he shouldered his pack, he said, "I need all my energy concentrated on this job today, so not too many questions. Don't rile me, okay?"

"Is that supposed to be some kind of joke?"

"Save it for our cowboy friends, hotshot, you're gonna need it. They've invited us for a visit."

"Why would we go?"

"Why not?" He turned away from her, used his boot to flatten a loose loop of barbed-wire fence to the ground, then gestured for her to cross. "For fun," he added. He took the lead again and she fell in behind. "And I may need your moral support."

"Mine? What for?"

"Don't talk now. Conserve energy. Didn't they teach you that in Girl Scouts?"

They got lucky. Or else last night he'd determined perfectly where to park and where to start hiking and in which direction to go. After a little over an hour, after maybe three miles of a pathless search for footing — constantly climbing then descending the sides of slowly eroding bluffs and crevices, filling their boots with loose dust or pebbles, scaring up a wasp's nest — the first time he pulled his receiver out to test for the signal, there it was, dead ahead. But at least six to eight miles away, judging from the volume. And by that time they'd be somewhere in the jagged Ferris Mountains. In another half hour, the signal was still coming from directly in front, and the next time he stopped to check was the first time since they'd started that he turned to look at Leya again. Her face glistened, drops dangled and dripped from her chin, as though every freckle opened up and gushed sweat, and it was only 10 a.m. Her light blue cotton shirt was dark all around the straps of her pack. Her bare legs were covered with white scratches from tumbleweeds they'd pushed through. "Sit down," he said quickly. "Didn't you bring a hat?" Without waiting for an answer, he took the Robin Hood hat from his head, used a corner of his vest to wipe the sweat out of the inner band, then put it on her head. She was sitting on a rock about the size of a footstool. "You stay here, get your receiver out, determine the direction, get the line drawn on the map — I'll show you exactly where we are now."

She nodded, sticking a finger into her sock to scratch an ankle.

"It'll probably take me an hour, maybe two," he looked south through his binoculars. "I want to go about three or four miles this way, pick up the signal and get a direction from there, so we'll have the two axes to put on the map just to double check her location, and see how far away she is."

"Aren't you hot? Why'd you wear a *fleece* vest?"

"I'm a fool," he said briefly. "Go easy on your water, get a good rest, looks like we'll find her, but we won't get back to the truck 'til dark. And, uh, take care of yourself . . . you know . . . sleep, if you can." About twenty feet away from her, he turned back and shouted, "I'll fire a shot when I'm within a hundred yards."

Hot. And dusty. Sounding suspiciously like the Central California back country where your uncle hunted dove with a shotgun. How long ago would that have been, before houses and communities were too close to allow hunters in the semi-arid region. You were all of five, so Diane would've been ten, the one time you went along — probably instead of an overnight with movie and ice cream, the story Diane told Mom. Mom already, by then, had become regularly demonstrative if Diane did anything that smacked of the unfeminine. You were supposed to pick up the birds, wounded or dead, and pull their heads off, drain the blood before it solidified in their bodies. Even a five-year-old hand has the strength — put your fingers in a ring around the neck, pop your hands apart. Why didn't you refuse to do it like the Daktari did? The Daktari was there undercover, working with the local African game warden to stop the poacher. Not once did she look at you with any accusation as you continued to fetch the birds. She put a hand on the back of your towhead as you

*walked in the dust at the poacher's heels. Then he did shoot
an egret, he claimed by mistake, and as he buried it, she said,
"You're in trouble," but she didn't know who to tell.*

Doubling his pace, Brian got his axis plotted and
returned to her in an hour, stopping on his way back
where he'd left a pile of rocks as a marker to shoot the
rifle, aiming up but on an angle away from the direction he was going. It wasn't exactly prairie — a combination badlands and bare foothills — so he couldn't see
her until he was just about there.

While she added his line to her map, he ate a candy
bar and a stick of jerky. "While you were away," she
said, "I did a Girl Scout survival trick. Get four sticks
and sharpen them, plant them pointed-side up in the
ground, then took off my blouse and attached it, like at
four corners, to the four sticks, to make a little low shelter, so I lay underneath it in the shade."

"Why would you tell me something like that?" He
turned away from her, flinging the crumpled candy
wrapper into a sage bush. He bent, panting, then squatted, rested his forehead on his knees, smelling the funky
odor of sweat from his lap. She moved around quietly,
undoing the Velcro fasteners on her pack, shuffling
around, rubbing hand cream in her hands and up her
arms. The sweet smell passed by him as it was whisked
into the open grassy, sandy scent of the landscape. He
caught himself grunting softly with each breath, but it
kept him from retching.

"I didn't really do it," she said softly, "I thought
about it. I was afraid I wouldn't hear you come back
and you'd surprise me—"

He raised his head, closed his eyes against a flash of
dizziness, then sank onto his back, his arm across his eyes.
"Never mind. Let's just finish what we're doing." He took
his hat from where she'd placed it near him on a rock.

"Is something wrong, Brian?"

"Yeah, we need to get *going*." He stood and adjusted the .22 across his back, under his day pack. "Let's
just shut up and *go*."

He found the cougar from about sixty or seventy yards, from the other side of a gorge they couldn't've crossed anyway, at least not and still get back to the truck that day. By determining as exactly as possible on the map where the two axes crossed, then following compasses and estimating the number of miles they'd gone with a walking mileage meter, finally, when the signal on the receiver insisted they were within a hundred yards, he fastened the compass to his rifle, pointed it the exact direction indicated by the equations on the map, noted the landmark that was held in the sights—a particular color vein in the side of a bluff across the gorge—and used the binoculars to scour that area. There she was, pacing back and forth on a ledge about a third of the way to the top of the bluff.

"Is she stuck there?" Leya asked. She also had her binoculars against her eyes, standing beside him, but three or four feet away.

"No. A cougar is never *stuck* . . . unless she's treed or snared. See, the bluff smoothes out, that ledge she's on is a trail to the top." Without removing the binoculars from his face, his knees bent slowly, and he settled down into a squat on his heels. "God, she acts like she's in a zoo, though."

"Is she hurt or sick?"

"*Some*thing's wrong." He removed his hat and wiped his brow with a bandanna, then wiped the eyepieces of the binoculars. "She could've eaten a porcupine and have quills lodged in her throat, so she can't eat. Or she could've been in a fight and sustained internal injuries."

"Rejected by a man," Leya said wistfully.

"Rejected by a male mountain lion. Or even another female. This one's young." He found the cat with the binoculars again. The lion paced the length of bluff twice more, then flopped on one side, rubbed the back of her head against the rock. "This is probably the one . . . the culprit whose conduct sent all twelve of them to purgatory."

"What?"

"It looked like coincidence in the project proposals and early field reports, but doesn't take much to put two and two together." He lowered the binoculars again, rested them upright on his knees. "There was a young lion having inappropriate brushes with civilization in the back country of Southern California. So that's the place they happen to choose to harvest individuals for the experiment of relocating cougars to bigger, *safer* habitats. Safer for *whom*?"

"What do you have against this as habitat?" A breeze coming through the gorge made her words sound fainter, farther away.

"The only thing wrong with *any* habitat is who else is living in it." He recapped the lenses on the binoculars and put them into his pack. "In California, she shared with people. Here . . . if there were other lions already in residence, as I suspect there may've been, it can throw everything out of whack, she's relegated to the worst territory, or *no* territory. If she's not just killed outright. I think he didn't spend enough time investigating the new habitat he chose. Figured if he sterilized them it wouldn't matter. Bullshit. The early projects testing this type of idea spent up to five years just studying cougar ecology before moving in and messing with anything, and in that case they only moved them a couple hundred miles. I thought he was in on that project. I would've thought he'd at least know what was learned." He flipped his rifle strap off his shoulder, cradled the .22 between knees and chest and removed the compass. "If there were just a few cats already here, that's because the terrain only *supports* a few cats. They only reproduce to the level that the habitat can maintain . . . that might be why the males sometimes . . . do away with a younger or newer female . . . no one really knows." He nestled the rifle's butt plate against his shoulder. "But they've never been documented to have overpopulated their terrain."

"But it sounds like they were overpopulated in Southern California."

"What makes you think so?"

"Well . . . what happened?"

"The usual routine. Repeated sightings near a mountain resort, a dog got knocked around. Horseback riders got bucked off their mounts when she showed up on a trail. And . . . she knocked a kid off a pony." He closed one eye and aimed, putting the sights where he knew the cougar was. He couldn't see her without the binoculars. "She got too close to society and didn't know how to behave. That in itself proves there was something wrong with her."

Leya wasn't looking at him, still gazing through her binoculars. "You mean . . . according to people's arbitrary standards of behavior?"

"No, I mean a healthy lion just isn't seen, doesn't come around, wouldn't want to be close to human habitation. It's a *mistake,* and only lions with problems make mistakes. Maybe she should be put out of her misery."

"*What are you doing!*" she screamed, lunging to push him off his heels, but he raised his right arm and warded her off. "You can't kill her! You're a biologist, a *conservationist!*"

"This is a .22, Leya," he said gently. "It doesn't shoot that far."

Even though it was around 4 and they weren't back to the truck yet, he consented when Leya wanted to stop at a slow dribbling rivulet or run-off from an underground spring that had surfaced to waste itself in a tiny creek bed that would never reach anywhere before evaporating altogether. "This's no creek, it's a *gutter,*" he grumbled.

"It's cold and sweet." She was crouching beside the trickle of water. "I'm going to soak my feet."

"No."

"Why? What's wrong?"

He'd taken off his pack and put it on the ground, but still held the rifle under one arm. "You should never remove your footwear before the excursion is over. Your feet will swell." He sat on the ground, propped the gun upright on its butt beside himself. "You might not get them back on." He was almost leaning on the rifle like a cane. "Or are you looking for a way to force me to carry you back?"

She started loosening her hair from the French braid. "Honestly, Brian, sometimes I don't know whether you're teasing or just being . . . weird."

"Do you think I'm weird?"

"Maybe sometimes you're . . . unfathomable."

"Okay, just go behind that rock and do whatever you have to do. I'll stay right here. Maybe I need to be alone and I'm too shy to tell you." Then he grinned, but still didn't look directly at her. "You can even wash your hair in the medicinal waters of this creek you've just discovered."

She laughed lightly, but when he didn't say anything else, just sat there staring at his boots, she did get up and go to the other side of a boulder. Then he closed his eyes. The water didn't make a lot of noise. He couldn't hear her put her feet in, she didn't sigh or moan. There were little rustles in the bushes around him. Lizards, probably. Or small birds. Mice, kangaroo rats, gophers. The type of fauna that lives in the space from earth level to about three-feet above, almost always dirt-colored. The lioness, forty or fifty feet above the floor of the gorge, was tawny yellow. Her eyes probably amber, although the binoculars hadn't been strong enough to carry the color all that way. He'd seen her open her mouth once in a silent snarl. "Do you think everything should be fathomable?" he asked quietly, half expecting her to not hear him.

But her voice wafted back around the boulder, "Well, yes, eventually, on some level; maybe not the way you expect, maybe not directly, but one way or another things can be understood if you're open to looking at them in new ways."

"What the hell is that supposed to mean?" With his left hand he picked up pebbles and tossed them awkwardly toward the water.

Leya laughed, a tinkle of a sound like the trickle of water. "It means I've been thinking about . . . my life, I guess."

"What, *again*? Isn't once a week enough for that?"

"I admit, I'm a habitual self-evaluator. Or, no . . . I do habitually think in retrospection." She was sloshing something around in the water then wringing it out. "I'll give you an example. I never got a chance to tell you why I *thought* I was so qualified for this job. But now, in new light, I'm reevaluating that qualification and seeing that it's actually crap. I had *crap* for experience." She was silent for a moment, then the sound of her scooping handfuls of water, throwing it against her face, patting her cheeks with her palms. "So I'm glad I never told you, you'd've seen me as a pathetic poseur, a cheap entertainer."

"What did you never tell me?" He squinted toward the sun, checked his watch.

"About my experience with large felines. At the zoo, we had this cheetah, a male, hand-raised from a kitten. You might've heard of him, he was put in with a litter of puppies, then grew up with one of his litter mates — had this incredible bond with this golden retriever. Anyway, he was fourteen or fifteen years old. I mean *is*. That's twice as old as most cheetahs live to be in Africa." She made a sudden loud splash. "And whenever there was an important luncheon at the zoo, donors or some diplomatic group or whatever, we'd bring the cheetah in after dessert and walk him around on a leash, then have him sit and let people come pat his head. He would purr like rocks grating, he loved it. But he also always wanted to leave as soon as he could. So because I led this old cheetah around on a leash, and could give him his commands to sit, and could tell people how to pat and feed him . . . I actually thought I could understand something as profound and stirring as that poor bewildered mountain lion pacing out there on that ledge." The Velcro on her pack ripped apart, followed by the shred of a wrapper being torn off a granola bar. She bit and chewed. "But things have different ways of being exposed to you: maybe it's *because* of my ridiculous notion of my own experience that I *can* appreciate the immensity of what we saw today."

"It was quite a sight," he said softly. "An animal so perfectly and powerfully made, so able to survive, so ingeniously adept at living almost anywhere in almost any conditions. And yet obviously in some kind of trouble, which maybe we can't hope to understand, let alone fix."

"I never heard you talk like that."

"Sorry. Am I being a poet again?" He threaded a twig through his knuckles, then rigidly brought his fingers together, snapping the stick in three places.

"Don't apologize. You sound like a true field biologist."

"Or your fantasy of one."

She laughed again, like she was being tickled. "Afraid you can't live up to my high ideals and expectations?"

"Jane Goodall couldn't live up to your ideals." He realized he was smiling idly, staring at the rivulet where it bent out-of-sight around the boulder.

"I sure do a lot of talking about myself," she said almost too gaily. "What about you, besides your life as a biologist, where're you from, do you have a family?"

"That's a new-colleague-in-an-office topic." He laid the .22 across his lap, took his hat off and ran his fingers through his sweat-matted hair. "Interesting to neither the asker nor answerer." His hat perched on his knees, facing him, he traced the new sweat stain with a small stick. "I could just say I don't have one and let it lie at that."

"Denying you have a family is another way of not having one."

"Oh, cut that kind of crap, okay," he groaned, but still half smiling. "So, okay, I had a sister. She's been dead well over twenty years. She killed herself."

"My god," Leya gasped, "I'm sorry. How?"

"Shot."

"I— I'm sorry, I didn't mean how— I mean . . . why did she do it, do you ever ask yourself, you know, if you should've read the signs . . . ."

"No."

Far above, a commuter plane droned. Without even looking to see what was behind him, Brian lay down and covered his face with his hat. It smelled of wet hair and canvas. The rifle was balanced perpendicularly across his body. A small sharp rock chafed between his skull and the ground, but he didn't move it right away, just rocked his head back and forth over it until it moved aside. *You know what you should do? Right now, get off this, cut this crap and go back out and keep a vigil over that indisposed lioness, all night, by yourself, creep slowly toward her minute by minute, hour by hour through the astonishingly dark summer night, until you sit just yards away from her luminous yellow eyes, and she'll confide in you enough to stretch out and rest beside you, her untamed breath easing, trusting you'd never pervert her wildness by touching her.*

"How can you stand to go on using a gun after something like that?" Leya said. He could hear her standing up, her boots back on her feet, crunching stones.

"I don't use a gun, it's a rifle." Sparks of sun glinted through the coarse weave of the hat's material. "And I didn't start shooting until three or four years later."

"You obviously started shooting as a way of looking for answers. You're probably like me, always searching for that resolution."

"No, I don't think so." His voice still muted in the hat.

"I think it's one of life's basic needs. Just one step above food, water and shelter. Up there with the need for companionship and intimacy and closeness, there's a need to find a resolution for those interactions that don't work out."

He reached down to his waist, took the rifle in both hands and lifted it over his head, placed it on the ground above where his head rested. As the rifle passed between the hat and the sun, the little sparks winked.

"Well, that's where I'm at," she said. "Wanting that resolution. An apology, an explanation, an acknowledgment, an answer, a validation, a *resolution*. So my mind will stop working and *working* over it. Coming into contact with the other person isn't the only way to find resolution. That's good, since in some cases it's out of the question. But I haven't figured out where to find it, my resolution, how to be able to say *I just don't care about any of that crap anymore*, and get on with things, the future."

"Just say it," he said. "*I don't care about any of that old crap.* See, it's easy."

"You know as well as I do that doesn't count. You can't pretend everything's resolved, because it'll come at you again and again and prove you wrong." She sighed. "I think you know what I mean, too." When he didn't answer, she continued, "I mean, look at you, drifting through other people's projects, working for other people's studies, hiding behind your weird way of joking, but you're alone, Brian. If you'd resolved everything about your sister, you probably wouldn't be, you'd be able to establish some kind of closeness with . . . someone . . . ."

He jerked the hat off his face. She was half lying on, half leaning over the boulder, her chin on her hands, looking down at him. Her hair was loose, kinky from the braid but flying around her head and blowing over her shoulders.

Did you really kiss her? Did you hold her face with both hands, as though stretching her skin as tight as the braid usually does until her eyes fluttered shut as your mouth covered hers? Were her

*cheeks like the tiny bones of a bird under your thumbs, her
skin like the untouched underside of a newly unfurled leaf?
Did she welcome your mouth with a gentle draw of breath,
with lips parted and warm, pliant yet firm, wet and eager?*

*And what do you expect to gain by this behavior? Her
enduring friendship? Her compassion, some kind of intimacy
or warmth or devoted bond? Remember, those things can't be
yours. No matter that some recent weakness in you seems to
want them.*

*On the other hand, this definitely goes outside the pattern.
What did any of them ever do before their first victim?
What do the profiles say these psychos really want? Not a
companion, not someone to* TALK *to. What kind of vulnerability is required in the victim? For her to be unconscious —
drugged or asleep? Or hog-tied? And naked? How long to
keep her alive and terrified? How long to keep her aware that
the tool which will kill her is already or always in his hand?
And those tools: knives, hammers, crowbars, bats, logs, belts,
twine, the victim's own stockings . . . . Seldom a firearm. Why
is that? Probably the cool control needed for shooting, the dispassionate precision. They say snipers are sexually inhibited.*

*It's supposed to be more complicated — a rage against
society. A rage against women, against rejection by either or
both, a rage expressed as cruelty. Notice how many of them
weren't wanted, then live adult lives of rootlessness plagued
by thoughts of meaninglessness, blaming everyone else —
this thing called society — for their own inability to adjust
and adapt. Does that ring even the faintest bell? No. No one
could claim to be unwanted when his sister began pulling
him around the neighborhood in a wagon to show off all the
nursery rhymes he'd memorized before he could even walk.
Whose sister fixed every perversely mischievous thing he did,
from turning on a sprinkler in the living room to throwing a
handful of laundry soap into a pot of soup simmering on the
stove. Remember how she begged you to start being good because she was afraid Santa Claus wouldn't leave you anything? Did you feel rejected when it was sister chosen to be the
manifestation of your mother's secret torment instead of you?
Or when — as though time had run out on your little-boy*

*cuteness or she finally got tired of your inherent naughtiness
— her adolescence brought an abrupt end to your childhood
friendship? Or did your sibling's misfortune in being the
scapegoat for Mom's concealed mortification make* YOU *feel
safe, healthy and secure? Or did you simply get off on it,
without a psychological reason from an FBI profile? Then did
you try to hang onto your perverted pleasure by trying to
prevent her from ending her miserable life? Or did you* HELP
*her end it? The only thing you should've done, you didn't do.
You could've helped Daktari stop the poacher. You missed.*
WHY? *Already your adult life spent grappling with these
questions, and you want the definitive answers here and now,
this very second?*

*There's got to be something available in what you al-
ready know that can suggest an essential change in conduct.
To spare this girl you may've just kissed, to salvage yourself,
and to liberate that tormented cat pacing a six-foot trail out
in the dark badlands. Research has to be able to direct a course
of action toward progress or what damn good is it? Otherwise why not just give it up, simply leave Wyoming right
now and Gallway will never find you. Leya can go home to
her support group and trained seals. Is there really any reason to worry about Hathaway? But if you stay, you've got to
stop listening to whatever seems to be whispering to you that*
SHE *may be your only beyond-remote one-in-a-million possi-
bility to ever be close to a woman without hurting her.*

Dear Sal,

June 8

Our letters will probably cross in the mail, but I just had to talk to someone tonight. I had the most incredible day, astonishingly beautiful, confusing, inspiring, infuriating, and heartbreaking in more than one way. You should've seen the way he looked at this sick cougar we had to track down. (We only got about 100 yards from her.) As though he loved her enough to, I don't know, _kill_ her. And then later he told me he had a sister who committed suicide. Maybe it's no wonder he does and says so many out-of-the-blue eccentric things. I mean, I can't explain it _psychologically_, but, it's probably like he _never_ has a clear take on what's going on around him because he's always looking through a distorting lens caused by this unspeakable thing he's never dealt with. I don't know anything about it except she apparently shot herself. I don't know how old he was, but I'm guessing very young, he probably has been seeking resolution since he was a kid, and that's why it seems like he never learned normal social behavior. Maybe it's even why he works alone with wildlife. Of course he acts very nonchalant about it. I know, I analyze too much. Always playing junior psychologist, aren't I? He's told me that already too, more than once. I know I risk your profound disappointment, Sal, but I think I'd be good for him.

I _do_ miss you and all the kids, but I'm needed here.

Love, Leya

5
HER BEHAVIORAL SYMPTOMS

```
FROM:          BRIAN LEONARD
ADDRESS:       WRANGLER INN, RAWLINS, WY
PHONE:         (307) 678-0990
FAX:           (307) 998-0550

DATE:          June 9

FAX TO:        031/45 33 31

ATTN:          PETER GALLWAY

# OF PAGES TO FOLLOW:   1

CONTENTS TO FOLLOW:        MAP OF FERRIS
                           MTN AREA
```

COMMENTS: Circled X shows where
female #4 (red/white ear
tag) was located yester-
day. I'll be keeping an
eye on her daily (mostly
via fly-by radio con-
tact). She's in trouble,
no doubt. Will send her
behavioral symptoms. So
far she's pacing as
though caged (should've
realized the reason the
mortality indicator
didn't show—she *was* moving). If nothing im-
proves, what would be the
course of action? Going
in to get her? Or just
let nature have its way
with her? She's my 1st
priority right now. More
soon.
                Leonard

So how would this girl touch you? The slow, ardent, absent-minded caress of a hand on a pet's ear? The exploring, curious finger of a blind woman seeing with her hands? Or would it just be an implied touch that quickens your hungry, confused synapses, exciting your blood, as your mouth moves from her lips to her fine jawbone, her chin, her quivering throat where you can feel her moan without hearing it. Does your own hand know how she would touch you? Or should you stop, because you know you can't hold your dick without remembering your sister.

It doesn't seem possible she ever was the giggling, freck-led, stick-legged playmate, kneeling with a stuffed bear on her lap, manipulating tiny snaps and buttons with clever fingers. She was Jane Goodall and you were her chimp. She wrote the first words you read; she fixed the leg you'd carelessly broken off your glass horse statue; she made you a black cat Halloween costume with a papier-mâché covered coat-hanger tail; with four or five boards nailed into the pepper tree, she built the headquarters that overlooked the veterinary compound in Africa. How did it change, and when? When she was nearing twelve and Mom took away all her jeans and T-shirts, forbade her to cut her hair, and Diane started to habitually lurk in her room except required attendance at mealtime where Mom was the only one who spoke, a tape-loop on womanliness and behaving accordingly? She skipped the stage when a girl's likely to be a bored, teenage diary-writer, mesmerized by her image in the mirror, big-sister mean, hogging the bathroom while you danced to a full bladder outside the door. Long after choosing your clothes and creating your mudpie recipes and cleaning you off when you fell in the creek, long after playing Daktari had dwindled away — and you apparently hadn't noticed that you'd abandoned each other — how did she actually become nothing more to you than those resigned, slow, feeble footsteps padding down the hall, whispering your name on the rug past your room, whenever your mother's voice, after midnight, called to her, dark and low? Would you have ever known it was happening if the thick dead slumber of childhood hadn't become weakened by your own adolescence? Naturally you don't want anyone to find it balled up in the sheets like half-dried snot. So go into the bathroom. Like you always did. Since the first time. It's still automatic. Even after twenty-five years of abstinence. Your hand knows what to do, how you like it. Knew instinctively from the first time. When to go fast and hard, when to tickle and tease. —softer than a lullaby— Or do you even remember the first time? Thirteen, on the toilet, groggy, drugged with half-sleep but the other half pulled to consciousness by the fundamental need, until your head lolls back against the wall, too heavy to hold itself up and you only have two hands, one cupping your balls, the other pumping your little stick of a dick. But voices, on the other side of the wall, and your hand slows to listen, speeds up again when you hear: The whimper is Diane, nineteen-years-old, bone-skinny, and not much to say for herself, or to anyone else, the past eight years. I DON'T UNDERSTAND YOU, Mom says at the dinner table, serving full-course gourmet meals even on school nights, WHY DO YOU WANT TO LOOK LIKE A MAN, PUT ON SOME LIPSTICK, BUY SOME HEELS OR AT LEAST FLATS, GET OUT OF THOSE CLUNKY SHOES, ARE YOU SOME KIND OF DYKE? But OHHHH is the sound she makes at night. WATCH US, HONEY, THIS'LL MAKE YOU THINK TWICE ABOUT BEING QUEER. Who else might've been there? I SEE THE DANGER SIGNS IN YOU, SWEETHEART, BUT YOU CAN LEARN TO BE PLEASED BY A MAN. Is it a memory from dinner conversation or a voice through the wall? THIS IS WHAT IT LOOKS LIKE TO BE A LESBO, DIANE, IS THIS WHAT YOU WANT?

Did your sister still dream of a compound in Africa? In her room most of the day — not even interesting enough anymore for you to pester or call names? A closed door that for years you might've only heard open at mealtimes, and then again at one or two in the morning; when she's suddenly beyond merely interesting — she's part of what makes your dick harder, your balls tighter, the explosion like the tug of a rope extending up into your guts, sending the spasm to the tips of your fingers, the stuff not just bubbling out but blasting. Especially when her whimpers turn to cries, mom's voice rising, and you can imagine how your mother's hands hold fistfuls of some guy's or some woman's, eventually even Diane's stringy long hair. Why don't you ask your dick why it loves the muffled sobs, the broken-hearted wailing? Your already once- or twice-satiated dick swells again and says: more. And if you haven't come like that for 25 years, you know it's probably because no one's brains are splashing out as you simultaneously blow spunk from the end of your cock. Can memory actually satisfy you? Or only reawaken the virulent need? And who's going to scream as she faces the end of her life which gives your dick head at the same time? Diane could only service you once. Mom called, as usual, then the familiar gentle click of your sister's door, the swish of footsteps. Were they any heavier because of what she carried that night, hidden under her nightgown? You were immediately

*awake, well practiced by now at sixteen — attuned to even
the most hushed signal — and quick, closing the bathroom
door behind yourself even as the door to Mom's room was
squeaking softly shut and the radio clicked on.* **Colorado
Rocky Mountain high— fire in the sky—** *The moisturiz-
ing lotion taken from the bathroom sink, squeezed like icing
up and down your shaft, made the same slurpy sounds you
couldn't quite hear through the wall. As usual, lately — the
last year or two — theirs are the only voices, no other visitors
on display, no man or woman as educational tool to scare
Diane straight. By now Mom had become both tutor and les-
son, Mom herself the only educational tool, the only exhibit,
the only assignment. But finally,* Not tonight, *Diane begging in a twenty-one-year-old childlike whine. And Mom:*
Where'd you get that? *The intensity of this new develop-
ment pumping more blood into your already hard ax-handle
dick.* Give it to me. *Your mother's voice hot liquid sugar.
Your sister blubbering,* I don't want to. *Your dick straining,
upright and quivering, practically swaying, like a Geiger-
counter needle discovering uranium that was about to blow
sky high. Yet you'd hardly started, hadn't even closed both
hands around yourself. At the moment you did begin, her
protests rampaged into screams, the climax moved like hot
lead from your balls, up through the shaft of your fevered
cock, her screeching voice not even making words anymore,
until it became the blast of the gun, and the explosion of your
glands, the eruption of gunpowder and simultaneous detonation of your cock, a prolonged explosion like a mortar shower
or firestorm, splatter of cum and spray of brain and blood
coating two sides of the same wall. The blast died away, seeming to take forever, revealed your mother's shriek that took
over where your sister left off. And she never wondered — as
her raw screams lifted like fog toward the ceiling but couldn't
disturb the steady undertone of a song on the radio — never
questioned why her sleeping son was not in his bed but* there
*in the room in front of her. Holding the hot gun. Kneeling
between your sister's splayed blood-spattered legs, surrounded
and speckled by her brain tissue, every thought she'd ever
had — about teaching math to stuffed tigers and becoming a*

Daktari in Africa and her forgotten little brother — oozing down the wall, seeping into the rug, continuing to bubble slowly from the crater in her head.

So what more do you want NOW? For this sweet fanciful girl — for Leya to come and squat between you and the gruesome body of your sister? She might cup your face in two hands, her thumbs in your tears could clean freckles of blood from your skin, her lips softly touch your swollen eyelids. Moving closer, ignoring your dangerous cock, still steadily stiffening between your body and hers, her hands could slide into your sticky hair, catch your foundering head against her shoulder, stroke your neck, murmur into your ear. She could sit right down in the spreading pool of blood and hold you with both arms tight around your heaving ribcage. And it might be an accident, one soft, tiny hand, or even just a tender finger, touching it . . . . No!

His head and shoulder tried to bash the bathroom door open three times before his hand finally found the knob. While his bare feet groped for, then fought their way into moccasins strewn on the floor, his fingers — as though cramped or arthritic — fumbled to button his jeans. A light windbreaker, the first thing he grabbed off the pile of clothes on the bed, was all he put onto his upper body before snatching the key from the desk then the rifle from behind the door and slamming himself out of the room.

The Bronco lurched into the registration-only space under the awning of Leya's motel. Left with motor running and door open as Brian leaped the stairs three at a time to the second floor landing, hammered on her door with the rifle's butt.

"What!" The door flew open. She was barefoot, in cutoffs and a short T-shirt. "Jesus you scared me."

"You open your door *scared* without even knowing who's pounding it down?"

"Well, it's just you, isn't it?"

"Let's go hunting." He took a backwards step towards the stairs and beckoned with the rifle.

"*Now?*"

"It's a perfect time. I need you to fly the chopper. Believe me, if I could get *any*one else I wouldn't want you."

"But *now?*" She smiled and leaned in the doorway. The short shirt didn't quite come down to the top of the cutoff jeans. "How about dinner instead?"

"*Are you crazy?*" Several sparklers of spit flew sizzling from his mouth, falling somewhere between them. His hand with the gun rose slightly, bent at the elbow as though warding off a blow.

She blanched slightly. "Are *you?* God, what's wrong with you, Brian? Are you sleepwalking?"

"I don't know. Maybe. Okay, I'll go alone."

"It's getting dark. You'll kill yourself."

"Good."

"That won't bring your sister back."

He opened his mouth as though to scream something, but only made a little ticking sound in his throat. He gasped for air.

Her voice modulated into composed tranquillity. "I know what happened — we opened a can of worms yesterday. Now you're imagining all kinds of vignettes for how things could've been different, but it only makes it *worse*. I've been there, Brian." Her hand reached out for his arm.

He stepped back. "Just shut up," he rasped. "Shut up and do what I say." His voice rose. The curtain on the neighboring window parted a crack, then closed again. "You're being paid to *do what I say!*"

"I'm not going to fly that helicopter at dusk when you're this upset."

His vision blurred, then water streamed on both cheeks.

"You need to talk, Brian?" She opened her door wider and stepped back, exposing the doorway, as though she expected him to topple forward into the room, but he didn't. Her tone remained melodious and serene, "No one *else* is punishing you, it's just you punishing yourself. You need to allow yourself to mourn her without blaming yourself. To remember her life instead of her death."

He was dizzy from shaking his head over and over, harder, savagely snapping it back and forth as she spoke. "You don't even know what you're saying," the voice of a wild stranger.

"Your mind *can* help resolve the relationship with your sister, but not by trying to convince yourself there was a way you could've changed the course of events." She came out of the room onto the landing, leaving the door open. Her freckles standing out, almost throbbing in her pale face. Her lips colorless. Her eyebrows seeming to be arched higher than ever. "Do you want to come in?"

"*No!*" He whirled around, dizzy, caught the rail, panting. But didn't plummet clumsily down the stairs. Turned back to her, caught her with one hand by the shoulder, pulled her unskillfully against his body and opened his mouth against hers, their teeth cracked together then everything softened and dissolved into liquid heat which he sucked at greedily. But then they were standing apart. He held himself still for a moment, then moved as deliberately as he could, backwards, one step at a time, away from her. Fingers laced together over his heart, cradling the rifle there.

If all you wanted was to see if you could stay in the zone with a girl beside you . . . apparently the answer is: you can't.

Why did you go to her? Running to her right after remembering— It's lunacy. Is what it is. Yes, you need to find the zone . . . and shooting is what keeps you calm . . . but why couldn't you think of another way to shoot besides from the chopper . . . where SHE'D automatically have to be beside you the whole time?

No answer.

So you had to kiss her instead? For real this time? An instinctive drive to feel the stimulating ache and nausea of agitation? You can't keep turning fantasy into reality. This can no longer be a true reliable test. Or it stopped being one a long time ago. Or this is your answer: you're distraught, falling apart, back where you were over 25 years ago. You haven't even let yourself THINK *about that night . . . all of a sudden you're reliving it . . . vividly . . . and going so far as to experiment with putting this girl Leya there too? Are you planning something? Did your wayward cat design or dream the disemboweling of a baby horse, then set off to live it through? No. Planning, in these cases, is instinct . . . albeit gone awry. You didn't plan to kiss her. But you did it.*

Even without the binoculars, camera, compasses, radio receivers, walkie-talkies, data book, rifle and micro cassette recorder, there wasn't enough room to sleep in the helicopter. He would have to return to his room at the motel eventually. He couldn't even stay out long enough to wait for the room to be cleaned and restored by a housekeeper, since it was somewhere around 8 p.m., half a horizon still burning with sunset.

What served as a chopper pad — broken, crumbling asphalt behind a freestanding row of three small maintenance hangars, just off the near end of the runway — was not visible from the airport office nor the tiny dirt parking lot. This time of evening the single-engine two-seater planes were all landing, nothing using the runway for take-off. It wasn't the best place to clean a rifle. He'd removed the only shell that had been loaded, started to detach the telescopic sight, trigger guard, bolt, hammer and breech block, to clean and oil everything, but stopped, put it back together, sat it upright in the passenger seat. The sights would have to be adjusted tomorrow at a session with one of his targets and a fencepost. He opened a topographical mapbook on his lap. The map showed no trails, but several spots could be checked out as possibly being fit for landing the chopper, saving hours of foot transportation which ate into available time for observation and necessitated giving up a day of homing the other grids. If the chopper could get him into the Ferris Mountain terrain quicker, he could wrap up two or three hours of homing the scheduled grid in the morning, get rid of Leya, and spend the afternoon trying to get close enough to form some premise about the nature of female #4's problem. The map stayed open but his eyes closed. Somewhere amid the tiny elevation numbers, little crosses showing alpine peaks, and swirls of fingerprint-marks that represented the rise and fall of land masses — mountains, buttes, bluffs, valleys, ravines, gorges — a distraught cougar might be feeling natural nocturnal urges but for some reason no longer able to understand or follow them. Her gums white and skin puckering with dehydration, yet weirdly unable to answer the impulse to seek water? Muscles exhausted and atrophied from lack of food, but the reflex to hunt, as though in alien hieroglyphics, unrecognized? *Does she have no life other than her inevitable death?*

He heard footsteps on the sandy asphalt. But perhaps similar to the cougar's current scrambled instinct, Brian's synapses connecting his sense of hearing to the impulse to look toward the sound seemed to be out of whack, and despite being aware that someone was approaching, he still jumped a little when Hathaway spoke.

"Hey there, going or coming? Sorry, didn't mean to sneak up on you."

"No, you didn't, that's okay. Just thinking."

"Just getting back in?"

"No . . . ." Brian shut the mapbook, rubbed his face with both hands, digging his fingers into his eye sockets, then stretching the skin tight as his hands pressed backwards toward his ears. "Just planning . . . new hunting routes. Learning terrain. You know. Trying to think."

"Sometimes thinking's pretty hard in those paper-walled motels. Most folks don't use 'em to *think!* I can offer you a quiet afternoon at my place."

"Thanks, I'll . . . consider that." Brian's eyes cleared.

"I mean it," Hathaway said, re-tucking his shirt which looked like silk, black on his front , turquoise on the back.

"How about you?" Brian asked. "Going or coming?"

"Had to fly to Cheyenne this morning. Do all my banking there. Push comin' to shove on my loan application. I told you how all that insurance drained me dry."

"Can't you sell some of the horses?"

"And take a huge loss. Yeah, that's one option." Hathaway shook a cigarette out of a pack, offered it to Brian, then put it into his own mouth straight from the pack when Brian declined. "Thought I might ask your opinion about some other ways."

"I don't know anything about horses." He scratched flea bites on his ankles. "Or insurance."

"Come on out to the ranch. Let's talk anyway." Hathaway exhaled a cloud. "When you can take an afternoon away from . . . hunting." The tip of the cigarette glowed again as he sucked through it. "I hear you haven't brought in any tails for two or three days. Coyote cleaned out already?"

"I've . . . had some other concerns." Brian zipped the jacket all the way up. The nylon felt icy and clammy against his skin. "Hey, does your wife try to analyze you all the time?"

"You kidding?" Hathaway crushed the live cigarette under one foot. "Like asking does she have tits." He grinned. "Can I expect you tomorrow?"

"Day after. No, I'll let you know. So I can get some . . . you know . . . scouting done."

"Good. I'll look forward to hearing what you have to say," Hathaway said evenly. "Bring the babe too." He chuckled. "I don't think she likes me. She don't even know me yet."

"Me either," Brian said tonelessly. Hathaway boomed a pot-bellied laugh, turned and walked back toward the parking lot.

Brian stayed at the airport, in the helicopter cockpit, until 9 or 10, then drove back out to the interstate. He considered getting a room at the Winston Inn or Key Motel, just for one night, but, after passing through the motel strip five or six times, finally went back to his room. It was, after all, just the dark disheveled room of a field biologist, maps and books stacked on the night stands and dresser, videocam case open on the floor, 35mm camera with zoom lens nestled on the pillow, daypack with contents strewn on the bed, a radio receiver on each chair, flags stuck in a map on the wall making jittery shadows in the light of the Weather Channel on the TV. Radio spitting static from a tuning knob knocked askew. And the message light on the phone blinking.

Crossing directly above the Ferris Mountain area, her signal grew stronger then faded as he approached and passed over. He circled tighter and tighter on female #4's thus-far constant location, affirming that she was still there. There was a place to land the chopper that was half a day's walk closer than where he'd parked the truck. A tornado of dust rose as the chopper descended. Spring grasses lay flat, petals blasted off flowers, those that had already been fertilized had the added benefit of getting their seeds scattered farther than any sage or tiny flowering groundcover could hope for. With compass, map, receiver and camera, Brian left the chopper glinting in the sun and headed off in the direction of the thin, beeping signal. Bees, already recovered from the hurricane winds, buzzed around his boots, staying close to the ground where small straggly plants clustered around rocks, holding miniature yellow or blue blossoms up on thread-thin stems.

Once again without a trail, Brian had to concentrate both on where he put his feet and on the instruments guiding him. Stepping only on large immobile rocks or wide unvegetated or sandy spots would reduce the chance of discovering a wasp's nest or rattlesnake. Boots protected his feet and ankles, but other that than he was only wearing nylon bathing trunks and a thread-bare blue workshirt.

He didn't stop at the same place where he'd observed the cougar with Leya. Coming from a different direction, he arrived opposite the lioness's hideout at a spot where the small gorge was more like a shallow canyon, not imposing at all on his side where it would be a downhill hike rather than a rock-climber's descent. Certainly the cougar possessed an open view across the canyon — probably the path of an old flash flood — but her best protection was not the ravine in front of her but the more vertical plane of the higher bluff directly behind her. At first he didn't see her. Without two receivers and triangulation, the less accurate information still said that she would have to be anywhere in about a hundred yard radius. And yet his pulse hammered while he used the zoom lens as a telescope and slowly slid the focal point along the ledge where she'd been. A sick spasm of loss he may've never felt before. As though discovering that the ailing cat was no longer banished to this remote and unlikely lair would catch him in mid step over an abyss and render him unable to know where or how to put his foot down.

Since he was here earlier in the day, a shadow was still hiding part of the ledge, disguising the fact that the ledge did get wider, and that the terrain above her was easily accessible via the way the ledge itself turned into an uphill path leading to the top of the bluff. The cougar easily could've just walked away — even as he was approaching with his receiver beeping — but she was in the shade, lying flat on her side. Barely visible in the shadow-haze. Then the tip of her tail rose and tapped the dust.

Without lowering the camera, Brian bent his knees into a squat and filled his hand with three or four rocks. He rose again, then stood still, holding his breath to steady the camera, making sure he was still looking at her and hadn't slid the focal point sideways. Flinging the rocks into the canyon jostled his head a bit, so by the time he got both hands back on the camera and located the cougar, her head was up, ears alert toward the sound of the rocks spattering into the bushes. She lifted her muzzle higher to scent the breeze at his back that would surely carry his identity to her. Yet she remained imperturbed. Certainly they were looking across the chasm directly into each other's eyes, acknowledging, accepting, understanding. The clench in his body subsided, a sigh easing out through his pores. She yawned and abruptly bent to lick her shoulder.

```
FROM:            BRIAN LEONARD
ADDRESS:         WRANGLER INN, RAWLINS, WY
PHONE:           (307) 678-0990
FAX:             (307) 998-0550

DATE:            June 11

FAX TO:          031/45 33 31

ATTN:            PETER GALLWAY

# OF PAGES TO FOLLOW:     0

CONTENTS TO FOLLOW:       NONE


COMMENTS: Female #4 still hasn't left
          her outpost. No longer as
          agitated, not in as much
          distress. Recuperating? Or
          just too exhausted for out-
          wards signs of anxiety? But
          from what? I stayed to ob-
          serve her for several hours.
```

```
She knew I was there—didn't
run. Unusual, isn't it? But
could be useful, if she
starts to trust me. Is that
hoping for too much? Or not
even desirable?
                Leonard
```

It took at least half a day, usually longer, for thorough homing of whatever grid they were scheduled to cover. Grid #1 was the most varied, with Pathfinder and Seminoe reservoirs, the bird refuge, Seminoe and Shirley Mountains, and the strangely rugged Ferris Mountains. Grid #2 was the twenty-five hundred square miles directly above Pathfinder Reservoir, with Casper just outside to the east, veined with creeks coming down from the Big Horn Mountains to the north and Owl Creek Range to the west, offering the desolate Rattlesnake Hills as habitat. Grid #3 was to the west, sliding slightly south so it bordered the lower part of #2 and the upper side of #1, containing the Sweetwater River and Oregon Trail route, plus the by-comparison lush Green Mountains, but also the almost totally uninhabited uranium mining districts.

It was near 3 before they'd landed, transferred markers and dates to a fresh map for faxing, and headed out to Hathaway's ranch about thirty-five miles up US 287 toward Bull Spring Lake — the same highway, same direction they'd gone to circle around behind Ferris Mountain and hike in to find the cougar. Hathaway lived closer to Lamont than Rawlins. Located on a map, the ranch, Ferris Mountain, and the place Brian had found to land the chopper were in a straight diagonal line, Bull Spring Lake on the southwest end, his remote makeshift chopper pad on the northeast. The lioness's location was closer to the chopper pad, and most of the Ferris Mountains stood between her and Hathaway's ranch. Even so, Brian had refrained from flinching when getting directions to the horse ranch from the taxidermist, who likewise didn't react much when Brian handed him a bag with only two tails.

"You said you'd tell me why we're doing this," Leya said. She was staring at the highway out the windshield, arms crossed. The only words they'd spoken to each other most of the day had been locations on the grid using axis numbers and letters, and cougar identification using ear-tag colors, gender and number. Except when he'd told her the plan to visit Hathaway's ranch: she'd asked why, and he'd said *later*. The one word seemed to hold her off from saying anything else, although he'd caught her looking at him a few times, as though studying him to find the residual effects of a week-long bout of torrential flu. Ironically, he *did* feel that kind of vague weakness, that thready hesitancy to move suddenly, that foggy slow deliberation of the mind.

"Reasons I can't . . . . I like horses, don't you?"

"They're okay." She turned on the radio but just left it only partially tuned to a syndicated talk show.

"Didn't you train horses at the zoo? Or did you stick to exotics?"

"We had a miniature horse. It just walked around on a halter."

"Good trick."

"It was *educational*." Leya was sitting on one foot, her body halfway turned toward Brian, most of her face behind sunglasses. She began tuning the radio but before there was anything other than static, Brian reached across her and snapped the radio off. "Hey— that was rude."

"Sorry. I like silence."

Pointing south toward Rawlins, a truck was parked on the shoulder. A man was on the side of the road, puking. Bent at the waist, hands on knees, the vomit looked frozen, suspended between his head and the ground, horizontal, like a tiny fish net thrown out of his mouth. They were past him in seconds.

"I guess it was cowboy's night out last night." This time Brian broke the interlude.

"Can't you speak without the slurs?"

"Am I slurring? I thought I'd sobered up already." He glanced at her and tried to grin, but only her white jaw and freckled cheek faced him. He sighed, then covered it with a cough. "As long as we're talking about talking . . .," he cleared his throat again. "Keep quiet as much as you can today, okay?"

"Why? What do you mean? I talk too much?"

"I just mean . . . you don't need to say anything about what we do. You know, our job here, what we're doing most of the time."

"I'm a zoo-hack, how's that?"

"An angry zoo-hack."

"You want to hear why?"

"Not really. No." He turned onto a dirt road. There was a mailbox on the highway, but no house or barn in view yet at the end of the long driveway. "Look, let's just get some R & R out here today."

They were going west, away from the nearest mountains. Thunderheads boiled on the horizon. Left of the dirt road, the yellow and gray-green fields were sparsely sprinkled with dark cattle. They veered right at a fork, passed through a wooden gate with the ranch name swinging on the cross pole overhead. It seemed incredible that the seemingly flat rangeland could conceal houses and outbuildings. But the prairie, which in twenty-five to thirty miles would become the Chain Lakes Flats in the Great Divide Basin, rolled like an ocean — a tawny, velvety ocean bordered and criss-crossed with straight, bright white board fences. Suddenly there were five or six horses grazing on the downside of a soft swell, and farther ahead a dark oasis of trees, another gate to go through which entered into an oak-shaded ranch compound posing for a tourist postcard: raked corrals, parallel sets of long white barns and rows of rolled hay, garage with upper-level bunkhouse, three-story wooden house circled by covered porches; two hands

in big-buckled belts, Levi's and T-shirts, loading bales
of alfalfa from a flat truck into a shed. Turn and look
back to the east, the Ferris Mountains rise in sharp relief above the patchwork of white fences on rippling
gold grassland.

Brian's new corduroy shorts were just a little tighter
than his usual canvas pants or the swimming trunks.
He tugged at each leg where they had bunched up
slightly while he'd been seated. "Now I know what it's
like wearing a girdle."

"Women don't wear girdles anymore," Leya stated
flatly.

"Good, then it's high time *I* did." He turned to locate a low dog-calling whistle. Hathaway was coming
from the barns. "Hey there," Brian called, "y'all got a
hoss for this little gal?"

She pushed him so hard with one hand he had to
take a few steps sideways. Her voice followed, tight,
low, fast, "Why is it you always turn into a cartoon version of an asshole when you get around these guys?
How many times do you think this joke will be funny?"

"Haven't you figured it out?" he said mildly, despite the sudden throb in his temples. "I was raised by
wolves." Then he reached to meet Hathaway's ham-
handed greeting.

"Find the place all right?"

"Right where you said it would be."

"Looks like some boomers will roll in tonight, but
there's plenty of time for a trail ride." Hathaway
squinted westward.

"Doesn't it bother you that your cowboys wear ball
caps?" Brian asked, an eye on Leya, several yards away,
fingers in her back pockets, watching the two ranch
hands.

"Doesn't worry me 'til they turn 'em 'round backwards," Hathaway smiled. "But *you're* not exactly
decked out for a rodeo either."

"*She'll* ride."

"Good, we'll talk."

As Hathaway lumbered back toward the barns, Brian edged slowly toward Leya. She was leaning against one of three ornamental hitching posts bordering the large lawn beside the house. "You *can* ride, can't you?" he said. She was looking down, her hair pulled in a knot on top of her head, the back of her skull looked warm and small as a child's. "You won't go and get hurt on me, will you?" In an inexplicably unrestrained moment, he almost put a cupped hand on the back of her neck, but pulled away as she lifted her face and turned toward him.

"I work with animals." Her voice no longer harshly undertoned. "I understand them."

"Well, *that* might come in handy." His hands balled in the pockets of his shorts. The empty flat truck turned around, crunching gravel, then pulled out of the compound, going between the barns and Brian's truck. After it passed, leaving a plume of fading dust — and Leya made a string of tiny kitten sneezes — Hathaway appeared again from the row of barns, leading a cobby dun mare.

When he reached them, Hathaway released the bridle, slid his hand under the horse's mane. She rested her lips on his shoulder, eyes half closed. "This here's Honey, turned nineteen last month, one of my oldest, used to be my steady ride, one of the best. Long retired, but it weren't *her* choice."

Without moving his feet, Brian felt himself backing away from the scene. Leya put a small hand between the mare's eyes, slid slowly down to her nostrils. The mare's lips fluttered. "What happened?" Leya asked softly.

"Nothin' really. I outgrew her, you might say." The mare nibbled gently at Hathaway's hair. "Combination of my weight and her age. But I like her to have a day on the trails now'n then, when I kin find a rider. She loves it and could use the exercise."

"She's sweet," Leya purred, her face against the mare's neck. The mare suddenly lifted her head, ears pricked, towering above Leya, looking toward the barns where another horse and rider had appeared — a stocky buckskin and leather-faced blue-jeaned man, sixteen from the neck down, hands and face at least sixty. The horse and rider waited, then a second man came from the barns on foot, leading a lithe, leggy blood bay. The buckskin's solidness was sharply offset by the bay's skittery frolic. The rider took the lead line and headed across the driveway toward a gate the other man was now opening. The buckskin settled into a jog inside the gate — which was one end of a large oval track of soft dirt — the bay volting sideways until the rider urged his horse into a lope and the bay trotted, head high. They went out of sight over a gentle swell toward the far end of the oval.

"Honey watches each colt and filly go out for exercise, wondering when her turn'll come," Hathaway said. "There was a time I let her be the lead horse, but that time's passed for her too. Anyway, she's really a ranch pony, and she knows it."

The mare whinnied and stomped one foot inches away from Leya's canvas athletic shoes. Leya jumped back as Brian stepped forward. "You sure this is safe for her?" he asked.

"Will you quit worrying," Leya snapped, gently. She was smiling.

"Old Honey," Hathaway said, a hand on one of the mare's ears, folding it down, rubbing the inside with one thumb, "wouldn't hurt a baby. Thunder, snakes, dogs . . . even wild animals, if there're any out there today . . . nothin'll put a spook in this mare, these hoofs'll never miss a beat, steady as sunrise — heart, wisdom, and loyalty, all the things you want in your best friend . . . or your lover, ain't that right, Sweetheart?" Hathaway looked from the mare to Leya. Brian's pulse throbbed again, sudden and hot on his temples. He looked at his boots and breathed deep and slow. The beat in his head had an echo in his wrists, fingertips and groin. Bile rose in his throat, and far away thunder mimicked his heartbeat. He tried to think of a reason to go back to the truck, but nothing was there, not his hat, not even the rifles.

"It must've broken her heart to retire," Leya murmured.

"It happened gradual. She was my all-terrain vehicle. My place is over fifty square miles and this little mare covered it all hundreds and hundreds of times with me, musta rounded up a thousand wild rodeo yearlings. Several years ago I bought a coupla three-wheelers — more versatile than horses, can tow a little trailer for feed or equipment. Anyway, that's when Honey started helping to exercise the thoroughbreds, but it's also when I realized she shouldn't be asked to carry my weight anymore. We weaned her from work, but I guess it can never be gradual enough." With the horse and rider out of sight, the mare seemed to sigh and sag, her muzzle close to Hathaway's ear. Leya's hand was making slow circles on her chest. Brian watched, realized the mare was cougar-colored, felt a hand touching his own stomach: *his.*

"My Honey's stood by and watched me get hot and excited about each promising brood mare," Hathaway continued, "each flashy yearling, each magnificent stud — pushing her stall farther and farther down the row. But her eyes still get bright to see me, she still knocks my hat off and laughs, shows her yellow teeth. Don'cha, girl?" The mare lifted her head again as the rider and two horses reappeared, completing a tour of the track and beginning a second.

"Let me take her out now so she won't have to watch them anymore," Leya said. "I can't stand it."

Hathaway chuckled and came around to hold the stirrup as Leya mounted. The mare chewed her bridle and Brian touched her velvet upper lip with one finger. "Don't get lost out there," he said quietly, slowly, then added, "We don't wanna hafta send a posse out to find you."

"You weren't this worried when I could've killed us both flying the helicopter." Still smiling, she turned the mare's head and they headed down the driveway.

"If you *think* yer lost," Hathaway called after them, "just give'r head, tell her it's time for supper — she'll come home!"

Leya waved. The mare broke into a slow jog, bouncing Leya's head like a doll with a wire spring neck.

"She can give *me* head *any* time," Hathaway stage-whispered. Brian turned and puked in the dust.

"Hey, buddy, you okay?"

"Touch of flu, I guess." With his boot, he covered the spot, wiped his mouth with one hand.

"Hell, *you're* not the one I wanted to get sick." Hathaway smiled.

"Pardon?"

"C'mere, I got somethin' t'show you." Hathaway headed toward a paddock on the other side of the barns, away from the oval track. As Brian followed, he heard the hoofbeats of the two horses on the track, as though coming after him, hard, from behind. A lynch mob with a rope.

The small corral was occupied by two mares and their foals, not newborn but still long-legged and knobby-kneed. All four were chestnuts with white blazes and socks. "I don't breed for markings," Hathaway said, "but can't help but be proud of these. The four'uv them'll make a fine-looking chariot team. Not that winning chariots are made by matched teams. And not many winning teams include *brood* mares."

"There are still chariot races?"

"*Still?* It ain't that old. Growing sport. Mostly in the West. Circuit runs down to New Mexico, into California. Montana, Colorado, Eastern Washington. I haven't gotten into it yet. Still dreaming of the big leagues, a Wyoming-bred triple crown." Hathaway stopped at a head-high shed attached to the corral, opened it and took out a small stepladder. "Look here, maybe you can tell me if I'm doing this wrong." He climbed the stepladder and hoisted himself onto the roof of the shed.

Brian followed, but stayed on the ladder, the roof of the shed at his waist. A big U-hook was bolted to the center of the roof, a chain attached to it. The loose end of the chain was like a rusted iron foot-long safety pin.

"You'n me had the same idea," Hathaway said.

"How do you mean?"

"I heard how you put out bait for the coyote. I was already doing the same thing here, only I wasn't waitin' with a rifle."

"Poison," Brian uttered slowly. His stomach turned.

Hathaway squatted beside the chain, picked up and opened the big clasp. "I didn't want no dog or coyote to take the bait — not that I'm protectin' the coyote, but wanted to be exactly sure the bait was took by exactly who I intended should get it. I used fresh horsemeat. And this is the corral where my colt was slaughtered, I figured the cat would come back to the same soup kitchen." He scraped a piece of dried flesh from the rusted metal with one thumb. "It was never took, just dragged around back and forth up here a bit. D'ya think the cat could *tell* it was poison? Or does this cat *always* just take one bite and move on? D'ya think it got enough and went off to die somewhere? I never saw no buzzards. But now I'm glad it didn't work 'cause I got a better plan."

Brian stepped down from the ladder. Clouds coming east met the sun going west, and suddenly everything was in shade. He could see the trail where Leya had turned off the driveway. The trail disappeared behind the rows of hay. Beyond that were the usual soft swells of prairie, then a row of hogback hills. All that to the west. That's not where the lioness had come from. It was a good twenty miles northeast to the cougar's open-faced lair in the Ferris Mountains. She'd dragged her suffering body a long way before she couldn't go any farther.

"Hey," Hathaway barked. He was standing on the edge of the roof, looking down at Brian. "Y'aren't being much help here, Pal. Quit lookin' for the girl. Old Honey'll turn around and come back automatic in under an hour. You'll get yours tonight."

"I wasn't . . . ." Brian swallowed, then looked up at Hathaway, shading his eyes even though there was no direct sun. Hathaway was back-lit and mostly silhouette. The toes of his cowboy boots stuck out over the edge of the roof, just above Brian's face, like two arrowheads. "What is it you think I can do for you?"

Hathaway didn't answer for a moment. He dropped the chain which boomed on the roof like an empty oil drum. All four horses jumped, the mares trotted to the far end of the corral, foals kicking and squealing beside them. "You know," Hathaway said flatly, "I *could* send all my guys out hunting. Every day 'til the job gets done. With a depredation permit, the government'll pay *me* to kill her. But ranch work goes undone, and I think you and I can work out an even better plan."

"I said I was thinking . . . . I said I didn't know if I had the tools, the skills—"

"What tools and skills is it takin' you to fly that chopper in circles over-n-over? Lookin' for somethin' special?"

"What?" The residual flutter in his stomach became a weakness in his knees. His mouth went dry.

"One day yer over the Ferris Mountains, the next over Rattlesnake Hills, then the Greens, then back to the reservoirs. Too high for shootin' coyote. And ranging too far."

"We're practicing." The silver toe guards were each pointing into one of Brian's eyes. He stepped back, still shading his face. "I'm teaching her to fly." *The sky is so big, of course the chopper could be visible for miles. You look like a search-and-rescue team, scouring the same territory in a pattern like that.*

"That chopper yer teaching her in," Hathaway droned softly, like when a fly is all you can hear on a trail in Death Valley, "it the same one owned by that wildlife nut was here a year ago?"

"Who—?"

Hathaway hit the ground on both feet beside Brian, landing like a cat with knees bent, stood panting for a moment then said, "If the lion took another horse, even our Dr. Wildlife Professor would say OK to killin' it. The thing would've proved unfit to live wild and natural, right?"

"I . . . guess so." *When you sound that weak, you might as well be IN the sights instead of looking through them. God, get into the zone. What's the matter with you. She's not even in sight.* Hearing hoofs, Brian glanced toward the trail, but it was the two horses coming in from the track behind him, both steaming and dark with froth. "At least that's the justification in granting depredation permits."

"Well, here's what I think," Hathaway said, still casually, "the cougar kills one more horse, I win two ways. The government'll probably come shoot the cat *for* me — and pay me if I take care of it myself — but more important, there's the *in*surance on the dead horse. Twenty-thousand. Forty for a brood mare."

Brian's legs goose-bumped as the breeze — chilled by the western storm — picked up, swishing harmlessly through the oaks. *There's an important trick in competition: replace the stress, the threat of failure, with a bigger central idea: you only exist when you hit the center of the target. Except what do you have to aim at now?* "This has nothing to do with me," he said, the quiver thankfully inaudible.

"It *could*. Twenty thousand apiece. Take your girl on a cruise."

"No . . . thanks." He picked up a handful of pebbles and tossed one at a tree trunk. "I don't see how I could be of any help."

"I built a little shed out on the range," Hathaway said sleepily, as though telling a story to his grandchildren, "slapped it together quick and it'll tear down easy. What would happen to a horse locked up inside with a cougar? Even if the cat only made a few slashes, I might have to destroy the horse myself — it's *still* a cougar attack. Guilty cat deserves to be shot. I collect the insurance too. So . . .," hands in his tight pockets, Hathaway rocked back on his boot heels, "I need the cat captured *alive*. And I need someone who knows what he's doin' to *get* me the cat alive."

Brian threw another pebble. Missed. Tossed another. Scooped up a new supply. Little rocks the size of bullets. Threw a handful like buckshot. So far nothing had come close to the broad tree trunk.

"I ain't really *askin'* you no more," Hathaway said. He stepped between Brian and the tree. "What I need is some kind of fish-n-game guy who's trained to track these cats. But . . . I guess his career'd be pretty well wiped out if his granola-eating tree-hugging buddies found out he was . . . say, shooting coyote from a helicopter."

Brian's arm — cocked to throw another rock, but would hit Hathaway in the face if he tried — dropped to his side. "Am I supposed to be scared?" He winced. It sounded too forthright or innocent, as though he were honestly asking. "Of *that*?" he added.

"Well, how important *is* your reputation . . . Mr. Wildlife Professor?" Hathaway smiled a sneer. "Or maybe," the smile disappeared, "you'd prefer to become a missing person — with your reputation intact?"

It was as though Hathaway had timed his last statement with an increase of wind he knew was due. Cooler, stiffer, more deliberate. It raised and rattled the corrugated metal roof of the shed where the poisoned meat had been chained. Brian reached to turn his collar up, found only the damp neck band of his T-shirt, then disguised the foolish gesture by lacing his fingers behind his neck so his elbows jutted out in front of his chin like artillery. "D'you expect me to say something like Reputation is 'bout all a man can call his own?"

"Or his life is."

"When you offer a man a choice, you better make sure he *cares* one way or the other."

Hathaway moved so he was between Brian and the sun, between Brian and the wind. A darkened cutout whose voice was low and clear amid the surrounding whoosh and whistle. "Ain't too many *choices* in this part of the country, just necessity. And survival. That's how we make choices here."

"That's true for the cougar too."

"I guess you'd be the one to know." Hathaway's hair whipped around like fire. "Cougar *chooses* to survive by killing foals. I choose to survive by killing cougar." He pinched his lower lip as though thinking. "But we have one thing the cougar don't. *Opportunity.* We can sweeten our choices. We hafta find it where we can around here, but it's there, just like for bankers and stock brokers, if y'know where t'look."

"And somehow," Brian said slowly because the wind seemed to rip each word away before it meant anything, "*your* opportunity has something to do with whether or not I survive my time in Wyoming."

Hathaway laughed, like a ghost-town echo among empty dust-scoured raw-board buildings where tumbleweeds scurried. "Your opportunity too, friend. I was jus tryin' t'make it easier for you to choose. *Opportunity's* what we call choices we *have* to make. But it'll be an easy decision for you — won't it? — when yer looking a dollar sign in the eye instead of . . . say, a chopper that quits on you when yer five thousand feet up. I'd call that an obvious choice, wouldn't you?"

The two mares stood parallel, their backs to the wind, the foals sandwiched between them, both suckling. A wind chime on the house sounded hysterical. A screen door screamed, slapped shut, and two roan-colored dogs came capering across the yard. They dropped their noses to the dust, one lifted its leg against a fencepost.

"Thinkin' about it?" Hathaway smiled. Back-lit, his grin seemed toothless. "Well, I tol' you my plan. Alls I need's the cat. Alive. And brought to that shed I put up out in Sage Meadow. I'll take it from there if y'have no stomach fer it. I'll produce the mauled horse carcass, I'll produce the cougar — shot clean, hunted down after the attack, see. I'll bring'm both in, open and honest, t'the proper authorities. They kin wire the photos to every newspaper in the state, I don't care. Vermin-kissing liberals kin write all the nasty editorials they want. There'll be no trace left of the shed. Insurance'll pay up, I pay my bills, it's over. Clean and simple. If it makes you feel better, donate your part to any bleeding-heart charity you want, then you can leave and never look back."

The wind hit a lull, and for a second Brian felt he'd been pushing a truck through mud, then the truck disappeared and his body, without the forward force, felt puny, atrophied. The two dogs stood with front feet against Hathaway's stomach. They each had a stripe of wrong-way hair — identical scars — down their backs. Hathaway scratched gently behind their ears. One of the dogs, the bitch, looked at Brian over her shoulder. She had huge light-brown eyes. She left Hathaway to come sniff at Brian's legs.

"I'm gonna giver t'you," Hathaway said suddenly.

Brian looked up, mouth open, but before he said anything — or even thought of what he might say — the wind picked up again. He saw the dun mare and Leya appear on the same trial where he'd last seen them. The wind buffeted his ears from the outside, his heartbeat the same from the inside. He could barely hear Hathaway saying, "These're Rhodesian Ridgebacks. Back when it first happened, I got me a dog book, looked at every one. This here breed was supposed to hunt lions in Africa. I figured, hell, those lions are even bigger and run in groups — a little cougar'll be a piece of cake! Drove to Denver to find a breeder and got me these two. Then the damn things slept on my bed while the second foal was mauled."

"What did you do to them?" Brian murmured, reaching to touch the disfigurement on the dog's back with a single finger, then gingerly placed his whole hand over the dog's shoulders and moved like a caress down the length of the scar.

"Cussed 'em a little, why? Oh!" Hathaway's laugh made the foals stop suckling. Brian's hand jerked back. "That's the ridge — they're ridgebacks. They *come* that way." Hathaway glanced over his shoulder at Leya and the horse, still approaching slowly. "You said you might need a dog. She'll do you more good than me. Might come natural t'her once she sees or smells the cat." Another glance at Leya. "Man needs company anyway. I take it you ain't gettin' any offa *her*." He indicated Leya with his chin. "That mare'll turn and come home after forty-five minutes. You can set clocks by her." The mare and rider disappeared behind the barns where the trail circled the outside of the compound.

"One thing," Brian said abruptly, his hand back on the dog's neck, then inexplicably oblivious, he sank to kneel beside the bitch, his arm snug around her body. "Leave her out of . . . your plans. Leave the girl out of your cougar maulings, your insurance pay-offs, your chopper crashes. Whatever happens, she goes home safe to California."

"Would that condition get me a live lion?"

"Hey!" Leya called from the driveway, walking, leading the mare past the barns toward the corral, like dragging a bale of hay. "Is she sick? Overly tired? She just stopped dead back there." The mare stopped again, opened her mouth and the loose-fitting bridle slipped off her head, making Leya sprawl in the dirt. Brian stood, fingertips on the dog's head. He felt like he was far away and out of breath.

Hathaway laughed. "She knows the way to her stall, darlin', she don't wanna go *past* and hafta turn around and go back. Just let'r go herself. She knows the way. The stall door's still open."

"Why isn't she scared of bones?" Leya asked as she got near, while the mare went the opposite direction, turned the corner and went down the barn row. "Aren't all horses scared of bones? I heard that somewhere, or read it."

"Well, that's a good example of how everything gets screwed up in books," Hathaway said mildly. "Foals *do* often spook at bones. But they're not scared because it's *bones*, only because it's something they never seen before. A foal only knows what he's ever seen or smelled, the finest-bred foals might be scared of *every*thing they never seen before. You gotta bring'em along slowly, let'um see the world's fulla stuff that won't hurt'em."

"Oh, that makes sense." She was casually extending a hand toward the male dog, lying in a fading patch of late sun, although not really looking at him. Brian stood as though anesthetized, the bitch still beside him, beneath his fingertips like a guide-dog. The male got up, wagging, approached Leya, then leaped against her, hugging her with his front legs. She shrieked, or laughed, or both, as his pelvis began to gyrate.

Hathaway's repetitious laughter, the wind's hoarse wail, the panicked wind chime, the screech of the weathervane, and Leya's voice all were instantly muffled, sealed in a tin drum. *God, do you actually have to have a rifle in hand to maintain composure? You've been able to conjure the zone by imagining a target, what's wrong with you? You don't need to see a piece of cardboard with black-and-white rings — put it behind the bastard's ear who's humping her.* Lightheaded, enervated, he couldn't find his breath, as though all his oxygen left his brain and lungs and muscles and rushed along with his blood to his groin. The male ridgeback slid down Leya's body, remained clutching her leg, and quickly Hathaway kicked it away, saying, "God, and he's *neutered*."

Brian hardly realized he'd taken the bitch with him until they were back on the paved highway and he realized Leya was chattering blithe nonsense to the dog sitting between them.

The explosion of thunderclaps, marble-sized hail hurled against the glass slider and drumming on the metal roofs of cars parked just outside, the unbroken howl of wind — none of it will hide what you're thinking. What you're doing while you're thinking. What you're thinking of doing? If she appeared naked and drenched outside your door this minute, would you swathe and rub her with thick towels, wrap her in blankets, ease the wet wisps of hair back from her fluid eyes

. . . or would your breath be the only warmth you'd offer,
your hot mouth closing over her white breast? Please don't
do this! But it's much too late to beg. Maybe the storm blew
the roof off her motel while she was in the shower — idiotic
premise to get her here, as unprotected as possible, wet, nude
. . . and of course terrified . . . and, naturally, she comes di-
rectly to you. Please don't. Don't touch her. Send her back
out into the deluge, let her pale skin be stung by the hail, let
her crumple and sob, bite her knuckles. Watch her from in-
side, from the window, from the binoculars, through the sights,
but please don't touch her. When the sun returns tomorrow
to raise steam from the sodden foothills and plains, maybe
you'll find her, curled, moist, humid and warm, in Hathaway's
horse barn, the mare's breath making condensation like dew
on her belly. Either that or she'll be out on that unprotected
bluff with the lioness, crouched at opposite ends, hungry and
disoriented, each waiting for you to come get her, Daktari.

The hail spattered against the side of his face like a
spray of gravel as he bolted from the room, clutching
the plastic ice bucket with both arms to his chest. His
breath caught in his throat like he'd been punched in
the stomach, and he crumpled beside the ice machine,
heaving, gulping for air. He hung his head inside the
machine's ice receptacle, the hail pelting his back and
shoulders.

As he returned to his room, the dog was standing
with her head poking out the cracked-open door, looking for him, her brow creased. Her concern eased when
he got closer. Her ears lay flat, her eyes smiled. The slight
sway of her head meant that inside the room her tail
was wagging her whole butt back and forth. He went
past her, his hand on her smooth brow, crawled on the
bed and lay stupefied while she licked rainwater from
his hair. His hand searched for the ridge of stiff reversed
hair on her back.

```
FROM:          BRIAN LEONARD
ADDRESS:       WRANGLER INN, RAWLINS, WY
PHONE:         (307) 678-0990
FAX:           (307) 998-0550

DATE:          June 13

FAX TO:        031/45 33 31

ATTN:          PETER GALLWAY

# OF PAGES TO FOLLOW:   3

CONTENTS TO FOLLOW:     GRID MAPS


COMMENTS: Main concern is still fe-
          male #4. Apparently there
          may've been some inappro-
          priate contact with civili-
          zation. Won't act until I
          have your OK, but am con-
          sidering the possibility
          I'll have to drug her and
          use the chopper to move her
          40 miles north to the Rattle-
          snake Hills (adolescent male
          #5 found near there last
          week). Checking on her again
          tomorrow.
               Leonard
```

He'd already long ago gotten his wake-up call, show-ered, loaded the camera and a rifle, fed the dog a pack-age of cookies from the vending machines, walked her, replenished the daypack with food and water. Had been humming a tune he couldn't name since 4 a.m. The phone was ringing again. Perhaps he'd asked for a second wake-up, to remind him to keep moving, if he wanted to get out to the cougar before 11.

"Hi, Brian?"

"Day off." Sweat broke in his armpits.

"Wait, listen. I just picked up my mail from yesterday, and this friend of mine sent me something I think you should see."

Brian met the ridgeback's calm gaze. She was always looking at him, steady and patient. "Can't it wait?" He held out his hand and she sniffed his fingers delicately.

"Wait for what? What're you doing, I thought we were taking a day off?"

"I'm . . . . Let's make it fast, okay? I'll be at that breakfast place, downtown, at the counter in ten minutes."

"Which breakfast place?"

But he didn't answer. The dog leaped up onto the truck seat like it was home, sat upright while he drove, instinctively leaning and bracing her weight on the corners. He turned and glanced back just before going into the diner, and she was still sitting there, following him with her gentle chocolate eyes until he disappeared. The place was called Square Shooters Eating House. From the counter, he could still see her through the window, but the dog continued staring intently toward the front door where she'd seen him go.

Why couldn't you say no? Why'd you have to come here? You have to stop testing. If that's what you're doing. Haven't you already gathered sufficient results to analyze? You're some kind of nut every time you're together. How much more of an answer do you want? One more try to make it different?

"It takes longer than ten minutes to walk over here," Leya said, breathing heavily, sliding onto the stool beside him.

His adrenaline lurched. Sweat trickled behind one ear. It was not an overly warm morning, only 6:30, the storm clouds had broken and were clustered on three horizons, like high white mountains with flat dark bottoms. To the southeast, fifty to a hundred miles across the prairie, rain was falling, as though someone had combed the cloud, at an angle, until it touched the earth.

"What's so important?" he asked tonelessly.

"What's with you, sleep under the bed?" She was pulling folded newsprint from an envelope. "My friend — we worked at the zoo together — she's interested in what I'm doing. Of course I haven't told her *every*thing. Anyway, she thought this would be a minor curiosity to me, but I actually think it's *crucial*." She spread a full newspaper page on the counter. Even his cursory glance couldn't miss the headline announcing the killing of a hiker by a mountain lion in north-central California, in the foothills of the Sierras.

"Brian, this is written so . . . *biased*. Listen: '*Anti-hunters want lions protected and allowed to live completely free, regardless of how many pets or livestock they kill or how many children they maul.*' Do you call that fair, objective reporting?" Her hair had been put into the French braid while still wet, again seeming to pull her eyebrows up and out, her oblique eyes hot and bright, her thin finger jabbing at the newspaper where she was reading, "'*With lions protected and their numbers at a 20th century high, Dept. of Fish & Game records show that the killing of mountain lions is close to what it was in the bounty days when there were no limits and an award paid for every pelt.*' Can you believe this, now they issue things called depredation permits every time there's an incident, and the lion is hunted down and killed by hired guns, almost 800 in the last two decades!"

"Just a second, put your picket sign away. Let me see it." With his finger, he snapped at her hand as though flicking an insect off the newsprint.

"Where'd you learn your fine social graces," she retorted severely, drawing her hand back toward her body. "Jeez, you act like . . . I don't know . . . where'd you grow up?"

"What kind of kill was it?"

"You morbid thing — which, the cougar or the hiker?"

"Here, they found the body a hundred yards from attack location, covered with leaves and twigs. A hundred yards, you realize how far that is? This cougar was storing a cache. She had no idea her prey was off limits to her. How could she know? I'll bet she had a cub." He seemed to be talking faster than usual, in a higher voice.

"Brian, they didn't give her a trial, they *already* found her guilty and gave her the death sentence."

"*Every* lion has a death sentence, as soon as they make their next, or first mistake." He had to lean toward her, over the newspaper, to scan the quotes. A hunting advocate suggested that a lion-hunting season would solve the problem by giving the cougars the fear of man they seemed to have lost. The soap Leya had used that morning stung in his nose; his eyes watered, his nerves starting to quiver. *Can you still trust imaginary target practice to maintain some equilibrium? Maybe not, but what else do you have to turn to? All that training . . . getting ready for national shooting championships, there'd be days and weeks of exercises to proof mental stamina and focus. Make it work now, make it pay off. Just see that long tube between your eye and the pin-point hole where the bullet will pop.* He slid the paper out from underneath her arm and centered it directly in front of himself.

"I suppose we should remember, a person was killed," Leya moaned, biting a fingernail. "He probably had a family, maybe children too. This's why people hate environmentalists, we act like we don't care about the human story here. We can't win."

"Environmentalists? Is that what we are?" he said, his voice echoing down the imaginary tube. "Here's how you compete: next time there's a homicide, get your environmentalists to go out to track, corner and kill the murderer on sight without asking *him* why he did it." He didn't look up. "*He's* lost his fear of man too, he gets to write books in jail, sell paintings at New York galleries—"

"What are you talking about?"

"You know, art shows by notorious killers." He'd read the same sentence of statistics four times: 30,000 square acres, 600,000 visitors a year, twenty mountain lions. That might be fifteen lions too many. The article said nothing about Gallway taking his dozen lions from Southern California four years ago.

"I swear, Brian, can't you take this more seriously?"

"What makes you think I'm kidding?"

"Okay, more *scientifically*."

"Oh, it's more *scientific* to worry about environmentalists needing a new PR man."

"You know what I mean. God, you make me so *infuriated* sometimes." Finished peeling the fingernail, she was wadding her napkin down to the size of a golfball, then blurted, "Didn't you have a father?"

"Obviously. Unless you think I'm a result of spontaneous generation. I sprang to life from a worm drowning in a sidewalk puddle."

"I mean a father *parent*, someone who raised you, a male role model."

"Why?"

With unusually rigid, straight fingers, she smoothed the crushed napkin flat again. "You're just . . . different from most men, and not really in a good way, like you don't know how to . . . ."

" . . . be a man? So that's the reason, huh? No father? I always wondered." He folded the newspaper page in half and held it up like reading a menu. "No, I didn't have one. My mother had two illegitimate children, might've even gone to a sperm bank. She was just out to prove she was straight."

"What an ugly thing to say about your mother. How do you know?"

"How could I not know?" The newspaper in his hands was shaking, fluttering. He held on tighter. "Look, I know I'm pissing you off royally, and I can't seem to help it. That's why I thought you needed a day off. Get away from me for a while, okay?"

"Gladly." She snatched back and folded the newspaper, then started to put it back into the envelope, but her flourish of fury was also awkward and clumsy. She couldn't seem to get the newspaper to slide in easily with the envelope's other contents.

"What's that stuff?"

"Just other articles my friend sent."

"About cougars?"

"Actually no," she softened and slowed. "Cheetahs. Interested?"

He shrugged. He scanned the breakfast specials posted on the wall above the steaming coffee makers, stacks of glasses and rows of soda nozzles. Belgian waffles with sausage. French toast and bacon. Short stack, egg, bacon or sausage. Two eggs, hash browns, biscuit. The early-bird crowd was growing, truckers and vacationing families getting ready for another day's drive. They had become surrounded by fragrant plates of eggs, biscuits, gravy and meat. He hadn't noticed the sound of clattering dishes, orders called out to the cooks, children's sing-song voices, or the door chime ringing until this moment. He could also hear Leya's breathing.

"Want breakfast, long as we're here?" he said softly. The microwave beeped. The coffee maker finished sending a stream of dark liquid into its carafe, heaved a long sigh, then a waitress whisked the carafe away so the last few drops spit on the hot plate. Leya cleared her throat, quietly, as though seated in a dark concert hall during the delicate silent moment between movements of a symphony. "Okay," he said, "tell me about your cheetah."

"Actually, we have two cheetahs getting ready to be in the Kritters show," she practically blurted. Paused and smiled. "I mean *they* do, the zoo does. They're six months old, learning to walk on leashes, sit and accept people patting them, take treats from people's hands. But they don't really *like* being fussed over and all these people who want to touch them at fundraisers and luncheons, so they're being introduced to this lab puppy about the same age who they'll hopefully bond with, and he'll then be their life-long friend, like another littermate." She looked up at a waitress and accepted a cup of coffee, drank almost greedily, then touched her lips with her palm. "*Hot*. Anyway, ideally what'll happen is when they do the show and go to special appearances, the cheetahs will cue off how relaxed the dog is, and also the dog loves getting gushed over by people, so he can take the brunt of the attention."

She had unfolded another news clipping, this one with a color photo, a smiling half-grown dog play-bowing to a grinning spotted cub who was about to bat the dog's head with a soft paw. Brian realized he also had a cup of coffee in one hand.

"That's my friend Sally," Leya said, pointing at the indistinct dark-haired woman in the background of the photo. "She wants me to come back and help this come out right. It's exciting and challenging, something *happening* every day. But also because I was so close to Rita . . . ."

He sipped his coffee. It *was* hot. The point of his lip felt swollen like a beak, throbbing gently. Leya passed her hand like a caress over the photo, smoothing the creases, looking down at it, mouth pursed slightly. It seemed her freckles were taking on the elliptical shape of her eyes.

He said, "You ever seen your male cheetah hold his lips back from his teeth and gums, like panting but exaggerated?"

"I don't know, why?"

"Big cats, they have sensing glands in their gums. So when they're in rut, they've always got these big shit-eating grins—" He broke off. Her eyes were glistening. "Okay . . . who's Rita."

"Our last dog. She was 14 when she died last year." She touched the tip of her little finger to the corner of one eye. "She lived her whole life as the bosom buddy of our first cheetah, the old one I told you about who we always took to the zoo fundraisers and publicity events. They're retiring him now. We thought he wouldn't make it when Rita died. He was miserable. They were so close, they'd *never* been separated. Sally . . . she thinks that's one reason I left, like a last straw after my divorce . . . because it was so . . . *empty* in the training area without Rita." She wound a napkin around one finger like a bandage. "But that's not it." She looked up and met his eyes.

He checked his watch, but whatever time it was didn't register in his mind. "I . . . uh . . . ." He fished ice from a water glass and held it against his lip. "I don't see how people will give any attention to the dog. They can pat a dog *any* time, how often do they see African wildlife close enough to reach and touch? I don't think they'll even see the dog."

"You're right, that's one way we've screened applicants trying to get a job as a zoo trainer." She stroked her brow with the back of one slender wrist. "We introduced them to the cheetah and dog — because the two are always together. The applicant's first test was to recognize the dog as a living thing desiring and deserving of love and attention, despite the fact that the dog is ordinary and the cheetah exotic. Anyone who sort of brushed the dog aside to get to the cheetah was immediately eliminated."

"Good idea." He swiveled on the stool to look behind himself out the front window, through the hand-painted *Breakfast All Day*, to where the dog in the Bronco sustained her vigil, watching people go in and out the door of the restaurant. "Look, I gotta go." He slid from the stool.

"Where . . . what are you doing . . .? I mean, is it part of our job?" She clasped her hands around one bare knee. She was wearing khaki shorts and hiking boots, as she did most days. "Don't you need any help?"

He put on sunglasses, smiled without showing any teeth, looking over her head. "Man's gotta do what a man's gotta do, know what I mean?"

"Yeah, I *do*." She picked up the news clipping so quickly, it ripped. Then she crumpled it. "Like kissing me?"

"What—?"

"Okay, I haven't asked, I've waited to see what you'll say or do, but now I'm asking, what was that kiss all about anyway?"

"I . . . ." He uncrumpled the clipping, ironed it flat gently with one hand. "I'm sorry, it was wrong of me. It wasn't professional, and you have a right to be angry." Concentrating on the newsprint, he lined up the torn edges. "I hope you'll forgive me and not give it another thought."

"Is that why you're afraid to take me with you today?"

He folded the two pieces of newspaper, slipped them into the envelope, put it into her hand and watched her fingers close on the white paper. "It never occurred to me that fear has anything to do with my decisions."

Three hours later, pulse thudding as though in terror, he scanned the ledge for the tenth or twentieth time. But she was gone.

"Can I go to sleep now?"

No, I'll be too lonely.

"You spend all goddamn day alone."

Don'cha think it's time you listened to some sage life experience from your older-and-wiser sister?

"Some life experience *you've* had . . . high school."

How about our senior prank. You ever hear about that in the hallowed halls?

"I don't think so."

Really? Paula and I dressed that school statue, you know the noble and too-brave-for-his-own-underwear matador guy. We helped him to step out in drag. Mom had made sure they put me in the home-ec sewing class, so I spent the semester making old matty's wardrobe: chiffon blouse and tailored business-style skirt, but with a big honkin' slit up the side. We used paint for his make-up and painted-on his black pumps too, hung one of Mom's old purses on his arm. Then we made a cartoon-character speaking bubble — made it out of hangars shaped into the outline then the frame covered with white papier-mâché, so it would be hard, and painted in "Hi, Boys! Yoo hoo, girls, wait for me!"

"That's dumb."

It really is, isn't it? Wow, that's depressing. It's really stupid. God, the things you think are funny when you're seventeen, the things you think are clever or outrageous or even that make a statement. Christ, it's pathetic. Dumb-ass moronic.

Imagine if that kind of crap was all you really did to make your mark on the world. See? Like I said, we'll have to be different than this someday. **When we meet again— La la la la laaa —Just don't let on that you knew me—**

"Diane . . .?"

No, I'm not crying.

"That's not . . . . I mean, you can if you want."

No, I don't want. It's a waste of my bodily fluids. I've got to save up, like a camel.

"Remember, like you said, someday we'll be sitting around talking about, you know, our jobs and . . . other stuff . . . we won't even have to . . . I mean, everything from now will be like dumb stuff from high school that doesn't mean anything."

Yeah, and for you, little bro, wow . . . by the time you finish college, there'll be a lot for us to talk about . . . like maybe a highpower shooting championship, a pilot's license, and rich. Well, maybe not rich. But you'll certainly be able to afford another rifle if you want. This time you go ahead into the match rifle category, custom made, free of regulations, front and rear sights, repeatable settings, and, for competition, a new adjustable sling with arm cuffs. What the hell, you can buy two, go for it and get another better service rifle, an AR-15. Are you ready for a semi-auto or want to stick with bolt action? You'll be old enough — juvie records, or anything else they've got on you, are expunged — you can buy from a gun store and no background will ever come up.

See, maybe it turns out you do have an inheritance, a trust fund that is suddenly sprung on you when you turn twenty-one, our mother's apology, her sorry-it-didn't-work-out payoff, not a million dollars, but makes working continuously not all that important. Still, you're prudent, little bro, like all average guys. You won't turn into some dilettante. On the other hand, maybe you will be. Can you be a dilettante wildlife biologist? One who rents an airplane and heads off to Alaska to photograph eagles or bears — you never decided which. But how about that speck-of-nothing feeling you get circling McKinley in a single engine plane, and yet at the same time just the opposite: there's EVERY*thing out there — vast glaciers and unreachable peaks, the meaty clouds sucked up against the mountains, the valleys of tundra, the brown rivers of caribou, the icy ocean and bottomless fjords and slick rocky cliffs — and there you are, in the middle of it, but not humbled by it, not an insignificant ant wailing away against the ferocity of nature, because you're soaring through it, untouched but also unrestrained, no need to conquer it or commune with it or be reduced to animal basics by it, that's real independence.*

"Until your plane hits any kind of weather."

Okay, okay, Mr. Unromantic, Mr. Pragmatic. So what do you do with all your sensible logic when you're finally situated with your enormous zoom lenses in the bear blind, and it's dusk but you haven't gotten a good shot yet so you're hesitant to leave. Your stinky insect repellent makes your eyes water and the viewfinder slimy so you're going to have to clean everything before you slime it up again tomorrow. Millions of bugs make a constant zinging sound — nighttime is so noisy compared to midday. The river is just twenty yards out in front of you, and both bears and eagles are supposed to come there to gorge themselves on salmon, dead or alive, but the few bears that showed up today were almost outnumbered by guys with cameras like you, and you only managed to get shots of their big round butts. So maybe you're practicing for tomorrow, what angles you'll set up for, where in the river you're guessing the animals will splash through, batting at the fish surging upstream. Maybe you're going to stake out your spot, stay all night and have the best place on the riverbank tomorrow — forget those warnings about trying to leave the blind. So, when you hear something — native dancers? someone being killed? someone having sex? — that biggest jumbo lens is pretty handy, you swing it around toward the dark woods where a campfire a hundred yards away isn't too difficult to spot, and what else does your curious eye discover? Two guys dancing around their fire without their pants on. Naked as long-legged frogs below their puffy sleeveless camping vests, hooting and hollering and laughing like cackling old ladies. But they're not dancing with each other. It's a rite of passage, they're braving the elements, which this time of year is a cloud of mosquitoes that moves like a big floating amoeba, and they're leaping through it and dodging it like bullfighters. Know what you'll do, average man? You'll pack up your gear and fly out the next day.

"What would *you* do, go join them?"

Don't you know me better than that, little bro?

"I don't know, Diane. Do I?"

What's that supposed to mean?

"Never mind, I don't know. It's just . . . . Never mind. Hey, cut it out."

You're still ticklish, huh, Bri?

"Knock it off, I mean it."

Why — you afraid of me?

"Maybe *you* should be— I mean it, I'm serious, knock it off, Diane!"

Shhhhh, okay, okay, shut up, okay? Don't worry, you're just slow, you think girls still have cooties. You'll like girls someday.

"But not my *sister—*"

You still a virgin? Huh? Thought so. No shame, Bri, you'll catch up. You know what they say, those who lag behind, catch up and pass everyone. And you know what? The wait'll be worth it. You don't want some bubbly, peppy, but touch-me-not sweet-sixteen. She'd probably clench her legs together like she has to take a pee, shut her eyes so tight her sockets look all wrinkled and empty, brace her hands against your chest so you can't get any closer than two feet. She should be teaching rape protection classes. My average-boy wouldn't know what to do with her without hurting her. But a real girl, Bri, should be warm and wiggly — and leaky — as a puppy, kissing with her tongue, and doing it all over. There's nothing softer, more knowing than a tongue. A tongue feels you, tastes you, smells you, and she'll make you writhe with something you can't name, cause it's not only lust you're feeling but complete acceptance, you're completely wanted, completely desired. And she won't feel like she's made of dry LEATHER *inside. She'll be slippery and welcoming, a steaming bubblebath that'll seem to snuggle and draw in your whole body.*

"I don't want to hear this."

Getting excited?

"No!"

It's okay, Bri, I'm sorry. But girls are great, you'll like girls, how could you not?

"You don't mean you *like* what Mom—"

I think I won't dignify that with an answer.

"Good, then just let me go to sleep."

I'll just lie here quietly for a while, okay?

## 6

SWEET LITTLE BUNNY

It was the wind itself that was difficult to see through. When the gusts had begun picking up, the deluge of rain the night before prevented a dust storm, so the atmosphere was relatively clear. But his eyes couldn't focus through the rushing current of turbulent air, like not being able to see the pebbles or fish on the bottom of a swift transparent stream. His shirt billowed and snapped like banners strung over a car dealership. Every step and arm movement actually met with resistance. His skin felt tight, his face frozen in a grimace, dry, stinging from microscopic particles driven horizontally at forty or fifty mph. He unbuttoned his shirt and hiked the neckline and collar up over his nose, then rebuttoned. The dog stood with her muzzle turned to the side, eyes closed. One ear was blown inside-out over her head. The other fluttered out away from her like a flag. With a hand on her neck, he guided her toward an outcropping of rocks, a small moraine, then he crouched, and the dog lay down. Brian put his forehead against the warm granite. Directly below his eyes, the dog slowly licked one paw, looked up at him and her tail tapped the dirt.

They'd been tracking the lioness since a little after 10 a.m. when they'd arrived on the canyon rim across from her lair and were unable to detect her there. By 11 they'd picked their way around the gully and walked back and forth along the small ledge where she'd stayed for so long. He looked back across to see how she might've watched him standing there with raised binoculars. He would've seemed no bigger than a jackrabbit to her. No more important.

He located scat and scratch marks on the small rocky plateau above the ledge. Relatively sure the stiff wind and wet earth were keeping the temperature down far enough to inhibit snakes from coming out to sun themselves, he'd given the dog plenty of time to sniff around the cougar's lair and scat pile, then turned her loose to see if she would use her instinct to track. They'd followed the cougar as much by the transmitter and his eye — spotting more scratch marks on a few of the spare, widely spaced pines, and shallow footprints in the sandy mud — as the dog's nose. She was keen on every rustle of sage, every rattle of pebbles, every wafting scent. But as the wind increased, as the terrain became steeper and rockier, he lost visual signs of the cat, and the signal on his receiver grew weak as though the wind also blew radio contact into chaos. Her battery might be dying. Or she could've doubled back on her own trail, then veered sideways, so, following the tracks, he'd actually been getting farther away.

"Not your fault, girl." His words weirdly calm in the quiet of the boulder's shelter. "You probably think you're supposed to find a pride of cats lying in the shade out on the savanna."

The dog sniffed at the front of his shirt hanging
from his face. He removed the daypack and rifle from
his back, then turned and put his spine against the rock,
his butt on the ground, knees bent and pulled close to
his chest. His loose swim trunks sagged toward his hips,
exposing newly pink upper thighs. The rifle on the
ground beside him, under his left hand; the dog on his
right, her velvety ear between his fingers. It was sparsely
wooded terrain, giving the wind enough room to keep
its speed and whistle softly in every tree. Dry bushes
scratched against the large granite boulders. But it was
still a type of silence. He could hear a fly buzzing, hovering over a tiny sand flower. He could hear the dog's
tranquil panting. *The type of secluded hush where you think
you're hearing your own heartbeat, but you only feel it.* Occasionally the dog stopped panting and raised her muzzle
slightly, sniffing rapidly through her nostrils, tasting the
air. *A dog . . . or any other animal might find this spacious yet
secluded, arid desolation to actually be teeming with sensation. Their ears and tongues, their noses, even their gums sa-
voring things you'll never know.* He ran the dog's delicate
ear between his thumb and index finger. The sense humans alone seemed to have evolved to use with any degree of nuance: touch. *Maybe you'll never sense the primal
gratification of breathing in the aroma of warm sand where a
bitch has peed . . . but you can know what it feels like to graze
a woman's skin with your fingertips . . ., or if she touched . . . .*
He released the dog's ear and moved his hand to his lap,
then the pads of his fingers slowly traced a line down his
leg. Stiff hair, razorback of muscle, bony knee. *It wouldn't
be like that.* He let his hand return up his inner thigh. Again
the scrape of hair, and the sunburn stung. And the nylon
lining of the swim trunks, which usually hung like a net
inside the baggy garment, was filling with him now. His
fingers eased inside the leg, reached under the nylon,
touched himself. *It won't feel like this either.* Gristle, rigidly autonomous, stubborn resistance, toughness. His
teeth chattered suddenly as though the wind turned icy.
Fist closed in a strangulation grip. Something beyond a

mere physiological reaction, and the excess adrenaline, as always, brought nausea.

She wants to be kissed again.

The dog raised her head, ears cocked forward, pupils pinpointed, nostrils twitching. His left hand was still inert on the rifle. In one motion, his fingers closed over the breech, the rifle swung across his body, his right hand found its place at the trigger, and he put a bullet into the back of a fleeing jackrabbit's head.

She took back her life — underweight, probably weak, but ready to find her place again. Not an excuse to lose the rest of your feeble hold on borderline poise. You're really languishing, in trouble, and you've got to pull yourself together. Sure, you can still shoot with dead-on accuracy when alone. Paper targets. But now, live running things can be picked off without a second thought? What if she'd been with you?

A rabbit. A brown and gray Mister Blister. Put out of his misery before a hawk or coyote carries him off alive . . . or swarm of bees . . .? Who're you kidding. Sacrificed for your momentary release from pressure. Mister Blister . . . prophetic name, but you were a dumb and dirty toddler, when she says "What'll we name Mr. Bunny?" And MISTER BLISTER must've been the first idiotic rhyme to fly out of your uninhibited four-year-old mouth. What did she trade for him, the doll sofa she'd made of cardboard and upholstery scraps? The minnows we'd netted in the polluted creek? The tiny blown-glass animals she bought in the zoo's gift shop with her allowance? But not the doctor kit. Daktari's backyard compound in the shade of the pepper tree had its first authentic animal occupant, an albino white rabbit in a wire hutch elevated on bricks. She donned secondhand hiking boots, green Girl Scout shorts and camp shirt, raked her compound's dirt floor with a bamboo broom while you climbed the branches above. Checked Mister Blister's Gatling-gun heart-rate with her plastic stethoscope while he crunched celery and carrots filched from the refrigerator. Then the compound's first emergency . . . could

*it have been your fault? So this time you left no question.
This time you killed him directly. So what'll she say about
this misuse of your dominion, misuse of your technological
superiority, your wanton disturbance of the ecological chain?
You'll have to say you're sorry, somehow. You can't bring
him back.*

He stalled while the taxidermist helped a customer
choose bass lures. The bulletin board had no new photos, but he was now able to recognize a few of the people
with deer and elk as guys who sat at the bar on Friday
nights. Then as the door tinkled shut behind the fisher-
man, Brian put his daypack, stained with dried blood,
on the counter.

"Been awhile," the taxidermist said. "How many?"

"No tails. This is a separate job for you. I want it
stuffed . . . you know, mounted, whatever you call it."

"What is it?"

"A jackrabbit."

The taxidermist unzipped the bag and looked inside but didn't pull out nor touch the rabbit. "Some'uv
the guys'uv been wondering where you been, what'cha
been doing. They ain't gonna be happy t'hear you came
in with one puny rabbit like you lost yer mind or
somethin'."

"I've been busy. I'll do a hunt soon. Believe me, I
need the money. I think the coyote have learned the
sound of the chopper, so I have to use other means."

"They been talking," the taxidermist leaned over
the counter, practically touching the bloody pack with
his chest. "We could have that yearly hunt like they do
lots of other places. And then also have a coyote-dog
contest. Even with prizes, they'd wipe out hundreds
more animals for a fraction of your price. Plus local
merchants cash in a little—motels, restaurants, bars."
He toyed with the unzipped opening of the pack. "What
they're hopin', though, is you're able to concentrate on

this area, really clean out just the surrounding range. A big hunt tends to fan out hundreds and hundreds of miles."

"I got me a dog now. Maybe she can be a coyote-dog." Brian stared at the tip of gray ear showing in the mouth of the daypack.

"Coyote dogs are trained. I never seen one, but heard'uv it down in New Mexico. Greyhounds and wolfhounds from Russia, dogs like that, they'll run down and kill an adult male coyote. Wouldn't believe it if I hadn't read it in the paper. Don't you got you a lion hound from Harry Hathaway?"

Brian jerked slightly. "Was it news on the radio or something?"

"We got our own wire service," the taxidermist grinned. "So whatcha got here?" He slid the dead rabbit from the sack. "Want me to make 'er into a jackalope? I turn out dozens of those for tourist gift shops, sort of my specialty."

"No." Brian turned away. "Just make it look like a sweet little bunny."

"Present for yer girlfriend?"

"Well . . . ." Sweat popped on his brow. "Maybe, sort of . . . like an apology gift. God, but d'you think she'll just see it as one of those dumb, insensitive things men do?"

"Not too many guys round here bring dead rodents to be mounted fer their girlfriends . . . nor wives neither." The taxidermist chuckled. "You want your pack back?"

"No. I'll need a new one."

"In the front, t'yer right."

"You don't happen to have bicycle pants, do you?"

"Them things that look like a wetsuit? Try the sport department at Alco."

While the taxidermist took the rabbit into the back room, Brian chose a new pack, light gray with an insulation padding, made for carrying a picnic. He also picked up three more boxes of shells.

"I got packs for dogs too," the taxidermist said when he returned. He rang up the pack without even looking for a price tag. "Not selling too well cause most hunting dogs go in the water, but I don't figure you're out for duck at the reservoir. Specially since it's not season."

"No thanks, she'd better keep her whole mind on what she's doing."

"Which is . . .?"

Brian gazed around behind the counter as though he hadn't heard the question. Finally he said absently, "Hathaway's got a nice place. How long's he been there?"

"Always. Was his father's and grandfather's." He put the shells into a small brown sack. "Not many'a them left, y'know, family ranches passed on generation to generation."

"He fly his own plane?" Brian folded the top of the sack down so the boxes of shells looked like they were a package wrapped in brown paper.

"Think so, why?"

"Nothing. Ranchers have to be able to do it all, don't they? Animal husbandry, run a business, predict weather, fly a plane, fix anything that breaks . . . be a mechanic . . . ." He took a bill from his wallet.

"Yeah, that's the long and short'uv it."

"He maintain his own plane too?" His fingers pushed through his hair. Grains of sand were still imbedded there, gritty on his scalp. "I wouldn't dream of opening the engine compartment of that chopper. Would Hathaway have a hand I could go to . . . someone who knows when an engine is looking okay and when it's likely to quit?"

"There's probably someone at the airport—"

"But if I was out . . . his ranch is pretty close to where I . . . might be."

The taxidermist looked up from the change tray and stared at him. "I guess. Harry's got a guy who's a pretty decent truck mechanic, don't know if he's ever touched the Cessna." He handed Brian his change.

"Thanks. I'll have some tails soon. I'm scouting to find better locations, you know? So I can put the bait where I'm likely to attract ten or twelve at a time. I think near Hathaway's place, up that way." He'd already put his wallet away so he made a wad of the bills and coins and pocketed them.

```
FROM:       BRIAN LEONARD
ADDRESS:    WRANGLER INN, RAWLINS, WY
PHONE:      (307) 678-0990
FAX:        (307) 998-0550

DATE:       June 16

FAX TO:     031/45 33 31

ATTN:       PETER GALLWAY

# OF PAGES TO FOLLOW:   3

CONTENTS TO FOLLOW:      Grid maps

COMMENTS: There'll be a time gap be-
          tween this information and
          the next fax. Going ahead
          with plans to drug and move
          female #4. No change. Also,
          male #2 and adolescent male
          #5 haven't turned up in grids
          2 or 3 since last found
          within half a mile of each
          other in the Rattlesnake
          Hills. Before moving female
          #4 would like to locate these
          two animals.
                    Best, Brian
```

Three days of dense hovering fog grounded him. A valium at night kept him dozing until 9 the next morning. Three mornings in a row Leya made a 10 a.m. call to ask what was on for the day — although she should've already known there'd be no homing since not only had there been no pre-dawn honk of the Bronco's horn outside her motel room, but nothing was going in or out of the airport. His voice cloudy, thickened with abnormal sleep, he muttered, "Take a walk, keep in shape, there's a long haul ahead soon."

Even indoors, the air seemed lead-colored. In his room with the heavy drapes pulled across the window, one small reading lamp spread a yellow circle over his maps: weather maps, topical maps, hiking trail maps, detail government land survey maps. By now the lioness could be anywhere. Covering five to twenty miles a day, she could be in the Green Mountains along the Sweetwater Creek, either gaining her strength and senses back on grouse and fawns, or emerging from the forested hills to stroll stupidly down the all-but-deserted streets of Jeffrey City in broad daylight. She could've picked her way, without stopping to eat, through the Seminoe Mountains to the state park and recreational areas at the reservoir, knocking over trash cans for bones of fried chicken, jelly donuts, watermelon rinds, blending in the shrubs just off the trails to contemplate each passing hiker or backpacker, her yellow eyes dazed and distrusting. She could be sharing mice and rats with the snakes in the bleak Rattlesnake Range, fifty miles north, and appear suddenly in the glare of sunlight in a uranium mining camp. Or she could be habitually searching for and following the equine smell she'd memorized, unknowingly going farther and farther onto Hathaway's ranch.

The dog slept behind him, stretched across both pillows. When she thumped off the bed, lay at the door and sniffed the crack of light at the baseboard, Brian let her out, pushed the drapes aside just far enough for one eye to watch her squat in the strip of white rock landscaping that ran between the sidewalk and parking lot, then cracked the door open for her to return. He kept the TV and radio off. As he reread Gallway's articles on cougar behavior, his fingers traced over and over the weal of stiff backwards hair on the dog's spine.

The fog didn't lift like a curtain, it tore, separated, left part of itself still on the ground like hovering smoke clinging in the grass, and the black trees seemed to grow out of it as though in a swamp. Then, finally, it dissipated the evening of the third day. Abruptly at sunset his room turned luminescent, and he became aware of squealing children splashing in the pool, laughter, car trunks thudding, keys jingling and people whistling, semis sighing, TV sets jabbering happily . . . as though the nearly three days of darkness had turned the interstate village into a ghost town which came back to life with sunlight.

Leya called. "Homing tomorrow?"

"No." His fingers encircled the dog's tail, moved with the grain of hair to the tip. When his hand slipped off the end, her tail thumped, her eyes smiled at him. He did it again. Cleared his throat and sighed, "Haven't we followed them around enough? Let's give them a little privacy . . . it's not a very fair game of hide-n-seek, let's give them a better chance to hide."

"But I thought we're *supposed* to know where they are all the time." Impatient. Maybe bored enough to give up and go home. "It's not a contest between us and them."

He let a moment of silence tick past, then said, "Sorry I haven't paid you lately. We'll do a coyote hunt tomorrow . . . dusk. I'll pick you up at four. I have to check the chopper tomorrow morning."

"Check it for what?"

"For . . . anything that might've gone wrong. It's sitting out there in the open where anybody could fuck— sorry . . . tamper . . . ." The dog licked his ear, went to the door and looked back at him. "Don't you ever check your car's oil or brake fluid? Or was that your husband's job?"

"Relationships don't have traditional roles anymore, Brian." Her voice was suddenly mellow, almost whispery.

"Okay, whatever. I'll see you tomorrow."

He used the utility rope in his gear to take the dog out along the interstate motel row. The signs, tall enough to be seen by cars on the freeway, were silhouetted in the maroon sunset. A train whistled and moved slowly, mournfully toward the west. Plastic grocery sacks rattled against fenceposts. A cross-country vacationer in striped Bermuda shorts and huge sunglasses walking her pair of terriers stopped to ask him what had happened to his dog's back.

"Cougar tore her open," he smiled, almost expecting to feel Leya whack his arm.

He took a sleeping bag and a flashlight, tied the dog to one of the helicopter's skids, spread the bag beneath the chopper's canopy, then drifted between shallow sleep and dizzy immobile weariness, floating on the far-off yips of coyote, an even more distant howl of a ranch dog left outside, and the closer, colder sound of a rusty hinge on a loosely chained gate creaking as the wind blew the gate back and forth as far as it would go. Finally he slept with dreams of confusion and panic, but no specific people nor action.

A blood-red sunrise woke him. The dog wandered out as far as the rope would allow and peed on the sandy tarmac.

He checked everything he knew how to check: were the belts and hoses whole, was the gas tank unpunctured, were electrical wires—as far as he could trace—unfrayed, uncut. He siphoned the gas into a can then replaced it with fresh fuel. There was no way to lock the engine, and installing some sort of car alarm was doubtful.

A little before noon Brian left the airport to pick up bait — steer entrails purchased from a slaughter house the taxidermist had suggested several weeks ago — then chained it down in the vacinity of the new state penitentiary south of Rawlins. After that, he returned to his motel room, fed the dog a can of hash from the vending machine, doused his shaggy head in a cold shower, and pushed his legs into new bicycle pants, like outfitting with a bullet-proof vest before going on duty. He meant to shave, but sagged on the bed for a moment and suddenly the digital red numbers of the clock were flashing 5:32 and Leya's delicate knuckles were tapping gently on his door.

"Brian? You in there? You okay?"

He didn't answer, but let his feet thud on the floor, pulled his canvas pants up over the spandex, ran water into the ice bucket to leavè for the dog, took his rifle, vest, and the new daypack, and slipped out the door so she wouldn't be able to see into the room. But she'd stopped knocking and was waiting three or four steps down the sidewalk, closer to where the Bronco was parked.

It was a noisy time of day. Interstate travelers bobbing in the pool, children unable to communicate in anything lower than a screech, cars with their windows down and radios clamoring —*Wake up Maggie, I think I got*—

Brian said nothing on the short drive back to the airport. Every time Leya looked sideways at him — dropping her lashes, hardly turning her head — a mosquito-tongue pinprick sent something hot-and-cold into his veins.

She wore the big headset as she took the chopper out of the airport, left it on even after she'd signed-off contact with the control tower. Usually she would exchange that headset for earphones connected to the transmitter, but they had the antennas pulled in and the transmitters off. She'd become proficient with the helicopter, and with one-word instructions — "south," then "west," as he directed her to the bait trap.

"Hover," he shouted over the noise, strapping on the harness and lifting his rifle. "Go in at about two-hundred feet until you see them. It's right over the next mesa in an arroyo." Picking shells from the vest, his hand shook. She was watching. "Did'ja see what we passed over back there?" He pointed north with the rifle.

She shook her head. She didn't look. Her eyes still on his hand.

He took a deep breath then quickly loaded the shells. "The state pen. Maybe they'll hear the chopper and shots. Maybe it'll induce a sweet memory of freedom. Or a painful one — of the day freedom ended."

Leya didn't answer. She raised her chin and met his eyes. Between the two massive headphones her freckled face was small and unusually pale. Her eyes a lighter, clearer brown. Her fingers resting softly on the controls.

"Imagine," he said, looking through the sights, holding the rifle too tightly, his fingertips white, "what it must be like to be the object of a manhunt and have these things circling above you with spotlights."

"What's the matter, Brian?"

"Huh?" He had his right knee braced against the rear edge of the open doorway, half his butt still on the seat, right elbow on his thigh, most of his upper body leaning outside under the thudding beat of the propellers, holding the rifle in a rigid, locked aim at nothing. "Okay, *go*."

But the chopper continued to hover. "Brian . . . ." Having to rise over the sound of the blades, her voice seemed more of a wail than a shout.

"*Go*."

"No, I don't think you're ready."

"I'm *set*, let's *go!*" Screaming, his words spread out and all but disappeared, not only into the tumultuous whirlwind directly below the chopper, but across the huge hazy pre-twilight panorama of empty rangeland stretching out around it as well.

"You're obviously upset about something."

"Yeah, I'm upset you won't get going before we run out of gas and fall like a meteor!"

"Brian!" Again, calling over the noise, her voice sounded like the plaintive cry of a night animal. "It *is* me, isn't it?"

"Yes, you're driving me crazy, okay? Now let's go!"

"Does it really make you this nervous to be developing a . . . friendship?"

His left hand like a talon holding the edge of the seat, he lowered the rifle's sights from his eye but didn't bring himself all the way back into the cockpit. His eyes slits in the buffeting wind. His body flinched at imagining the freedom of diving out the door.

"Brian!"

Usually, both wearing headsets, concentrating on the thin beep of the transmitter, they couldn't talk, she couldn't screech at him in her wounded bird-call voice, making him hear, for the first time, how his name rhymed with his sister's. *As a marksman, you don't just learn to shoot* DESPITE *the hair raising on the back of your neck — you shoot with precision* BECAUSE *of it.* On the ground, a ring of dust moved away from the midpoint below the chopper like ripples in a pond, like a crater being formed. Like a huge bulls-eye.

"Brian! *Listen*— because of your sister, you're not letting yourself have any sort of close association with *any*one. That relationship is still unresolved, and it's grown enormous and distorted until there's no room for anyone or anything else. Can't you admit, 'I loved her, but *I* need love too.' Denying you need anyone else won't make the pain of that loss go away. We can't just pretend you didn't kiss me!"

"*Shut up!*" His shriek spiraled down and away from his mouth. "Not here, not now." The rifle flailed outside the helicopter as though two people were struggling over it. "If you don't shut up, I'll jump out the fucking door!"

"Jesus, okay, calm down!"

She took off over the eroded, low mesa. In the arroyo, buzzards circled the bait, some sitting on the pebbles in the dry creek bed, lifting their bodies with slow beats of their large wings as the chopper swung into view, rising to circle with the helicopter as though it was a bigger, hungrier rival. Brian fired wildly at the birds while Leya shouted "Stop it, will you — *please* stop!"

"They heard us hovering over there, probably heard your goddamn screaming, and they all took off."

"How do you even know there were any coyote here in the first place?"

"Put it down."

"Will you promise to calm down? Will you promise to . . . talk?"

"*Put it down, put it down,* this goddamn noise is making me *crazy!*"

A wounded buzzard flapped in circles near the chained entrails, was blown ten or twenty feet further away as the chopper approached and landed in the arroyo. Brian hit the ground almost simultaneously with the helicopter, ran doubled-over until he was out from underneath the blades. *Easy easy easy easy. Why isn't there any relief — there* SHOULD *be relief — that there won't be a killing today? How complete, how dangerous is your apparent growing acclimation to live targets?* There were a few coyote prints in damp sand, the burlap bag of guts ripped open and scattered farther than the buzzards could've accomplished in a few hours. Probably just one, at most two animals. The low sun stretched long shadows from every bush and skinny tree, rippling over the smooth rocks where just days ago water from the storm had made a river here. The blades of the idling chopper slowed to a lower gear, and Leya came to sit beside him where he was leaning against a boulder that must've divided the current when there was one. "How many got away?"

"Not many." He moved away, stood with his back to her, a bloody mess of severed steer hooves and fatty intestine near his feet. When he touched it with his toe, flies and meat-eating wasps rose angrily toward his face.

"Maybe we'll see them on our way back."

"It doesn't matter."

"I'm sorry, Brian."

"Forget it."

"No, really . . . I'm . . . ."

"Forget it, okay?" He turned, forcing a smile. "No big deal." He batted at flies, then unloaded the rifle.

"Maybe . . . I mean . . . I still meant what I said," she said softly.

The chopper blades beat five or six times, then he said, "Fine. You don't need to repeat it."

"But Brian . . . things need to be said."

"*No.*" He was grinning, but it felt like the cracked-open mouth of a toothless old man. "You know, this's why guys like their dogs. They don't hafta discuss everything — give her a scratch behind the ear, pat on the butt, she's happy to sit there and be quiet."

"It's good to hear you try to be funny," Leya said, still soft and calm, "but I'm not joking, Brian. We need to talk."

He licked his lips, rubbed his hand against the stubble on one cheek, turned away. "Or maybe I need a divorce-therapy group."

"Damn straight," she snapped. Then she sighed. "Okay, I deserved that. But, really, sometimes groups make it easier, give you a chance to own up to what you feel. To admit things to yourself. If you could do that . . . you might be ready to . . . talk to me."

"What do you think I'm supposed to be admitting?" He looked at her. Her legs were crossed. An elegant length of lean flesh between her boots and khaki shorts. He closed his eyes but still saw the swimming patch of light that had been her white shirt, open at her throat, with the long, slender neck emerging.

"What you're afraid is happening between us."

He answered quickly, "Nothing's happening." Again he turned away, looked at the bait. The long shadows had reached and covered it. Suddenly he could smell it, fatty and rancid. The buzzards had returned, flying far overhead. The wounded one was still.

"I know, I'm supposed to forget it ever happened. So okay, maybe you can admit why you've never had a close friend." She paused. "And that you'd like to."

"How do you know I haven't?"

"Oh, Brian, it's so obvious." She laughed weakly. "Isn't it a relief to have someone notice, acknowledge that they've noticed, and tell you it's okay, that they understand?"

"What are you talking about?"

"Just that you don't need to pretend with me anymore."

Brian stepped over the bait. His feet kept lifting and going on, five, six . . . eight, ten steps down the rocky arroyo. *Easy easy easy*. Behind him, the chopper throbbed. Every footfall put the engine, the thud, the wind from the propellers farther in the background. The dead buzzard was in front of him now. Sage, rocks, old limbs of trees brought here on a flash-flood current — everything was tinted a firelight crimson. Then, like a final dribble of blood, the sun dripped behind the soft hogbacks far away in the west. His head tipped back, his mouth opened. A long, low wail came from his throat. It didn't stop. Louder, not quite a howl, not a bellow, a sound only a man can make. It spread into the sky, moved out away from him like the ring of dust caused by the chopper blades. Then he stopped, sucking in another breath and holding it. A tiny echo of his cry fell away, and Leya's boots crunched behind him. He moved forward and spun around before she could touch him.

"What time is it?" he asked quietly.

"I don't know. Sunset." She looked into his face. The colors of her eyes were translucent, almost taking the place of the sun, everything else growing drab and flat now that direct light was gone. "Let's go have dinner, Brian."

He looked down at the dead buzzard on the ground between them, nudged it with the end of his rifle. "I guess his friends will be out here tomorrow morning to eat him."

"Come on." She stepped back and turned slowly, looking at him over her shoulder. The rims of her eyes and nostrils were slightly red. "Let's go eat. Okay?"

He watched his boots walk back to the chopper, the rifle still cradled in his arm, pointing down, barrel hovering above his right toe.

In less than an hour he dropped her off at her motel. "Come back in fifteen minutes," she said. "I'll check the yellow pages to find a place for dinner."

Looking forward through the windshield, he didn't answer, didn't nod, waited for the door to close; then drove, as though impassive, back to his room, washed his face and shaved. Let the dog out, watched her do her business, called her back in, kneeled and held her in both arms — his brow pressed down against the hard top of her head — before he went back out the door.

Leya had brushed out the French braid and put on a denim skirt, clean white camp shirt and flat sandals. Then the restaurant she'd chosen had tablecloths, candles, cloth napkins, menus in leather folders. Brian stopped in the foyer. "Are you out of your mind?"

"Don't worry, we'll go Dutch."

"Are you crazy? What was wrong with *Country Kitchen* or something? I thought we were just getting a quick bite? And what you're *wearing* . . . ."

"Sorry, it's the only skirt I brought with me. And lookit *you*," she grinned. "Did you join a street gang or something? How many of these canvas balloons d'you own?"

As though mule-kicked in the chest, he took a clumsy step backwards, muttering a weak, "Just these." The spandex underneath was simultaneously cold and hot.

"Come on, we're here now." She winked. "It's Rawlins' best, and we're obviously as duded-up as we can get, let's give it a try and see how it rates."

The waitress wore a short frilled skirt, like a square-dance costume. She poured water from a plastic pitcher, then set it on the tablecloth where it made a wet ring while she took their orders. He mutely pointed to steak and fries. Leya requested stuffed trout with pilaf. "How would you like that steak?" the waitress asked.

"Huh? Oh, um, rare." He was holding his fork, pressing the points into his palm. After the waitress picked up the menus — she had to reach across the table to take his from his plate — he blurted, "No, wait, make it medium. Um . . . medium *well*."

Leya smiled and when the waitress was gone said, "You changed from rare to almost well-done in ten seconds. Don't you know how you like your steak?"

He drank half his water. "Long day. I don't think we'll be able to home tomorrow either."

"Truthfully, I don't mind the break from it, but I thought maybe we'd do something *else*, like hike in again somewhere, I don't know . . . try to get some photographs?"

"I'm not much of a photographer."

"Taking wildlife photographs isn't much different than hunting." With one hand she pulled a loose lock of hair over her shoulder "In fact, some hunters have turned in their guns for cameras. There's even a publicity campaign to try to get people to do so. It's the exact same activity: track, trail, hide, point, shoot. But your trophy is so much more—"

"*Rifle*."

"Gun, rifle, they do the same damage."

"A rifle is a precision instrument of environmental conservation."

"That's NRA bullshit." She leaned back in her chair, shoulders squared, chin up, glaring across the amber globe that held a flickering candle. The waitress brought a basket of bread, and Leya glanced up, smiling warmly, said, "Thank you," then the smile faded as she looked down and slowly buttered a roll, as though painting a piece of china. "I never know how you really think," she said softly. "Which side you're really on. Are you a wild-life biologist or is it just a job. Do you care about . . . any-thing?"

One elbow was already on the table — his face fell into his hand, his thumb rubbing one eye socket, his fingers in the other. Momentarily he dove into the dark place made by his cupped hand, the tinkling, murmur-ing sounds of the restaurant were in another dimen-sion now. *It's the kind of raw fatigue that tells you: up to now you haven't ever experienced being tired.* His neck felt like a pipe cleaner supporting a boulder, his aching joints hot and tight. Wished he could just stay sequestered in a place as secluded and gloomy as his own fist, but he could still hear her breathing. "Please . . . . I'm hungry. I'm whipped. Let's just chew and hum along with the Muzak." He raised his head, blinking as though the bug candle was too bright.

"I thought we were going to . . . talk."

"I'm exhausted. We talk so much."

"No, Brian. I'm sorry to seem so insistent or unre-lenting, but . . . we've been working really well together, yet you're so often agitated and upset." She lifted the roll to her lips but put it down again, unbitten. "Are you afraid I'll hurt you if we . . . were more involved?"

"Oh god." He closed his eyes, feeling himself bal-anced carefully on the chair like a stack of wine glasses. He heard his own voice moaning softly, so he forced it to become words. "Everything's fine. All animals are cautious . . . *you* could stand to be more . . . careful. Don't we have this conversation memorized by now? I don't have the energy to hold up my end this time."

"Brian—"

"Why do you say my name so much?"

"I don't know . . . . Maybe I think I have to get your attention all over again every time I say something. Am I right?"

"Oh lord . . . probably . . . I don't know. Why can't we just eat? I need a few days."

"You just spent three days in your room."

His eyes opened a crack. His arms moved slowly, elbows and shoulders aching, reaching out to hold his hands over the candle like a campfire.

Leya smiled somberly. "Are you cold?"

"I should've been doing this last week. With a real fire, out in the hills. I should've been keeping a closer eye on her." His hands lowered slowly to the tabletop. "She's not there anymore."

"Our cougar?" Leya's eyebrows lifted, shaped like the wings of a soaring gull. She wore no make-up, her eyes nakedly exposed, too accessible in the freckled and pale face. "Do you think she's okay?"

"I don't know . . . . If she isn't, I'm responsible. I didn't stay on it well enough, I didn't . . . . Maybe you're right, I didn't care enough."

"But you *did*." The seagull wings became a descending hawk, but the eyes beneath were just as undefended. "Don't beat yourself up. I know how you felt about that animal. I felt it too."

"*Feelings*. Why do women talk about feelings? Nobody knows what anyone else *feels*, we barely understand our own basic . . . urges."

The eyes facing him sharpened, intensified, finally slammed a door. If only for a moment. Then she said softly, "You're allowed to have feelings, Brian . . . for the cougar, or anything else. It's because you haven't worked out or understood your relationships in the past that makes you think you're not allowed to be . . . emotionally intimate."

"I can't discuss this again." Meant to be a groan, it was almost a whimper.

"You *can't*? That's precisely why you *need* to discuss it."

"I don't need anything . . . except a steak and . . . quiet."

"What about those urges you're so afraid of?" Without being rigid or severe, she folded her lithe arms under her breasts, her head slightly cocked, her eyes pure and direct. "Brian, loneliness is an urge too, but nothing will change until you admit . . . that you *want* more than a working relationship . . . with someone . . . even though you're fearful of the thing you want."

Again he was moaning softly before he spoke. "What I wanted . . . . I wanted to get close to that cat. To meet her eye-to-eye and have her perceive I was not a danger to her . . . . You don't understand."

"But I *do*." She scooted her chair around the table toward him. "Maybe this will make you feel better." She took a piece of folded newspaper from her breast pocket and opened it on top of his empty plate, pointing to the photograph like a kindergarten teacher, reading aloud, "*'Two cubs found near attack site. Wildlife officials in Northern California believe these 8-week-old mountain lions are the offspring of a cougar, killed two weeks ago, that attacked and killed a hiker.'* Brian, they cared enough to go find the babies when they realized the dead lion was nursing."

He looked vacantly at the color photograph of a spotted kitten digging its talons into a handler's leather glove.

"But some of this article makes me mad." Her voice puffed against the side of his head. Hackles raised on the back of his neck, then the chill came out in bumps on his arms. But he didn't move away. "Listen to this, *'When conservationists questioned why the adult lion wasn't drugged and moved to a new, more remote habitat, the answer from the F&G was that such programs are too expensive and haven't yet been proven to work.'* Doesn't that make you furious? *We're* the ones who should know if it's working—"

"I don't know," he murmured. "It's probably *not* working." He reached for a roll, clutched it in one hand, didn't look at her.

"Brian . . . ." Her sleeve brushed his forearm — she was leaning forward to try to see his face. "I do understand your apprehension. *I* thought I could never trust a man again, but . . . ."

"God, don't start with *me*."

"Brian . . . ."

"Stop saying my name!" It was a whisper, but urgent. He turned toward her. There were no freckles in the skin beneath her eyes. Fragile and pale, protected by sunglasses most of the time, a small pulse might tap there, probably dampened occasionally by tears — of exertion or irritation . . . melancholy . . . or unnamable fear. Only to be freshened again during her guileless dreams. Limp, in sweet slumber, her hand half curled like a new flower, her throat and delicate collar bones warm and white in a shadowy motel room at dawn . . . . The bread was mangled in one hand while the other was awkwardly stretching, reaching, holding the side of her face, his thumb lightly sweeping over her cheekbone.

"Brian—"

His chair crashed backwards. He was standing, arms held out to his sides, palms open, as though to prove he was unarmed. A water glass, hit by his knuckles as his hands swung away from her, rolled off the table and smashed itself on the floor. A dark wet spot ran down the side of the tablecloth. The waitress was frozen behind Leya, steaming plate in each hand, her mouth open and eyes wide, but not alarmed. Yet he had absolutely no idea if Leya was aghast, appalled, shocked, angry, or . . . . He didn't look at her face again. The water glass crunched into even smaller pieces under his boot as he edged around the table to get to the door.

Silly, idealistic girl doesn't realize: when the cougar makes a natural kill, but of forbidden prey, transferring the cat to new territory likely WON'T solve the problem. Conventional understanding says moving her farther away doesn't accomplish anything because she's already acquired the taste, she's discovered how easy a trapped or caged prey is, she's memorized WHERE it's most likely to be, she's learned to recognize and now seeks THAT *scent as the object which satisfies her needs. Is it* HER *fault? Regardless, she's the criminal whose behavior doesn't fit in polite society. The ideal solution: prevention — don't let her learn to want what she shouldn't have or how easy it is to get the prohibited thing she isn't supposed to want in the first place.*

Don't ever smell, taste or touch it, you won't know it's there. Then you won't find the tables turned — it's YOU *being hunted down because your appetite strayed and your instinct for normal, natural behavior failed you. But your cat's problem is compounded by the limitations of her tiny brain. Yours shouldn't be. She has no other choice. Homo Sapiens have options. You thought, or hoped, that if you could work a project like this one intently, if not passionately — instead of being obsessed with yourself — you wouldn't need anything else. And you thought if shooting remained a central activity, you'd stay in the zone. But it didn't happen. It was already noted, long ago, that this isn't a controlled test anymore. You can't keep lingering in the same conditions until you panic —* THAT'S *too late.*

What little sleep he got was accomplished sitting up in the stiff arm chair, still fully clothed, the dog snoring softly on the ugly bedspread that matched the curtains. A semi arrived after midnight, its engine idled until one, then it was throttled and pulled out of the parking lot. Two trains went by without blowing their whistles. Somewhere far away a thunderstorm rolled in and moved on. At 6 a.m. he was already at the airport checking the helicopter again. He tried to leave a hair balanced across one of the belts, and another on the gas tank cap, the way older brothers in movies tested to see if siblings were borrowing the razor. But the warm breeze removed the hairs as soon as he tore them from his head and put them in place.

The taxidermist was sitting behind the counter so that only the top of his head showed. He rose when the door tinkled, chewing a mouthful of a sandwich he held in one hand. "Your bunny rabbit ain't done yet." The sandwich was sardines and onion.

"Why's it taking so long for one puny jackrabbit?"

"Ran into some problems."

Brian stopped approaching, stood six feet from the counter. "Me too. I was right. Damn coyote know the sound of that chopper now. On to plan B, I guess."

"Harry's lookin' for you."

"Now?" Brian wiped his brow with his palm. The sweat in his hair had already dried stiff, but his skin was damp again. It was close to 100 degrees at 11 a.m. "How can you stand to eat something like that in this heat?"

"This?" The taxidermist looked at the ragged edge of the sandwich where the back of a sardine, dorsal fin still attached, was clearly visible. "Never thought about it."

"Doesn't it remind you of all the dead fish you stuff and mount? God, I'd be a vegetarian by now. Or at least stick to ground meat and tuna. Something that doesn't look so . . . *whole*."

"What's made *you* so queasy all of a sudden?"

"Maybe this heat. Where'd all that lovely fog go? It was keeping things cool."

"That fog ain't good for nobody, believe me. It caused Harry t'lose a foal."

He could almost taste the raunchy smell of fish in the glob of spit he swallowed, moving too slowly down his throat. "What? How? Was it . . . uh . . . coyote?" Brian took a step back.

"No. Mare due to drop was in a paddock, fog so thick that no one could see her, just on the far side." He bit deeply into the sandwich. "Foal suffocated in the bag, mare didn't do her business."

"God, that's too bad."

"He's down at the Lincoln."

"This early?" Another step back.

"The day he comes in t'see his mother."

"Oh, yeah."

The temperature might've climbed another five degrees while he was in the store. By the time he walked down to the tavern, his limp shirt was sodden, the canvas pants felt like they were made of lead, his feet swimming in his shoes. He stopped outside the door, took off his boots, threw his drenched socks in the sidewalk trash can and put his bare feet back into the boots. If the beer smell wasn't thick enough yet in the tavern, they'd smell him coming.

Hathaway was hatless, his hair slicked straight back, wearing a pale peach silk shirt, light blue jeans and loosened white tie. His cowboy boots were new, black lizard skin with silver toe guards. He was at the bar, had one foot on his other knee, polishing the boot with a paper napkin, watching a rerun of a black-and-white comedy. Brian sat two stools away. Shook his head when the bartender approached. The TV show became an advertisement, and Hathaway, without turning around, said, "Been sick, pal?" He continued to polish the boot, pausing to dampen the napkin with his tongue.

"No. Well, maybe. The heat."

"Hasn't been too bad 'til today."

"Yeah. Fog kept me grounded, though. By the way, sorry to hear about your colt."

"She was a filly. Bay. Four white socks. Pity."

"Was it . . . insured?"

"No." Hathaway swiveled his bar stool so he was facing Brian, licked the napkin one more time for a final buff on the bright toe guard, then balled the napkin and put it in an ashtray. "Insuring a fetus — of any age — is too damn expensive. The rates drop when the foal is twenty-four hours old. If you wait six weeks, it's even lower, but that can be too late. You gotta pick and choose where and when and with whom you're willing to gamble."

"Makes sense." With one finger, Brian pulled a bowl of peanuts closer.

"Does it?" Hathaway smiled, fondling his tie. "Well, I can't figure out why you'd want to take such a gamble with that pretty girl."

"Excuse me?"

"Why would you risk her . . . safety?"

Brian smelled gasoline on his hand when he pushed several peanuts into his mouth, so he sucked the nuts without chewing until the wave of nausea passed. "This seems to be a sticking point in this negotiation," he said, the peanuts still whole in his mouth. Then he crunched them carefully and swallowed. "She'll have nothing to do with . . . *any*thing we've talked about. So her safety isn't even an issue."

"Wrong, pal." Hathaway tightened the tie. "If you aren't smart enough to be concerned about your own skin, maybe you'll worry about losing your fresh little squeeze. If you won't help me out, her safety *will* be an issue. Can I say that any plainer?"

"I've said she's to be left out of it. How plain is that?"

"Fine, you just do this one favor for me — let's say next week, or the one after — and she'll stay in her happy little world, protecting flowers, bees . . . and bunnies from extinction."

Brian could smell himself. The rancid odor of adrenal sweat was far more powerful than any ordinary perspiration. And a fan on the end of the bar put him up wind from Hathaway. He licked salt from his lips.

"How's that hound workin' out?" Hathaway asked.

"Not sure yet, but . . .," his voice was hoarse, he cleared his throat, "I'll keep you posted."

"You do that." Hathaway put money on the bar. "My mom's expecting me. Maybe you'll come on over in an hour or two?"

"I'll see." Possibly the shrill female laugh in the kitchen covered his throaty voice. "Maybe."

Hathaway put a hand on Brian's shoulder as he passed him, leaving the tavern.

WHAT IF the engine just sputters and cuts out, the blades go dead, an unnatural half second of gliding balloon-like silence, and she realizes . . . turns to you, huge eyes lacquered with tears, her sobbing heart beating on the outside, hands reaching . . . for YOU . . ., mouth open in one last anguished cry . . . calling out to YOU . . . but you can't hear it over the . . . no, the blades have gone dead, you can hear everything . . . YOUR NAME, of course, again and again, screeched at you like a falcon's deathcry . . . . And would you feel this same sick, eager flush? Or worse? Would you be panting with feral pleasure? Lunging to shred the blouse off her body while the chopper drops like a bomb and she's practically retching her guts out of her mouth . . . begging YOU to save her?

WHAT IF it takes even longer, the motor doesn't die immediately — spits, skips a few beats, runs rough and uneven, ripping itself apart as it struggles to keep the blades turning . . . and you're not even there, you're watching her panic from . . . from . . . from . . . how about from where you're lying now . . . face down . . . . Can't your perverted thrill be just as acute? If it all just happens in your head, with your dick in your fist — wouldn't this be a viable option? At least she'd be alive tomorrow. Then go on, let go, LET yourself dream . . . .

. . . while you're lying on top of the clear cockpit, under the rotating blades. She's still inside. Her mouth moves. You can't hear what she's saying. Can't tell if you're flying or not. She's not wearing the head-set. She's not holding the controls. It's just her face and white throat you see . . . and one shoulder through a ripped blouse. How'd it tear? As you were climbing out, she grabbed, held on to keep you beside her, to spend her last moments in another desperate kiss, and in the struggle, you took a bit of cloth away in your fist . . .? Wondering about that small frayed opening, exposing the freckled skin, so vulnerable to harsh environments . . . and suddenly realizing: YOU'RE naked. And she must be seeing all of you, pressed up against the clear bubble, and her mouth opening must be her screams. But you hear nothing. How well you

know, even a rabbit finds a voice at the moment it hangs between vigorous life and violent death. This sudden silence is the chopper screaming. Maybe you went out there trying to make repairs before it crashes. But instead, a vulgar hard-on smashing itself obscenely against the glass right over her face.

WHAT IF this scenario isn't distorted at all by the pills you took . . . an hour ago . . . half a day ago? Hey, if you want to prevent Hathaway's promised disaster, why aren't you sleeping at the airport again, standing guard? Or why aren't your hands, instead, holding the smooth breathing reality of the hound while you sleep? Why aren't you controlling yourself? WHY ARE YOU THINKING ABOUT THIS?

Dear Sal,

                                    June 20

Thanks for continuing to forward my mail,
even if it is all junk. Sometimes I think
that's all I have left to call my own, my
junk mail. How melodramatic. I'm expecting
something from Mitch or my lawyer. And
double thanks for the clippings--elixirs for
the soul. Believe me, more than you know.
In fact, last week I thought I might have
to call you and say come get me. I thought
he was going to abandon me and run away in
the night. He was so depressed, I never saw
anything like it. Actually, I probably
didn't even see the worst of it, he didn't
come out of his room. But what I do see is
plenty. When his infuriating flippant
rudeness goes away, all you can do is want
it back because without it, his stark
misery is just so exposed. But he seemed to
recover a little, after a bit of purging
out in the middle of nowhere. I won't bother
to describe that part. The clippings help a
lot by giving me a chance to get him to
listen--giving me an opening so to speak,
giving us something to share feelings about,
so thank you thank you thank you. Oh,
sorry, he doesn't like that word. Feelings.
He's so male, know what I mean? Like, it's so
cute the way he gets flustered when you
notice his clothes. But I haven't gotten to
the best part yet. I think he does want
something more with me. He's so afraid of
being vulnerable, it's so touching. He even
ran away! Left me with the restaurant bill. I
brought his dinner to his room, knocked but
he wasn't there, left it outside the door,
and in the morning, mixed in with my mail,

found an envelope with $20 inside. I won't
tell you where the money comes from, it
would upset you, like it did me at first.
Still does, but I can't do anything about
it. I know you don't want to be hearing any
of this. Thanks for being worried about me.
But don't be.

I'm glad the new puppy you found is
starting to get along and form a bond with
Ben and Jeri. Maybe it's good I'm not there,
though. I don't think I could ever feel
about a dog the way I did about Rita. That
reminds me, Brian has this dog now, someone
gave it to him, and this full-grown dog
bonded to him completely and instantly. She
never takes her eyes off him when they're
together. You can trust dogs' judgments,
can't you? It must say something about him
to have that dog be so devoted to him so
quickly. They must communicate on some
alternate level. But, anyway, back to the
cheetahs, just remember that Daphne _only_
had Rita, but Ben and Jeri have each other,
so their bond to the puppy may not be as
strong. Also, I'm not too happy that your
new Ken-doll assistant seems to have an
instinctive way with them. Find something he
can't do, okay? I still may need to come
back. I hope not. I do miss _you_, though!

Love, Leya

7
PRECIOUS AS WATER

Does it matter if it's the sleeping brain creating the violence that produces the arousal? The brain and penis are inexorably linked, so if one is abnormal, the other can't be healthy. Are you showing clear signs of impending action? Some COUNTER-*action might be called for. Something* BESIDES *a stealthy pre-dawn skulk outside her door, even if it was for the seemingly innocent purpose of paying your debts. Twenty for a touch on the cheek, or is that the previous kiss and touch combined? How much would she charge for that scene in the chopper you designed in living color last night? No, don't try to ease your own total accountability by trying to make* HER *into a whore. But* DOES *she share some of the liability? For repeating your name. For breathing on your neck. For boring holes into you with her seemingly harmless eyes. Never mind, the changing course is still your responsibility. And there's also a similarly targeted lioness who needs help just as imminently.*

The note said: *Missed you at Mom's. She was disappointed you weren't there to try her cactus jelly. There's a semi trailer behind the gas station in Lamont, 10 miles up the road from the turn-off to my place. Noon tomorrow. Don't want to miss you again. HH*

As though in answer, Brian tore off the blank bottom half of the Wrangler Inn stationery that Hathaway had used, and wrote: *Homing canceled until further notice. Coyote hunt tomorrow 5 p.m. or the next day same time. If no honk by 5, hunt canceled.*

On a midday walk with the dog, 103 degrees in the shade, he took along the note in an envelope with her name and room number, and as they passed the roadside mailbox in front of her motel, he stopped to slip it inside. The dog sagged to a slow trudge beside him. Her shoulders undulated like a feline's under her smooth red-brown hide. Her head hung, sleepy eyes half closed, long meaty tongue dripping from the side of her blood-engorged mouth. His joints were jello, his arms hanging limp, empty. He let his fingertips graze her spine as they plodded back to their room.

It was 11 and already 105 when he arrived at the chopper the next morning. He spent twenty minutes adjusting his harness to fit the dog, then coaxing her to lie quietly behind the seats with the harness fastened to either side of the cockpit and tightened enough so that she couldn't get up and try to go anywhere else. There was no time left to check the engine nor replace the gas in the tank.

"We just might go down in a blaze of glory," he shouted to the dog as they lifted off. He circled Ferris Mountain, flipped down the antenna on his side of the chopper and turned the receiver to her frequency, and found it, weakly, probably at least fifty miles away, but he didn't have time to determine in which direction she'd gone. Then, after he found the state highway to the west and followed it south, he shouted, "I guess no fireball crash today, girl. I guess he really wants to see us."

The gas station was easy to spot, the semi trailer sitting in a large back parking lot crowded with tumbleweeds that hadn't yet broken loose to roll and spread their seeds. In this heat it would be a matter of days. At the front of the station, a pick-up finished gassing up and pulled out onto the gravely road into town. As Brian descended into the back lot, some of the tumbleweeds did pull loose and scatter. Hathaway's truck was parked behind the gas station, and Hathaway stood in the open, hands on hips, watching the chopper come down, his head bare and hair whipping. Brian clutched and disengaged the rotors, finishing the descent in auto-rotation, so that after the skids hit the asphalt, the blades wound down on their own, and everything was quiet.

The clear cockpit immediately began to heat up, so after he unbuckled the dog's harness, it was almost a relief to jump out. He left the rifles in the rack.

"I like a man with a spectacular arrival," Hathaway called, approaching with his hand extended. Brian released the eager dog so she could leap against Hathaway's chest, attempting to lick his face. The handshake was aborted as Hathaway laughed, filled both hands with the dog's ears, gently shook her grinning head — to her obvious delight — then let her bound away to sniff in the parking lot.

"She missed you maybe," Brian said.

"She loves *every*one, she's never without a best friend. Sort of promiscuous of her, don't you think?"

"Don't underestimate her loyalty." The dog squatted to pee and turned to look back at them as she did. Brian squinted in her direction. He couldn't wear his hat while wearing the headset in the chopper, but he'd forgotten to untie it from the gun rack and put it on when he got out.

"Well," Hathaway grinned after a pause. "I know we're not talkin' 'bout your little girlfriend!"

A white flash blinded him for a split second. "What . . .," he hesitated, both hands at his brow, visoring his face. Then continued as his eyes cleared, "makes you think Leya's not loyal?"

"Just a little joke, pal. I'm sure she is. But, you know . . . she sure as hell isn't *promiscuous!*" Hathaway laughed out loud.

"Is this why you wanted to meet out here — baking our brains and frying our eyeballs in the closest thing to hell I've ever seen — to talk about what Leya is and isn't?"

"In a way, yes."

Brian took his hands away from his face, his arms dropped to his sides. "Hey, I told you—"

"Calm down. I know what you told me. Maybe we don't have to discuss business here in the sun if you're uncomfortable." He gestured toward the semi trailer.

"That place'll be an *incinerator.*"

Hathaway pointed to a thick electric cable running from the gas station, across the parking lot, disappearing under the trailer. "Has its own little A/C, working since dawn to keep you cool and happy, friend."

"What's in there?"

"It's a who. And it's a *she.*"

"Huh?" Brian extended an arm, beckoning for the dog to return.

"Sheila won't go far. Leave her be to explore."

"Who's Sheila?"

"Didn't I tell you the dog's name?" Hathaway put his hands in his pockets and rocked back on the heels of his boots, the toes pointing up and glinting in the sun. "What'cha been callin' her? *Yo, Bitch?* Save that one for Deb. She likes it. Just kidding. C'mon, I'll introduce you."

"Wait." He looked at the chopper; looked at the dog trotting nose down along a weedy trash-strewn fence.

"It's okay, pal, my treat."

"Um . . . no thanks . . . I don't . . . . I mean . . . not that way."

"Any way you do it is pretty much the same." Even though buckled below his big belly, Hathaway's pants were so tight, it looked like the edge of the pocket might sever his hand where it was stuffed to the knuckles inside. "B'sides, Deb'll be pretty insulted if you don't at least say hello." He continued rocking back on his heels and then forward again. "What's the matter, you got bigger problems than I even figured on?"

"What?" The haste and volume of his voice brought the dog's head and ears up for a moment. He waited until she resumed sniffing around a rusty oil drum used as a trash can. "I just . . . I'm surprised, I guess . . . that this is why you wanted me to come out here."

"Okay, so why *did* you come out here?"

"I . . . was in the neighborhood."

Hathaway stopped rocking. "Out looking for my cougar?"

Brian opened his mouth slightly but didn't answer. He could feel perspiration drip from the ends of his hair onto his shoulders. A rivulet ran down the center of his sternum. The saturated underarms of his threadbare shirt stuck to his skin. He wiped away the sweat that collected on his upper eyelids.

"C'mon, Deb's waiting," Hathaway said, starting to walk past Brian toward the trailer, even taking Brian's arm and trying to turn him around to likewise go toward the trailer.

"Not today." Brian ripped his arm free, backing away.

"Buddy," Hathaway said softly, crossing his arms and settling his weight onto one leg, the other cocked out to the side, "I think you just can't think straight 'cause yer not getting any off yer girlfriend. So I've took care'a that problem for you, so you kin set yer mind straight again and git back t'business."

"This is . . . . There's no word for it. You really believe what you're saying?"

Hathaway was walking backwards, as though holding out a steak to coax a shy stray dog to follow into a cage. "A frustrated man can't think, can't make an informed decision. I discovered that years ago."

Brian realized his feet *were* following, and they were getting closer to the trailer.

"Hey, pal, don't worry. I pay her doctor bills twice a year when she goes fer tests, she's got a clean slate."

A rusted metal set of stairs on wheels was pushed up against the trailer, leading to a windowless door. Hathaway's feet made a hollow metallic boom on the steps as he climbed, but the door opened before he knocked. A low, husky but mellow female voice was laughing and said, "You two gents been discussin' business out in the sun? Come in and get cool, I got beer chilled f'you here, wadda y'been standin' round outside fer?"

"Sorry, Deb, wanted t'take care of our mantalk so we wouldn't bore you to death." Hathaway crushed the woman Brian still hadn't seen to his chest. They shared a long noisy kiss, then she broke away, laughing again, and pushed Hathaway on into the trailer.

"Lemme see yer friend, Harry!" She wasn't very old, but no girl either. There was a cowboy look to her face, lean, brown, sun-lined, but not coarse nor sour. Her eyes crinkled when she smiled. Two teeth overlapped slightly in front, a small scar split one eyebrow. She wore a sleeveless calico sun dress that came to her shins, her feet were bare. She held out her thin strong arms to Brian, but he skimmed past without touching her.

The inside of the trailer was made up into living quarters, except without running water, so there was no bathroom. One end, about a fourth of the total space, was completely taken up with a four poster bed. The posts were thick with softball-sized knobs on the tops, the cover was a patchwork quilt, and on top of that, spread decoratively in the middle, a black and white cowhide with the legs pointing to the four corners of the mattress. Deb was fishing two beers out of a half-sized refrigerator on the other end of the trailer, where there was also a chrome and Formica kitchen table and chairs. That's where the boombox was, the soft music a folksy harmony —*they say he's not your kind*— *he'll leave you cryin'*— Hathaway, after a long drink, patted the woman's butt, left his hand there in a long caress. She laughed, pushing his hand away. "I reserved time fer yer friend, Harry."

There were other cowhides all over the trailer: tacked to the walls in lieu of pictures, draped over the back of the small sofa, spread on the floor as rugs. An old-fashioned yellow-shaded lamp stood by the bedside, the kind with an ashtray attached to the pole about halfway up. A stained-glass Tiffany lamp sat on a nicked-up side table. The air conditioner was mounted in a hole cut in the back side of the trailer. Churning away on a high setting, the A/C caused the metal wall to vibrate, making the hum louder and more palpable, sometimes covering the low music. He felt it in his stomach and fingertips.

"Brian, is it?" Deb said, coming toward him to offer the beer. He was still standing about six feet inside the doorway where he'd stopped after edging sideways into the trailer. "Brew?"

"No, thanks."

"Maybe it inhibits his performance!" Hathaway boomed, his laughter crashing around the small space.

"Get outta here, Harry."

"No, don't bother, I'm not staying," Brian said, his throat dry, almost cracking.

"Relax for a second, Brian," she said. "Harry'll leave, we'll cool off. I gotta TV, a little one, but it works. Or we'll listen to music. Pick out any tape you want."

Hathaway hitched up his pants, although they settled right back where they'd been below his gut. "See ya later, pardner. You can find yer own way home, can't'cha?"

"I . . . ." Brian put his hand flat on the wall where a red and white cowhide was mounted at an angle. "I heard cowboys get their rocks off with sheep . . . and cows . . . ."

He saw Hathaway put his beer down, hard, and start toward him. Deb's husky voice hardened, her eyes became slits. "Who're you calling a cow, mister?"—*blow you old blue norther—blow him back to me— He's likely driving back from—* Then Brian heard the boom of vibrating metal almost before he realized Hathaway had slammed him up against the wall. His ears rang. One of Hathaway's legs was lifted, a bent knee jammed against the crotch of Brian's safari shorts. His hands were around Brian's neck. His beery breath on Brian's face. "You treat your woman as shitty as you want, pal. But you're a guest here, and our women are as precious t'us as water." The pressure from both the knee and the thumbs on Brian's throat increased. "I could squash your balls like berries right now, but . . . ." Hathaway gathered saliva and spit in Brian's face. "Y'ain't even got enough gumption t'fight back . . . and I still need you next week."

—Loves his damned old rodeos as much as he loves—someday soon—goin' with him— Brian's heels slid down the wall, joined his toes on the floor as Hathaway slowly, eased the pressure and backed away. "I'll need to hear what you have to say soon, I need an answer, one way or t'other," Hathaway continued matter-of-factly. "You have my fax number? Use it instead of the phone."

"Don't hold your breath."

"You wanna hold yours indefinitely?"

"Go on, get outta here," the woman cut between them to go open the door. "Both of you. I don't wanna hear this crap. And I kin take care of myself, Harry."

"All our women do, Pal," Hathaway said, pausing as he stepped out the door. "Does *yours?*"

Brian's fingers were still trembling as he buckled the dog into her harness in the chopper, the blades already beating, blowing faded newspaper pages and dust into the corners of the lot.

And as though they'd trembled themselves into exhaustion, his fingers didn't seem to want to hold the rifle with their usual expert dexterity. At least not for more than two or three minutes at a time. They kept locking up, cramping, and he would have to release the rifle and kneel, quickly stretching out then closing his hands, staring into his palms as they flashed open and balled into fists again.

After 6 and it was still over 90 degrees. The sun didn't even seem close to the western horizon. The decades-old ravaged skeleton of a station wagon was about a hundred feet west of the chained bait, so, hopefully, the setting sun would back-light the junk heap with a blinding glare thereby hindering the coyote from detecting any movement behind the car, which was where he and Leya were lying in wait. The abandoned car was several miles east then north down a parallel-rutted dirt path that turned off the airport road, way out past the chain-link yards of rusty equipment. He'd laid the trap, another batch of guts from the butcher, at about 4, plenty of time to draw flies and bees, a few scavenging crows and buzzards. But the coyote, whose voices he'd heard when driving to and from the airport at night, and whose tracks had been plentiful on the dirt ruts of the overgrown road, had yet to appear.

"I still don't get it," Leya said, yawning, "why we're doing this."

Important questions constantly seek answers. Repeated questions mean the answers haven't been adequate, or reasonable. How can you explain yourself, except the simple diversion? "I thought you understood, Gallway isn't sending enough money for two. It costs something to sit in our rooms watching the weather channel."

"We haven't gathered data in *days*." She scratched the dirt with a stick. "Is that what you do in there, watch the weather channel? Any hope for a break in this heat?"

"I don't know." He propped the rifle against the car and let his hands hang limp from his wrists, shaking them a little, then letting them hang again.

"We have a timber wolf in the Kritters show. He's like a big puppy. How could you kill a puppy?"

"Be quiet, okay?"

"You wouldn't kill *her* would you?" Leya put her hand on the ridgeback who was stretched out in a line of shade created by the car's bumper.

Brian stared at Leya, then at the dog. His hands throbbed. Because the sun was at their backs, there was no shade for them. His shirt was sopping for the fourth or fifth time that day. *If you don't drink enough in this kind of dry heat, you're apt to experience dizziness and headaches, momentary blindness, muscle weakness, disorientation or even hallucination.* He shook his head, his ears ringing as though he'd already pulled off a dozen shots. *Easy easy easy easy easy* but the mantra didn't do anything except change the word into the taut thin buzz of an angry insect. Likewise his body was a humming hot wire, ready to jolt himself and anyone who touched him into fiery convulsions. "Okay, you need to understand this: The ranchers, they get suspicious of wildlife studies, especially protection programs or relocations. Like how they're screaming about wolves being reintroduced around Yellowstone. So we show them we're on their side too. We show them that we don't value every single animal's life over *their* livelihood."

"Well, despite the ecological reasons to value every animal's life, to do so is to value our *own* livelihood."

"I said be quiet. Please." He watched Leya run the twig in her hand gently over the dog's ribs. The dog had her eyes closed but was breathing quickly, opening her mouth to pant a few breaths every minute or so, then sighing again but continuing to puff heavily through her nose. "I hope she's in condition for a long day of tracking," he said.

Leya looked up expectantly. "Are we finally going to go find that cougar?"

"We may have to." He reached for the insulated pack that was sitting on the ground between them.

"Good. I've been looking forward to something like that." Her eyes were hot and radiant.

He'd been planning to get a drink from the canteen in the pack, but he suddenly moved several more inches away from her, lying down again and positioning the rifle through a wheel hole in the single rear fender. Crept forward as far as he could, so she was more behind him than beside. He licked his chapped lips and swallowed. A dry wad in his throat felt like a whole egg moving through a snake. "It's not that exciting," he mumbled into his elbow as he looked through the sights.

"Maybe you'd better fill me in on the procedure."

"You can just follow and watch."

"Brian!" She playfully tapped his shoulder. He almost dropped the rifle.

"Cut it out! I'm try'na get steady here."

"Old grouch." Her voice was blithe. She hummed airily and tunelessly for a moment, then said, "What's the dog supposed to do? She won't kill the cougar, will she?"

"Oh god," he groaned. "The cougar goes up a tree. As soon as the dog is close enough for there to be any kind of chase, the cougar trees itself."

"Do you have a gun that shoots tranquilizer?"

"*Rifle*. Actually, in this case you're almost right, it's usually a specially modified shotgun. I don't have one. We'll use a jabstick. Okay? Satisfied? Now be *quiet*."

"I don't think I'm scaring off anything."

"You're scaring off *me*, okay? I'm going to run screaming out into the desert any second now."

"You're cute when you're annoyed." She touched him again, this time on the small of his back.

"*Shut up!*" While he shouted, his finger spasmed and the rifle fired. The bullet pealed through the fender's brittle rusted metal, the shot reverberated off the hills to the east.

"You should learn to handle compliments better," she said quietly when the echo died down. "You're the one who'll be scaring everything off."

The dog had lifted her head when the rifle went off, but was still half up, her ears pricked. Then she lifted the lower half of her body as well, the hair on her neck raised to match the ridge on her back, a low growl in her throat. She wasn't facing the bait.

"What is it?" Leya whispered.

Brian sat up and turned, swinging the rifle around, looked at the crouched posturing dog; then glanced at Leya, kneeling, bent forward, clenched fists against her stomach. Her eyes stayed on the dog, but Brian heard the rattle. He turned the rest of the way toward the west where the snake was coiling itself, ten yards away. Two or three shots hit the dust around the snake. He kept reloading and firing, his shouted curses lost in the rifle's detonation. Four, six shots. The snake writhed and twisted, wounded, not dead. He heard Leya shout something and grab the dog as she started to lunge forward. Seven, eight shots. The snake lay in two mutilated pieces. He shut his eyes and sat panting.

"They don't die easy, do they," she breathed.

"Nothing . . . dies easy, but . . . I was *missing,* dammit. I'm not supposed to *miss.*"

"Sorry, that was insensitive of me to say something like that." She touched his knee. "Why were you missing?"

"How should I know." Eyes still shut, his thumb felt the polished brass of the trigger. He wasn't sure if there were any more shells still loaded in the rifle. "I guess it's not true, then, that you can't help but kill a snake on the first shot because the snake strikes out at the bullet and gets hit in the head every time. An old wives' tale."

"More like an old *fart*'s tale," she retorted. "Where would a woman come up with stupidness like that?"

Eyes open again, he blinked at her through swimming colors. Then got up. "Hold the dog. Don't let her go." A predictable dizzy flash hit him on the first step, so he stopped for a second, face toward the ground, took off his hat and fanned himself.

"Can I have the rattle?" she asked sweetly.

He didn't answer until he was standing over the mangled snake. "No, I want it."

"Why?"

"Maybe . . . to remind myself not to *miss*." He touched the dead snake with his toe. "Flies'll be eating us alive if we stay out here much longer. I . . . ." Bending too swiftly, bringing the dizziness back, he fumbled to open his pocket knife, hacked off the rattle, then stood to kick the snake into the bushes and cover it with dust.

"What were you going to say?"

"I . . . need a drink."

She handed him the canteen. "It seems a *little* cooler now."

"Let's be quiet, okay?" He picked up the rifle and took the dog by the collar with his other hand, kneeled once again, coaxing the dog to lie down between himself and Leya. The dog sniffed at his ear. He turned slightly and let her lick his mouth and nose. With one hand he felt the creases on her brow.

"You really love that dog, don't you?" Leya said softly. He didn't answer. Again tried to swallow the dry egg in his throat. "Isn't that Hathaway character going to want her back eventually?"

"With interest," Brian muttered.

"Pardon?" When he didn't respond, she went on, "I mean, it's good to see you can feel that way toward *some*thing, but . . . maybe you subconsciously knew it wasn't a relationship you would have to commit to, so that's why you let yourself go. You know, since you already know how and when and why it will end, the end isn't a threat, so the relationship itself isn't a threat."

He crushed a spider on his knee with one palm, then ground it into a smear on his skin. "There are many ways to end something." Surprised he'd spoken, and words he'd never have expected. He clenched his jaw, pulled his hat lower, pressed the top of his head against the warm rusted metal.

"I know your sister's choice hurt you, but, Brian, that's not *why* she did it, to hurt you."

"You don't . . . know . . . *anything*." His voice as unfamiliar as an owl's cry in sunny daylight. He released a heavy breath, his chest tight, his hands still holding the rifle across his knees. Precariously balanced one moment, maybe already in a free-fall the next. Wheezing as though beyond winded, fighting to catch a breath, *easy easy easy easy.*

"Brian—"

"*Shut up!*"

A breeze rattled a dry leaf against the metal. Leya jumped. Then together Brian and the dog picked up their heads at the distant but approaching yips and yawls. *Maybe they've learned the sound of a rifle means something has been killed. Food.*

The half-dozen coyote came up over a ripple of prairie, partially surrounding the bait. In summer coats, they looked in poor condition, patches of thick matted fur still being shed out on their backs and throats, thinning and gaunt around their ribs, hips and loins. One lifted his muzzle to send his string of thin laughing barks into the air. The ridgeback growled, her fur still bristling. The other coyote joined the vocalizations, and, after the lead male advanced to assault the burlap bag holding the bait — shaking his head as though breaking his prey's neck — the others approached, some slinking, others posturing their degree of dominance. The animals handled stings from the meat wasps with mere shakes of the head, refusing to give up a mouthful or piece of hide, and amid the growing noise, the entrails began to be spread over an area about ten to twenty yards square.

"They look awful," Leya whispered. "We should be out here giving them a proper diet. I wish they didn't have to eat garbage."

"Carrion." Brian's answer was monotone, through clenched teeth. "A critical part of the food chain — as precious as water."

He lifted the rifle. Lowered it again to reload. Aimed. Froze. Followed each animal in the sights. Released the trigger mechanism to wipe his sweaty palm on his shirt. Resumed aiming. Then began firing, right hand back and forth between bolt and trigger, squeezing off shots, moving quickly across the targets left to right and back again. *And so it is, after all, getting easier to shoot to kill.*

Because of the echo and the indiscriminate spray of bullets, the coyote ran in circles first, unwilling to completely abandon the cache. One was limping. One, screaming, shook his head and sprayed blood from the stump where his ear used to be. The rifle continued resounding, pausing to be reloaded, then cracking again. The ridgeback was barking, rapidly, rhythmically. Leya was screaming something. She grabbed Brian's shirt and the material ripped as he wrenched away. The animals were scattering, carrying off pieces of intestines and feet.

WHAT IF she tried even harder to stop the rifle . . . tried to stop the bullets? What if she grabbed and clung to your arm like a small monkey, rode your back, could you shake her off? Would she then break from cover to help the targets to escape? To hold herself hostage for their safety, for their innate right to live in their own habitat and follow their own behavior? Could she scream something as involved as that between shots? Maybe while you're reloading? Will you look up and find her out there shielding their wealth of food? Unaware she could soon become part of their supply. WHAT IF you did scatter shots in your mother's bedroom that night — and, suddenly freed, like a mare returning to the burning barn, what if Diane had run forward to once again protect you from your natural roguishness . . . and took the bullets . . . the bullets that were MISSING their intended mark . . . and maybe it sent you into a paralyzing ecstasy, a shot cracked and she simultaneously died . . . . So would you expect to writhe again in excessive gratification if Leya drops to the bloody dust where they've scattered the coagulating guts . . . . You're not supposed to MISS.

Bullets peppered the dirt between sage bushes and rocks.

"Brian . . . they're all gone."

A brief touch of his shoulder. The rifle clattered out of his hands. "I can't shoot anymore, can't hit anything, what's wrong with me, *it feels like something's choking me!*" Then silence and dusk returned. Like a light going off, a thin shadow crept up over their backs. The temperature seemed to drop ten degrees in ten seconds.

"Maybe you missed on purpose . . .?"

He snatched up the rifle again, turned it over in his hands. "That's idiotic. If you don't have anything intelligent to say, shut the *fuck* up."

"I'm going to ignore that misplaced hostility."

"What makes you think it's misplaced?" He got up, slammed the pack over his shoulder and turned his back. "It's aimed *right* at you. And at my*self.* I was wrong to bring you out here. Go back to your goddamn husband."

With the dog beside his leg, he strode back toward where the Bronco was parked a little way down the dirt road, but Leya's voice followed him like a whining fly staying close to his ear, "That's just cruel." Then she broke into bona fide weeping. "You're hurting so you have to hurt someone else. *I'd* never tell *you* to bring a picture of your sister hunting with you, instead of me."

He stopped, his back still to her. He heard a few more of her footsteps, then she stopped somewhere close behind him. "Well, you just did, didn't you. So now we're even."

When they turned off the rutted, bumpy dirt track onto a paved two-lane road, she said, "I'm sorry," almost too softly to hear.

Was it . . . could it have been the searing weather and sus-
pected heat stroke . . . jumbled your neurological signals,
thus the choking sensation . . . and . . . . More evidence of
weakening or deteriorating . . . shooting no longer stabiliz-
ing you. No longer fabricates normalcy . . . . Some mutant
exigent need has overcome the ability of disciplined precision exercises to hold it at bay. What is it about her that has
set both your voluntary and involuntary functions and responses in such turmoil? Your behavior has gone off the
fucking chart. But you're able report it calmly, perfunctorily,
like that cat who lay nonchalantly gazing over her private
canyon, patiently waiting for her body's sickness to fade,
unconcerned at the impaired behavioral drive that led her into
this trouble in the first place. So now she prowls again, unaware that she still has not answered for her crime, and her
sentence could be to force her to repeat it, in bloody detail,
then die amid the gore she creates. Will any attempt to save
her be at the expense of yourself? Or if you WERE to partici-
pate in Hathaway's pre-planned torture and death, would it
be enough to satisfy you? Yes, YOU, the sharpshooter . . . who
have now cupped the two small globes of her white buttocks
. . . one in each of your big hands . . . holding her, drawing
her, as though she was supposed to be part of YOUR body and
you were pulling her back into place . . . every sensation keenly
distinct . . . silken inner thighs brushing against your hips
. . . dusty citrus scent in her hair . . . salty darkness of her wet
ear in your mouth . . . then her mouth . . . sucking your thirsty
tongue . . . holding your shaggy head in her hands during the
desperate bottomless kiss . . . yet soft as a life raft . . . "easy,
easy," her feathery whisper when your breathing turned to
frantic grunting, feverish sweat on your face she stroked with
a light dry palm . . . the delicate pale breast and pointed nipple
standing upright between your lips . . . all her smallness,
softness, delicacy, but nothing weak, you slid forever between
the strong, slippery walls that allowed you in, that held and
protected you . . . .

Who will protect her?

Who was it, WHO made her cry out, who WAS it? — any one of Mom's anonymous visitors, man or woman, then Mom as well, then Mom alone. And she ended up eating a bullet.

But your rifle still in the back seat of the Bronco, perhaps jolted to the floor when the truck skidded off the road, across the gravel shoulder, zigzagging and boomeranging in a strip of tumbleweeds beside a barbed wire fence . . . a last sliver of daylight slicing surgically through your sun-stroked eye into your brain, couldn't find the brake, the truck shooting forward, veering left then right, the wheel meaningless in your disoriented hands . . . her disembodied shriek registering nowhere in your baffled senses . . . and when the motion stopped, her secure hands pushed you just far enough to one side so she could drive the truck while you leaned in near fevered delirium against her . . . led your clumsy stumbling boots into her room, shoved your thick throbbing head under a cool waterfall then led you to the bed and . . . . Didn't she peel your threadbare shirt away and dry the rancid sweat of sunstroke from your body with her sheets . . .? Tease the drops of water from your chin and ears with her tongue . . .? Wrap her body around yours without fear your searing skin would either flame or liquefy against hers . . .? "Is it tomorrow?" you woke mumbling. "Is it okay? Does anyone know it was me?" The slow breathing behind you broke into a moan then a whisper as she woke and murmured, "Feeling better?" You knew that would be impossible, to ever feel any better than your dry flesh against the healthy heat of hers . . . but she rolled away from you and came around the bed, fully clothed, to open the heavy curtains and let a mid-morning sun expose the dim shadows of where you lay on top of the rumpled bedspread, also fully clothed, filthy, dried stiff with sweat . . . except your boots lined up beneath the night stand, socks stuffed into the tops to prevent scorpions from crawling in to lie in wait. "I'll shower first, then you can use it, then we'll have to get you something to eat."

But you picked up the boots and walked barefoot out to the truck as soon as the bathroom door shut and the spatter of water hit the tile, her body enveloped in steam. Why should you be afraid? Will your apology ever be enough?

As soon as Brian came up the aisle, the taxidermist left the counter and hurried into the back room. Then an apprentice came out with a covered package, set it in front of Brian, and he too hurried to return to the back room.

The stuffed jackrabbit was encased in a thick Plexiglas box with a polished oak base, a much more expensive setting than Brian had ordered. Looking at the expert way the corners of the clear box had been glued together without showing a seam, he didn't notice, at first, the rabbit displayed inside: Standing half upright like a predator dinosaur, the rabbit's front feet had been outfitted with talons taken from a hawk or eagle, and its rodent teeth replaced with feline fangs — the same size as a small cougar's. The tip of one fang was painted an unbelievable red. In its clawed front feet, the rabbit held a piece of torn stained cloth.

When Brian tried to lift the Plexiglas cover off the oak base, he found the cover glued into place, and also found the little gift card taped to the bottom of the base: *I admire a man who only fucks one pussy at a time. Hope all remains well with you and your main squeeze. Give her this one for me.*

He clutched the display box to his torso, wrapping both arms around, hurrying, almost limping, to the Bronco parked at the curb out in the stupefying heat. The tires, softened by the scorching asphalt, screamed and left dark smears of themselves on the street. *What's that smell . . . the closed cab baking in the afternoon glare, a hot, dusty, clothy odor of canvas, stronger when it's damp or sun-warmed. And you can't breathe or move . . . .* The sun was knife-like coming through the windshield. Squinting, veering erratically within his lane, perhaps hallucinating again — on the frontage road near the interstate, he saw Leya jogging, stumbling forward along the dirt shoulder, going in the direction of his motel. He passed her, swerving practically into on-coming traffic, and saw her receding in his rear view mirror, frantically waving her arms at him, mouth open in a tiny, quickly dwindling cry. *The scream — was it her or the dying rabbit? You'd stopped hearing the buzz of bumblebees, wrapped and smothering in the hot, collapsed tent, not one stinger reached you. "Shut up," she shouted, but you weren't making a sound. "Lie still," she murmured. What were you struggling for, to breathe? to get out of the hot canvas? to see? To see the white rabbit with his ears full of angry bees, stinging, stinging, getting as close to its brain as they could get. What was that tingle in your tiny stomach? Your sister threw you into the tent, collapsed it on top of you, held you down inside the thick canvas, and something was screaming. You'd never before heard a rabbit's deathcry. She'd set up her borrowed Girl Scout pup tent near the rabbit hutch, with a bamboo rake swept the compound's dirt floor, used fist-sized rocks to mark off paths . . . to the compound kitchen, the examination rooms, the exercise areas, the sleeping quarters. But the veterinary compound in Africa under the pepper tree in the backyard was in complete turmoil from the attacking bees, Daktari saving those animals she could while the rabbit, Mister Blister, with his blood-gorged vulnerable ears, was sacrificed. She never found out what had been going on in the compound while she was away gathering supplies. The natural granite was plentiful, and with a pocketful of ammunition, you'd waged war on the bumblebee nest hidden somewhere under a pile of old lumber. You'd spotted the fat bumblers coming out then returning, landing on the warmed wood and crawling beneath it through a knothole. Your six-year-old arm may not've been powerful, but the dead-on aim of a future sharpshooter was certainly at work . . . by the time Diane returned with carrots and lettuce and peanut butter crackers, the air was full of the menacing drone and the zigzagging bees looking for signs of their enemy. The first shriek was hers, crackers and vegetables tossed like confetti, two stings on her arms, but the swarm was already zeroing in on the rabbit hutch, Mr. Blister shaking his head and throwing himself from one side of the hutch to the other. Were you immobile, still in the sharpshooter's zone? In the second before she threw you into the tent, with absolute slow-motion clarity, you saw a bee land on the tip of a white ear and make its way into the pink canal, out of sight. What was that bright tingle in your gut and between your legs, the hot adrenaline-blast — something dying a few yards from your blinded eyes and smothering skin, and your sister saying "Lie still" but you couldn't . . . you couldn't . . . you'd never heard a scream like that.*

His pouring sweat was mixed with tears when he finally burst into his room. The dog had heard the Bronco and was already at the door. He pushed past her, a wild, unfamiliar voice panting, *"I'm sorry, I'm sorry . . . ."* Crashed to the bed, bouncing the rifle to the floor, the dog sat eerily at the door, refusing to come closer to him. He stared at her. "I don't blame you," a hoarse whisper. "I'm sorry, girl. Everything will be okay."

From the cracked-open door, a line of light streaked to the bed, rippled up the side of the mattress, diagonally across the bed, then continued up the wall. When he rolled to his back, the beam crossed his body at his navel, dividing him. His eyes in a shadow. Above his waist in daylight, below in dusk. He counted ten, twelve, fifteen, twenty deep breaths, each inhale five seconds, each exhale twice as long. Pushing the air out with his diaphragm. His muscles became heavier, as though he were sinking farther into the mattress. Like a feather tick that might rise up all around his prostrate body and he would disappear. But even as his muscles slackened, a drum beat continued, down below the band of light. Thick, slowly quickening, focusing his concentration. *Is there really a phantom, mythic rhythm, a hypnotic pulse that seems to be made on stretched skin with animal-bone implements — some intuitively received male signal, imperceptible by normal senses, constantly being sounded on an alternate frequency, and when you hear it — calling you to a war-dance — you make no resistance and ask no questions, but obliviously pursue it to where it leads? Do you lose yourself at this moment? They aren't* YOUR *legs, spread-eagle and rigidly trembling. It's not* YOUR *mouth open in a silent cry.*

It's not your sweat drenching your clothes enough to make a body-outline on the sheet. They aren't YOUR *hands reaching to hold—*

Outside his room, or outside his head, there seemed to be a convention of songbirds fighting for territory with crows and buzzards and barking dogs. Then a light tapping sound quickly approaching, growing louder, becoming a boom of fists on his unlatched door, and the dog's alarmed bark as the door is pounded open by same the demanding fists, and his own voice shouting *"Go away,"* but the interloper already barging through the door he should've taken the time to close and lock.

The thin stripe of sun flashed into a vapor spot-light.

You never even had to wonder, WHAT IF SHE SHOWED UP HERE NOW . . . . *As though on schedule, as though planned, as though* REQUESTED: *a raw image of fear and hysteria flies through your open door, becomes part of your episode. You never once locked the bathroom door either. An invitation to a fantasy-nightmare of pleasure-pain ecstasy-agony or-giastic death throes? But no one else ever came into the bath-room with you, and in* THIS *room it's an actual weeping girl coming in — Is she blind to what you're doing? — and you're pulling yourself back, your hands and knees and feet crowding toward your body, like a flinching snail, a startled tortoise, a touched anemone.*

He was sitting upright, his back against the head-board, knees gathered to his chest, the two pillows he'd grabbed as she came in the door were crunched in his lap. Leya sank to the floor, clutching the dog, crying into the smooth brown neck and one velvet ear. Her voice more a series of spasms than words, "Oh god, Brian . . . ."

His staring eyes felt trance-like, growing larger and zombie-opaque as long as he remained motionless, si-lent, dormant. Then she stood, her face a pale smudge, as though scrubbed free of freckles, leaving the red blotches of abrasion. Her eyes swollen to slits.

"He . . . instead of sending the money to my law-yer, he . . . used my old address. My mail was forwarded.

My friend . . . she sent it here. I thought it was just the check. I expected the first check. Everything's over, the divorce was finalized last week, there was no *need* to say anything else." She was standing at the foot of the bed, the corner of the mattress pointing between her knees. He stared there, one eye on each knee. The heartbeat in his throat ebbing and sinking, his jaw slack and lips parted slightly like a cadaver, his limbs and joints settling into icy rigor.

"But he couldn't leave it at that, he had to get in one more stab, one more wound, one more nasty last word." Crying softly, she opened a scrap of paper wadded in one fist. "Why do people have to do things like this, Brian, just when you think you're free and can forget . . . ." She dropped to her knees again and wiped her nose on the bedspread. It felt like his staring eyes were crossing, colors and shapes fading in the searing light gushing through the open door. Dazzling white blindness. Transported into a new zone. Blanketed in heavy inertia.

Her voice muffled in the bedspread and blankets, the words disjointed and distorted, "He couldn't seem to be able to just put a check in an envelope without saying . . . just listen: *'Giving you money is a hell of a lot less awful than having to think about you. Rebecca and I considered inviting you to our commitment ceremony so you could see what a real woman looks like, so you could watch me kiss someone who kisses* BACK. *And fucks with abandon, but of course she's not wearing your cast-iron chastity belt with* TEETH.'" The words were barely intelligible, yet for some reason he was almost straining to grasp each one. "'*God, life is wonderful after those six torturous years imprisoned with a cold, dull, rigid, bag of bones. Goodbye forever, this is the best day of my life!*'"

The dog, standing in the doorway, looked once backwards over her shoulder, then slipped outside.

"Why couldn't he just send the check?" Leya finished with a whisper. She rose, one knee on the mattress, head hanging and face tilted down toward the limp, crumpled paper still in her hand. And his arm fell like deadweight, fingers reaching to the floor beside the bed. "Please go away," his dry voice rattled in his throat.

Her sobbing turned to convulsions, turned nearly to wailing, she looked up once, eyes not visible through the matted lashes and swollen red lids, then she toppled forward onto the mattress, across the foot of the bed, and his fingers felt for the rifle.

He was holding it to his shoulder. "Get out." His finger finding the trigger. "Get out of here." His zombie eye staring sightless down the barrel that glinted in the glaring light. "*Get out.*" He lunged upright to his knees, and Leya, gasping, vaulted backwards off the bed. "*Get out of here, don't come here again, do you understand me!*"

The door slammed behind her and the dazzling light disappeared as though the sun exploded.

Long after sundown, when he emerged from his room, he found the dog lying across the welcome mat at his doorstep. The parking lot was lit by more than the dim yellow lights on the corners of the building. The moon was full, hanging nearly directly overhead. He was groggy from a valium that had only half worked, still damp from a shower, hungry, slightly stiff, and had a headache. But concentrating on these things, purposely thinking about your headache, your hunger, the ache in your muscles, instead of trying to ignore them, prevents the wayward mind from returning to any scene that is already, thankfully, over.

This time he crawled *in*to the station wagon carcass. There were no tires, no seats, no dashboard, not even a steering wheel, and two of the doors were lying fifteen feet away. He was sitting on hard dirt, pocked by a half dozen rodent holes, his head grazing the rusted roof, the rifle balanced on the bottom edge of a glassless window frame. The dog was also sitting upright, where the front passenger seat would be, looking through her own window hole. The light provided by the full moon was luminous, but shoddy, like floodlights temporarily mounted on tall poles for a rinky-dink makeshift rodeo or dirt bike races.

Enough of the entrails and steer feet were still scattered around to entice the weaker animals to return — the ones who hadn't been allowed to eat yesterday, who hadn't managed to grab anything to take with them before they scattered, or their bit of skin or white ligament had been quickly given up to an alpha. If they came, they would come quietly.

A shooter needs to be free of all anxiety and apprehension in order to achieve and maintain pinpoint accuracy. Right now — the way your guts feel vacuum-packed, the way there's not enough room to move around inside your skin — it's an obvious deterrent to cool precision. But the shooter must also be naturally detached from any adjacent tension and distress. Can you? Muster enough raw proficiency to overcome the ostensibly hopeless opposing forces? Pick off five or six loners as they come down the narrow moonlit wash, then feel the build-up of urgency seep out of your body like pee? Mark territory with their stiffening carcasses, one neat hole through each eye, then walk away with at least some restored tranquillity?

The animals came silently, single file down the sandy wash, a whitish path through the chaparral flatland. Their eyes turned to reflexive opaque orbs in the moonlight. Beside him, the ridgeback moved only the corners of her nostrils, tasting the musk of the coyote entering the area. The worried wrinkles were etched into her forehead. The zipper of backwards hair on her spine bristled slightly. Brian settled down behind the rifle's sights. He'd attached a silencer so he might get in four shots — hopefully four cold kills — before general panic and confusion ensued. They were five or six adolescent males, unsure of their positions, chased off by their mothers, not allowed to breed, forced to cower and submit to most other individuals, not daring to even steal food from a pup. With only a few halfhearted attempts at displaying for the alpha position among themselves, they fell to scavenging the food quietly. Brian drew a bead on each gray cheek. The barrel was steady. His hands didn't sweat. The leveling device didn't so much as quiver. The dim moonlight was suddenly resplendent, the targets sat as though frozen. With grace and ease, the bullets would make their soft thud in the center of each.

Brian raised his head. Lowered the rifle's stock. Slowly withdrew the barrel from the window ledge. He turned his back on the animals feasting in the full moon, their courage and voices rising as their claim on the carrion remained unchallenged. No impulse from his distraught brain had said *pull the trigger*. Strung just as tightly, still balanced on the edge of boil-over, the pressurized sensation that he was choking on his own body continued to fume, but all of a sudden no longer anything screaming *this! this! this! this!*

He unloaded the rifle, held the shells in one palm. *Tools to defray other impulses. Obviously if shooting has been serving as a dispassionate substitute . . . effective for literally decades but now no longer sufficient . . . then in order to avoid, or even postpone, the undesirable outbreak, the substitute might need sharpening — to raise the stakes.*

The large mammal in rut feels an indescribable drive, causing extreme restlessness, even uneasiness. Sometimes you hear nearly painful bellowing, whether from buffalo or wolf. The adult male non-human mammal can't explain it to the scientist observing behavior, but shouldn't men be able to empathize, understand this mysterious delirium by way of their own inarticulated experience? The normal, healthy male often doesn't eat during this time, the urge to hunt completely superseded by his other hormonal drives. Might it not be possible, though, that the unhealthy — the aberrant — male may misdirect his hungers and be driven to kill irrationally . . . sometimes even the female members of his own species whom he craves?

But if his brain were capable of any amount of lucid thought, when simple self-control is no longer the answer, might he not be able to redirect the misdirected urges and kill something ELSE *instead?*

But the transition from paper targets to running mammals has already been completed, and lately THIS *diversion appears grossly insufficient. Besides, you can't get satisfaction from a cool, clean hit if you can't hit anything. You can't hit anything because you're distracted, out of the zone . . . too far gone?*

But if surrogate targets, even live ones, are no longer keeping you in check, look at what the surrogates have lacked. You don't think about coyote day and night. The obvious solution: remove the superabundance of abnormal pressure distorting too much of your conscious thoughts, kill something you CARE *about?*

Are you really what you think you are? Do you at least have the balls to follow your sister? More cowardly now than then, when you staggered into the scene and, appropriately, guiltily held the gun, your culpable fingerprints on the brain-spattered grip. But weren't able to use it a second time the way you SHOULD'VE. *So you submitted yourself to the pattern of the rest of your life.*

Hours later, the last caterwaul was miles away. Up close, dry tumbleweeds scratched against the outside of the car's metal shell. Inside, the dog lay sleeping with her chin on his ankle. He continued to hold the bullets extended in an open palm above his lap.

Dear Sal,

June ~~23~~ 24

After midnight--a bitch of a day, hot as
hell, then the letter you forwarded from
Mitch (more about that later, but ever
notice how Mitch rhymes with Bitch?) and
then the weirdest episode yet with Brian.
He's far more messed up than I thought and
maybe you're right, I shouldn't play
psychiatrist, it could even be dangerous. I
hope I'm not making him worse or anything. I
mean, well, I'll start with the high point
of the past several days--and it's about the
highest point yet, as far as his behavior:
I don't think he's as capable of killing
coyote any more. I think it's no longer an
outlet for him. Believe me, Sal, this could
be a major breakthrough. I think his
immature fascination with his gun--excuse
me, rifle--is actually passing. I think his
habit of hiding his fear of emotional
closeness by shooting things is being
broken. And even though he pointed it at me
tonight (wait a second, put the phone
down!), I thought about it afterwards, and
I don't think he would've done anything more
than that. I really believe that. He said,
at the very beginning, no one wants to hear
someone else cry about their problems. So,
what did I do, went ahead and tried to cry
on his shoulder (not literally). I guess I
can't expect him to totally reverse a
lifetime of clinging to that gun in every
emotional crisis. I mean, it was a little
setback in the midst of a big breakthrough.
Okay maybe a big setback. He was pretty
upset. Okay no whitewash, he was thoroughly
upset by my hysterical outburst--he

obviously wasn't ready to be that kind of
friend even though I've been trying to show
him it's okay to show what you feel to
someone if you trust them. Anyway I'll have
to back off for a while, let him make all
the moves and call the shots (not
literally!), and only get as close as it
seems he wants me to be. He's been pretty
edgy, but I imagine he's never functioned in
his profession while handling all these new
emotions. Am I saying what you think I'm
saying? Yes, I do think he likes me, whether
he knows it or not! (Yeah, you only point a
gun at the one you love, right?) I mean, at
first I thought, this guy is _crazy_, I'm
getting out of here. But after thinking
about it, the gun was probably empty.

Yes it was the note from Mitch that set
me off. How could you know you were sending
me a poison-pen letter. Poison hardly
describes it. I'm not kidding, the animosity
was unbelievable. It was downright
malicious. When he first kicked me out
(asked me to leave), with all the bullshit
new-age reasons he gave, I asked if it was
really because I was a crummy lay. I _was_.
Sexually incompetent. (And, truthfully, I've
been sort of scared to even try it again
since.) But _he_ claimed that had nothing to
do with it. Now all his hatred is _only_ about
that. As if I did it on purpose. Why would
he want to go out of his way to make me feel
even worse about myself? Sort of staggers
you to realize someone could abhor you that
much. Funny, I think Brian could handle that
kind of hate--it staggers _him_ to think
someone could _care_. Boy are we opposites!

I'll try to get him to take a picture of
me with the cougar when we catch her. She'll

be asleep, but that's the best I can do! You
forwarded my mail without a letter--does
that mean you're busier than usual!? Keep
your hands in your fish bucket and off the
new guy!

    Love, Leya

FROM: BRIAN LEONARD
ADDRESS: WRANGLER INN, RAWLINS, WY
PHONE: (307) 678-0990
FAX: (307) 998-0550

DATE: June 24

FAX TO: 031/45 33 31

ATTN: PETER GALLWAY

OF PAGES TO FOLLOW: 0

CONTENTS TO FOLLOW: NONE

COMMENTS: Going in to get female #4.
          Will probably transport her
          to alternate terrain. Maps
          show two or three different
          areas of several hundred
          square miles with no cougar
          signals. Hopefully she can
          establish home territory
          there and won't disappear
          altogether.

```
FROM:       BRIAN LEONARD
ADDRESS:    WRANGLER INN, RAWLINS, WY
PHONE:      (307) 678-0990
FAX:        (307) 998-0550

DATE:       June 24

FAX TO:     (307) 690-4545

ATTN:       HARRY HATHAWAY

# OF PAGES TO FOLLOW:    0

CONTENTS TO FOLLOW:      NONE

COMMENTS: Getting started on my part
          tomorrow early a.m. Be ready
          day after tomorrow and ev-
          ery day after that until you
          see me. It's my way or not
          at all.
```

Ever think about being a hero, Bri?

"I thought you were going to sleep."

No, YOU were going to sleep. But I'm interrupting you again. Were you asleep yet?

"No, I don't have room for my legs 'cause someone's spread out all over the damn place."

Maybe YOU'RE the one who's growing. You'll be six-five by the time the alarm goes off.

"Well I think I have a right to stretch out in my own bed."

Nanny-nanny-nanny. With an attitude like that, you'll never be a hero.

"What do you mean by hero? Like an athlete or in the war?"

THE war? Like there's always going to be one, the same one, going on? Where've you been? We withdrew from Vietnam when I was in high school. Saigon fell, little bro, we lost. Jeez, you missed everything.

"I'm not the one who graduated three years ago and hasn't left the house since. Don't you wonder what *you're* missing?"

I've got everything under control, I know what I'm doing, I'm making some plans—

"Bullshit, she's controlling—"

Shut up, Brian. I'm trying to tell you something I've thought about. Unintentional heroes. Balky heroes. Dumbfounded heroes. Like a hero who never thought about it, but just because he is who he is — or who she is — it makes him do the right thing, or just do a thing that someone else says is a hero. It doesn't seem fair. Is this another of those things I think is so heady now, but someday I'll realize is another shallow teenage I-think-I'm-so-profound moment?

"Does Mom tell you everything you think about is stupid?"

I said shut up. But, anyway, about these reluctant heroes. More than reluctant, more than embarrassed, I mean . . . mortified. Why would you be mortified, Bri? It's not like you didn't do anything. Like, after you graduate, a crisp new master's in biology in your pocket, likely you'll spend a season working for the forest service. Of course, this means you won't be getting as much shooting practice done, so on your one day off, you're down on a ranch outside the closest desert town where you got permission to put some targets on fenceposts cause you're still going to Ohio for the national championships like you do every summer. Mostly your job is to make sure there's toilet paper in the outhouses, that no one's being too drunk-and-disorderly in any of the campsites at night, that no cars or motorcycles try to go beyond where the dirt roads allow, that no one tries cutting down any trees, and every day you pick up trash and empty the trash cans around the campsites. You're not the game warden, if anyone's catching fish with a net instead of a fishing pole, or taking more than the limit, there's not much you can do, but at least your official-looking green shirt and smoky-bear type hat helps scare them. You spend a day looking for rattlesnakes if any camper reports seeing one — but of course the snakes live there, so looking for them is just for show, and when you report back to the snake-scared camper, you give a little talk on "snake safety." You're working on the eastern side of the Sierras, on the dry side, opposite King's Canyon and Sequoia where the western mountains get more rain. I don't know, maybe because you're afraid of all that sheer, variant beauty. Not me. Africa, or wherever I end up, is going to be as spectacular as any nature movie ever promised. Or maybe it's the ignoramus National Park tourists you're avoiding, not that there aren't people camping on the Mojave Desert side of the Sierras, but not as many, and probably not as ignorant, since there are no showers, no flushing toilets, no RV hookups. Anyway, the part about being a hero, like if you're walking along beside the creek — it's not a gentle trickle, no babbling brook, this is an icy glacier creek that comes roaring, mostly whitewater, out of the mountains, especially turbulent in early summer when the ice packs at twelve-thousand feet and above are melting. Not really part of your duties, but it's dusk and you like the woods by the river, following the little trail blazed by decades of fishermen. Then you see a kid, maybe five years old straddling a fat old log that crosses the river. He's swinging his legs and singing a little song, perched right out there over the white-cold boiling river. The river is so loud you have to shout: "What're you doing!" And he says "Ridin' a horse." Of course, you fool, couldn't you see that? So, after you walk out behind him on the log, you tell him old dobbin needs to get back to the stable for his supper of oats and corn, and you straddle the log behind him, and tell him to schooch backwards until your boots hit the creek bank which is when you swoop an arm around him and swing him to the ground. He trots beside you down the dirt road toward the campsites, still holding his horse's reins and slapping his own butt, shouting "Get up, get up." And it's almost dark by the time you get to where the campsites are clustered.

You kind of go halfway into each campsite where most people are either sitting around the fire or eating dinner in mosquito-net tents with Coleman lanterns. You don't have to say anything, if they look up and ignore you or send a halfhearted wave, you know he's not theirs, but one guy, brushing his teeth with a coffeecup of water, finally says, "Down two or three sites, I think they're looking for him." Sure enough, a lot of panicked people are huddled around inside a lit-up trailer tent, and a few other forest service guys are there, and all hell breaks loose as soon as someone spots the kid. Not bad hell, like they're not accusing you of kidnapping — you're obviously a guy in a forest ranger costume bringing their kid back, and they never thought their kid was kidnapped in the first place, but maybe drowned in the river or lost in the forest, and when they suddenly see him coming back with you, before the search has even started — can't you understand? Their relief must be like summer arriving — like BOOM *— in the middle of winter's worst blizzard. They're hugging you and touching you and women are crying and they even knock your hat off in all the hand-shaking and jostling. But average-man don't like being in a spotlight — asks one of the other guys to do his shift tomorrow and goes down to the desert ranch to shoot.*

> "People don't understand, sometimes embarrassment is impossible to explain, can't be defined, has layers that can't be peeled, but . . . I don't know."

Talking in your sleep?

> "No, but haven't you ever had this, like, profound idea or answer in a dream, then when you wake up, even if you can remember it, it's . . . just stupid."

Welcome to my life, it doesn't even have to be a dream.

> "So are you not going to college, or doing anything else, to sort of spite Mom for being . . . whatever . . . like overly protective of you in high school?"

Overly protective is quite the gloss-over understatement, don't you think? She would've sent me with a handcuffed bodyguard, if she could. Think about the rock-and-a-hard-place she was between. Couldn't send me to military school, that wouldn't straighten-me-out, so to speak. An all-girls school certainly wouldn't do. Would she have tried an all-boys school? Would she have decided that letting me wear a brown-corduroys-and-blue-blazer uniform was a good trade-off for the other life-changing experiences I might have thrust upon me? She had no choice, had to leave me in public school, but took some things into her own hands.

"How could you let her?"

How could I NOT, she's my mother, she had a right to make my class schedule, choose my teachers, forbid me from extra-curriculars, maintain my dress code, instruct the librarian to report any books I checked out, demand that I never have to take a gym class — she signed a thing saying I was in ballet classes for my physical education, but she had no intention of sending me there either.

"No, I mean how can you—"

Her intentions, at the beginning, were maternal, sort of, she just doesn't want me to turn out like HER.

"But—"

Why do you keep trying to make this about me? I came over to see you, you know, to get to know my little bro now that he's past being a grubby gutter rat and is headlong into ado-lescence — a special kind of hell, isn't it? But why dwell on shit when there are so many wonderful experiences to notch in your belt, so to speak — don't get all weird again, I'm not being nasty. You don't even have to go to Africa with me. How about counting and taking data on burrowing owls in Arizona and New Mexico, mapping remaining habitat for the least tern on the West Coast, every few years helping to thin the non-native goat population on some of the Califor-nia coastal islands, there's the California desert tortoise habi-tat study and census, someone's study on Canada geese — how many still migrate as opposed to those who have stopped, and are the two groups becoming more and more separate gene pools? And someone else's project on elk migration routes through the Rockies — how much have they changed over *the course of this century, as compared to last century, using Native American lore as research. Wow, some quaint ideas for foundation grants, but hey, take the work!*

In between field work, there's always another shooting competition coming up — although don't bother with any local, little matches anymore, just the big ones — and other cool ways of keeping busy while working alone, be your own boss: With an original stake from the trust fund, one at a time buy houses on the outskirts of wilderness or semi-wilderness areas — outside the towns that are outside National Parks or near National Wildlife Preserves or even National Forests — then remodel and re-landscape to make them wildlife friendly, picture windows and observation decks on the house, and a yard that would attract the critters. Install waterfalls and ponds, or, if there's a creek on the property, use it, redirect it if necessary, dam or widen it, make a grassy reedy area or set off the banks with rocks, attract song birds and water birds, turtles, frogs, even fish, muskrats, whatever is indigenous. Create feeding stations with permanent high-quality feeders of every sort, and nesting areas for the right kind of native birds. Then plant and arrange the right kind of foliage, the right percentage of conifers and deciduous, high and low growth trees and bushes, and winter berry-producing bushes like holly and firethorne, maybe even a dead tree snag for hawks. Then advertise exclusively in environmental or nature magazines, sell to the environmentally-concerned-rich, like Ted Turner, but people one or two echelons down from Ted Turner who can't afford half a state. Not that there's a lot of profit to be made here, but enough to do another house and to stay occupied.

"Some hero."

Well, if that's what you want — I thought it wasn't — it's back to facing tough decisions. Decisions where there's no distinct right and wrong, or maybe where there is, but there are for-sure bad consequences, so everything's mucked up. And it's just you, average-man, no one to tell you what to do or even give you a hint of advice. It's not going to be as simple as fixing your sights and deciding when to squeeze off the shot, knowing exactly when you're locked on and you'll put another neat hole in the seven-inch ten-point circle. And not anything like deciding which pair of boots to buy or what field jobs to sign on for or which direction to take off down the runway or what tree to plant or should the deck be cedar or redwood. If you're so worried about being a hero — you sure that's what you want? — or maybe eventually it just can't be avoided anymore — those hard decisions usually involve another person. Besides you, I mean. So much for the benefits of you being your own boss and your boss having only you for an employee, right? So much for me, myself and I. And you can't even get off the hot seat by choosing to do nothing — that IS a choice, you see. Average-man gets strung up good and tight between hero and rogue. Hey . . . Mom's calling me.

"Don't go."

## 8

SLOW HEARTBEAT SIGNAL

Across the railroad tracks from town, in a long weedy lot designated, seemingly, for a commercial strip that never materialized, Brian set the Plexiglas display box on the ground near a spot of grease. He paced off nearly 50 yards, which placed him just off the shoulder of a frontage road, near but not too near the KOA. He set himself on one knee, his foot crushing the already life-less butts of cigarettes from an ashtray that had been emptied there. He removed the silencer. The first four shots shattered the box to smithereens and sent the stuffed rabbit spinning twenty feet to one side. The next four continued to obliterate the rabbit. The last four shots had little target to aim at. He could barely find the pieces of fur through his sights. He shot without haste, the echo of each died completely before the next rang forth. He reloaded slowly, aimed carefully. But no one called the police.

By himself, the day before, he'd located the cougar only about 30 miles west of her original location: in the foothills of the Green Mountains, on the edge of the Chain Lakes Flat in the Great Divide Basin, twenty miles due south of the lifeless Jeffrey City, and almost 30 miles northwest of Hathaway's ranch. A dirt road leading out of Bairoil would get them within five to ten miles of her. After that it would be trail-less tracking, this time carrying the jabstick, vials of tranquilizer, and dragging a large airline kennel on a wheeled cart over terrain that could preclude the use of wheels at all.

The Bronco was packed and ready. At 3:30 he honked outside Leya's motel.

The dog was sitting on the passenger seat. When Leya tried to coax her into the back, the dog stepped across the gearshift and squeezed her body into a precarious posture on Brian's lap. He remained like a statue, staring out the windshield, simply moving one arm to facilitate the dog's choice of position, then replaced that hand on the wheel so his two arms locked the dog in place.

"Can you see well enough to drive?" Leya asked. And when he didn't answer, "*Some*one's grumpy again today. Why do you insist on not getting enough sleep before important days like this? By the way, was that you I heard shooting yesterday afternoon?"

"Did you count the shots?" His voice robotic.

"Of course not." She was struggling with the seatbelt clasp. "Actually I heard it, wondered if it was you, then completely put it out of my mind. It's kind of creepy to realize that it's gotten so the sound of a gun hardly means anything to me anymore."

"I've never shot a *gun*."

"You know damn well what I mean."

"Do I? Do *you*?" Uttered hollowly.

They shared almost twenty miles of silent two-lane highway. The dog lowered her head and rested her chin on the edge of the open window, her neck and the beginning of the backwards ridge of hair slid just in front of Brian's throat. As they passed the turn-off toward Hathaway's ranch, neither Brian nor the dog moved, but Leya said, "Did you bring some antibiotics or something we could give her while we're at it, to protect her from infection from the needle, or any other wounds she might've sustained?"

Brian didn't respond, except to remove one hand from the steering wheel and put it on the dog's shoulder. Then his fingers slid down and held her foreleg.

"Or . . . I don't know . . .," Leya continued, not sounding particularly perturbed by his reticence, "shouldn't we take the opportunity while we've got her tranquilized to test her for plague or rabies, just for the sake of statistics or whatever, to answer every question we might have about her physical condition and why she's having problems?"

Again he didn't answer. But in Lamont — at the same intersection where the lone semi trailer sat in the empty parking lot behind the service station — when he turned off toward Bairoil, he said, "Let's just get this done and get out of here. When we're done today, we may want to get out of the whole damn state."

"What's that supposed to mean?"

There were only five more miles of paved road. Bairoil was dark and silent, as though boarded-up. Beyond the shabby buildings, continuing west, a dirt road began climbing the first of the Green Mountain foothills, forking off toward various ranches with wooden gates and rusty swinging signs illuminated momentarily by the headlights. Apparently regular use of the dirt road had gradually been limited to the eastern two-thirds. As they went west, more and more arid vegetation had taken root on the dusty tire tracks, until the faded *Road Ends* sign was practically buried in chaparral fifteen feet farther west than they were able to drive. Then the sign disappeared into darkness when the headlights went off.

The dog was the first out of the Bronco, slipping in a fluid dive out the window as Brian set the brake. He sat watching her walk slowly in front of the truck, nose up, eyes closed as though trying to prevent her other senses from distracting her from information carried in the air.

"Look, I'm sorry about the other night," he said.

"Day. That was daytime. You aimed a gun at me."

"Okay, I'm sorry for that too, and for everything. But I mean in your room . . . when I . . . ."

"Oh, that. Hey, you'd've done the same for me."

"But I don't know what you *did* do for me."

She smiled, "Then it'll be my little secret."

Brian wiped fog from the windshield in front of his face. "Let's go." But he didn't move. Leya got out, opened the back door, rustled around in the equipment. "How are we going to pack this dog crate in with us? I don't think these wheels are going to be of any use."

He cleared his throat and forced himself to answer: "After we triangulate, we'll carry it as far as possible. If necessary, I'll have to pack the cat back to wherever we leave the crate. Then I'll have to leave you there and come back in the chopper to lift her out."

"You can't carry her! What if she wakes up?"

"Don't you think I know how long things take?" Still pre-dawn, but the cab was already heating up and the first trickles of sweat seeped from his armpits. The dog continued to air-scent. Brian got out of the truck. He couldn't see Leya but could hear her putting her pack on. The water in her canteen sloshed. "Big cats air-scent with their gums," he said. "But they can only sense one thing that way: sexual signals from a prospective mate. They may look like they're grinning . . . or snarling . . . but they're exposing the sensors in their gums . . . searching."

"I think you've told me that. In fact, I know you did, because I remember wondering if that's the actual origin of the Cheshire Cat." She came around the truck toward his back. But he heard her and turned quickly, brushed past her to unload the crate and get his pack.

"Are you okay, Brian?"

He grunted, lifting the crate from the tailgate.

"I mean, I know no one's really okay at 5 in the morning!" She laughed, but stopped herself quickly, as though she also thought it sounded too odd in the hushed, partially moonlit clearing at the end of the road, surrounded by blackened rolling hills.

"Are we likely to run across tracks of other cougars?" she said. "Or are we listening for other signals? I mean, isn't this another animal's territory?"

"Why?"

"Well . . . why are we moving her? You never said for sure."

The dog came around to the rear of the truck and stood placidly watching him thread the jabstick through the vents in the crate. Leya moved closer to the dog, stroking her forehead with the tip of her index finger. "She's always so worried."

"But she doesn't ask questions."

"I have a right to know why I'm doing what I'm doing."

"We'll each have to hold an end of the jabstick and carry the crate between us. It'll be tough going." He gazed at the faint crack of light in the east. "Let me know if you want to bail out now."

"No, Brian, I just want to know why we're moving her. It doesn't seem in keeping with wildlife study to go in and mess with it, change the conditions, while you're gathering data."

He sighed, but she kept looking at him. He didn't exactly meet her eyes, just flashed across her pert persistent face as he swung to study the dark western horizon. "Maybe because she can't make resolutions like you did — she can't just chuck her old problematic life and strike out for a new place looking for life-fulfilling adventure, so we have to make that decision for her."

"I know you think that's supposed to come off like an insult, Brian, but I've done something I'm very proud of." She crossed her arms and lifted her chin.

He took out his receiver and turned it on. "You're staying here for a while. You want to keep the dog?" His receiver was already beeping, the slow heartbeat signal of the cougar, about six miles away. "Get your direction, get out your map and compass, and have a line made by the time I get back." He turned to leave, then stopped but couldn't tell whether it was literally his voice speaking toward the dark wilderness or just himself thinking from some newly cracked-open place in his head, "But have you ever actually chucked *every*-thing? Sacrificed *everything* to find out what you're really made of?"

Her motionless silence behind him was not an answer, neither to his question nor to whether or not he'd vocalized at all. He plunged forward, without attempting to pick his way around bushes or rocks, just letting his boots fall and crunch, each in front of the other.

You COULD *stop. Each step could be the last. But no one whose work is truly their life would experience, let alone examine, such full-blown thoughts of abandoning everything now, putting the girl back into the truck and driving away. How do you do such a thing? Easy: you just say "come on," you start the engine, you gas up in Lamont, you turn north, and then maybe east where the highway forks. And then where . . .? And to what end? What will you do somewhere else that's more important than what you're doing here . . . where you could finish this plague of apprehension . . .?* DIDN'T *you somehow help your sister splatter herself against the wall of your mother's bedroom?* DID *you finish your own indulgence and simultaneously, if symbolically, pull the trigger? Will recreating that level of terror finally secure the punishment you evaded? The shrinks and bleeding-hearts pitying and coddling you — but weren't* YOU *the one found holding the gun? Then rescued again from your fantasies of obliterating all of* THEM *in a matching holocaust of bullets, by a foster family that indulged and defended you even while you sought serenity at the shooting range. Not surprising, they said. He's working it out, they said. But now, isn't an impulse to flee with her nothing other than . . . a predator dragging his new prey to a farther, more remote, secluded lair. Because last time you made a kill, someone took it away. And took away the gun . . . . Carried your filthy, exposed body from the room, gave* YOU *the tranquilizer and moved you to safer habitat. Tried to tell you that you didn't do it. Can the aberrant individual ever be moved far enough away? Their studies and analysis of you were too brief, very flawed, never came close to guessing why the girl unlucky enough to have been born first, from the same uterus that produced you — the girl who customized a knapsack for you and lugged you on her back when she was seven, dressed as a safari guide for Halloween — ended up with what was left of her life seeping down the plaster, gurgling out of the hole in her face. And you never even thought I'M SORRY.*

The sun, emerging from below the horizon, hit as though sunrise and noon had become the same instant. His shirt already wet. The Robin Hood hat so low over his brow, all he could see were his boots and where his next two steps would land. His odometer, strapped to his ankle, told him he'd gone over a mile south. He half expected to turn and find he'd never even taken the first step into the brush off the faint dirt road. He rubbed his eyes then shook his head violently. The hat flew off and sweat sprayed from the ends of his hair. He found the direction of the cougar's signal, used the compass to plot it on the map, and retraced his steps. It was 7:30 when he got back, and Leya was dozing in a limp heap, leaning against a tire on the shaded side of the truck.

She seemed to pop awake when the dog rose, squeezed out from under the truck and came to greet him. "Do you think you went far enough away to get a good axis?"

"Farther than I intended. This close to her, a mile difference gives us a twenty to thirty degree angle on the two lines. That's plenty. Let's see yours."

"Sounds like you're feeling better?" She passed him her map, wiping a hand slowly across her brow.

"Better? That's a difficult concept. How about . . . determined . . . to get finished before this heat leaves the three percent of us that isn't water in a little turd on the ground."

"You have such lurid way of complaining."

"Thank you." He'd transferred her line to his map and was examining the axis point. "Well, a little four-and-a-half to five mile walk." He opened the truck and took out the hunting vest.

"Why are you putting *that* on, you'll get heatstroke again. And where's your hat, did you lose it?" She paused, looking at him, waiting for something.

"Let's go."

The crate, supported by the jabstick and hanging between them, didn't make it much farther than three-quarters of a mile. She started to need to put it down and change which hand she carried it with every twenty steps or so. The grassland had begun to give way to forest. The trees were thin evergreens that didn't produce much shade, the biggest with only an eight-inch diameter trunk, almost every one swarming with large ants gathering sticky sap oozing through the bark.

"We'll leave it here," he said when she stopped to rest again after going forward only five or six steps.

"I'm sorry."

"I have to come back with the chopper anyway. Here or a mile from here or five miles, it makes no difference."

"How'll you land here?" She looked around. The trees weren't abundant, but there wasn't a clearing large enough, and the ground was no longer flat.

"Leave that to me." He lowered his pack from his shoulders. It wasn't the new daypack but a bigger one, carrying tranquilizer, extra ammunition, a blanket, first-aid kit, flashlight, and the requisite granola bars, chocolate, beef jerky, and a full canteen.

The sun, which had already risen on the prairie, was just sliding above the last hill they'd crossed, as though following them, bearing down on them.

"God, this *heat*." She unbuttoned the lowest buttons of her shirt. Brian, untying something on his pack with his teeth, felt the dry canvas strap swell to the size of a leather belt in his mouth. She rolled the bottom of the shirt and tied the two tails in a knot above her navel. He dropped the strap from his mouth. Her stomach was not freckled at all, and they were only scattered lightly on her back. Her spine made a trail of smooth, fine bumps that melted away before reaching the waistband of her shorts. She suddenly turned and looked him in the eye. "What're *you* grinning about?"

Then he felt how tightly stretched his cheeks were, and the tautness of his lips, stretching out beyond showing just his teeth, exposing his gums as well. He swallowed and instructed his facial muscles to slacken.

"Sorry," she sighed. "That nasty letter wasn't the first time Mitch informed me how unattractive he found my body. I'm probably oversensitive."

"You'll get burned."

"I know, and I'm a bad risk too, but I just don't care, it's so damn hot." She reached behind herself to tuck the shirt up higher on her back. "So, *am* I a bag of bones? Is that what you were laughing at?"

"Laughing?" He lifted his pack again as a flash of heat-blindness made her look like nothing more than a shimmering mirage. "Come on, let's keep going."

Your voice could've, instead, said, Let's go back to the truck. It might not have seemed such an irrational surprise. Wouldn't she say something like, good, let's just leave her alone, she's okay now, she can survive, and if she can't, we shouldn't mess with nature. Or she might not even say anything until you turn the truck north instead of south toward Rawlins — and then what would she do? Turn the radio on and sing along while she takes off her heavy boots, peels down her socks and wiggles her toes? Not even notice where you're headed as she pours water from her canteen onto a handkerchief and begins to wipe it over the skin on her midriff, sighing with pleasure at the short-lived cooling relief. Would you drive off the road again, watching her? Then not even discern that the truck is tilting crazily in a gully off the shoulder or leaning up against a long forgotten sign post. Maybe you

can't help it because the few freckles on Leya's lower back
look remarkably like the tiny spatters of blood on your sister's
exposed body, her nightgown around her neck, as though half
taken off before the bullet smashed its way into the end of her
life. Enough material flowing down to cover her breasts. Her
little-girl flowered underwear clean, taken from the drawer
at bedtime as instructed. Her feet in large, ankle-high padded
slippers. Her legs bent, her body twisted like a discarded
mannequin, with those few wayward spatters of blood. The
rest of the blood had flown backwards, as it should, as the
police spatter-tests proved it would. Except for five, six, seven
pin-head dots on her back, you were counting, how many
times can you count to seven in a minute or two. Not I'M
SORRY, *but* FOUR, FIVE, SIX, SEVEN, ONE, TWO, THREE, FOUR . . . .
Using the gun to point and count, point and count, how long
did you sit there in the growing, spreading pool of her blood,
counting the specks, touching them with the short barrel . . . .
Instead of pointing it where it should've been aimed and kill-
ing the one who should've been eliminated.

The blue barrel of Brian's rifle glinted in the sun, rising from its carried position — pointed toward the ground — to touch the skin on Leya's side, just below her last rib. She shrieked, *eeep*, jumped forward and spun in the air, landed on both feet facing him, walking backwards because he continued to put one boot in front of the other in rhythm with the slow *beep beep beep* from his receiver.

He laughed, a dry, wretched sound.

"God, sometimes I wonder, Brian," she snapped, "was I wrong about you—*are* you some sort of lunatic?"

"I don't know," he said wearily, the unfamiliar tight chuckle long gone, the adrenaline rush passing. "I guess I'm just trying to lighten things up."

Her footfall wasn't regulated by the receiver's repeated signal. Neither did the dog breathe in rhythm with the pulsing tone. The rustle of small birds in the bushes, lizards scooting out of the way, boots on pine needles, rocks dislodged by their footsteps to roll downhill, the dog's fevered panting — the only unnatural noise was the receiver's mechanical signal. Except maybe also his blood pounding like whitewater in his ears. He cupped his hands on either side of his head, the dull chaotic roar intensifying, like listening to a seashell, until the fuzzy pulse almost started to crystallize into words, *who are you?*

Some sort of lunatic?

How long did they keep you in that loonybin hospital? Five, six days? A week? You BEGGED *them to keep you longer, forever if necessary.* WANTED *them to find out who you were. Waited for them to figure it out, waited for their eyes to level at you with dead-on condemnation. Six, seven, maybe eight dumbfounded days. How could they be so blind — to find you, no scars on your skin, your dick still hanging out, still holding the gun, and not recognize that* YOU— *But just looked at each other and nodded, as though* THEY *knew what happened. Your babbling culpable mother, shrieking about the blood bubbling slowly from* HER *thigh, which you only saw in the flashing micro second after the second gunshot. Your shot. Did you ever look at her again after aiming, so wildly, so poorly . . . and much too late? You were counting the new reddish brown freckles on Diane's back. Until someone covered her with a sheet stripped from mother's bed and dragged you out of the puddle of thickening blood. You said nothing — thought your aberrance would be obvious and they'd take appropriate measures. But they must've bought your mother's hysterically demonstrative claims:* PSYCHO BITCH, SCHIZO-PHRENIC DYKE, WANTED TO KILL ME! *Four, five, six days in a row you stared in disbelief at the stupidly benign face on the other side of the desk, not asking but* TELLING *you what had transpired, rebuilding a scenario you could only shake your head at in mute astonishment, a hitman's dream-come-true to be grilled not for a confession but to share* FEELINGS *about an* UNFORTUNATE UNHAPPY TRAGEDY.

He was leaning against a tree, one hand holding the trunk on the opposite side from where his face was crushed against the rough bark, his cheek seemingly stuck to the fresh sap oozing out in a slow-motion cascade. Leya went on several more steps before stopping, turning and coming back. She approached staring quizzically; opened her mouth, but slowly closed it again and didn't speak. Put her pack on the ground so she could dig inside, then stood up, unwrapping a candy bar which she thrust toward his face.

He flinched backwards, pushing himself away from the tree. "I don't need that."

"Have you been eating? Are you hypoglycemic or something?"

"Just not concentrating enough. Sorry." He checked his odometer, standing on one leg like a heron. "We've come about three miles already."

"*Already*? It's after ten o'clock."

"Is it?" He picked at the sap on his temple and in his hair.

The dog was lying in a strip of shade created by the tree. The narrow shadow ran the length of her body, but her legs were still in sunlight, as was her muzzle, cracked into an almost distorted grin, her tongue twice its normal length, hanging out one side, touching the dirt. Every once in a while she stopped panting to swallow saliva and spit out pine needles and other debris sticking to her tongue.

"We'll put her on the trail soon," he said.

"The cougar's trail?"

"No, *yours*." He shook his head, then alternately slapped both his cheeks as though waking himself up during a late-night cross-country drive. Dully, staring abstractly past her, "We have to let the dog tree her. We're not fast enough by ourselves — she can always stay far enough ahead of us to not feel any need to go up." He counted four, five, six beeps on his receiver, louder, more distinct, healthier.

"Is she running from us?"

"Not yet. But she probably knows we're close by. She's about a mile away."

"How can you tell?"

Five, six, seven, eight more blips from the receiver before he said, again wearily, "I don't know. I just do.

I'm trying not to get angry or upset at you this time, but please . . . just trust me."

"Okay, but . . . are you sure you're all right?" She looked down at the chocolate still in her hand. "Let's split this." Suddenly her glittering eyes beamed up at him. "Doesn't stress turn you into a chocoholic, or is that just women who get cravings?"

Her voice trailed away as he began pulling his lips back again, a contorted grin to rival the dog's. But his voice wasn't amused, "Now why would you ask me something like that?"

"Just . . . conversation." She took a bite of chocolate.

"Pick a better time."

"As though *you've* always said the most appropriate thing at the most appropriate time."

"Okay, I'm a boor, a vulgar brute." He took a tissue-wrapped lump from his pocket, crouched beside the dog and opened the tissue to let her sniff the cougar scat he'd collected several weeks ago. "This's what you're looking for, girl," he said softly. "If you have any instinct at all, let's use it now, okay? Get it, *get it*," his last urgings issued in an excited hoarse whisper. The dog bolted to her feet, ears trained but head turning frantically in every direction. "This way," he directed, pointing with the jabstick. He pushed past Leya and took the lead. The dog barged past his legs and charged ahead, stayed out of sight for several minutes at a time, then came crashing back to check their location. She continued to zigzag ahead of them, going in the same general direction, pausing in his path as she crossed over in front, taking a split-second look at him with her crazy tongue hanging from the corner of her lips, then continuing her criss-cross pattern, each foray off to one side getting longer before she turned to cross back, making diagonal progress northwest then southwest, an instinctive tracking pattern, searching to pick up a hot-scent trail.

"God, does she know what she's doing?" Leya panted, her voice coming from close behind him, as though whispered into his ear.

He startled inwardly, but replied quietly, "As much as any of us does."

"Well, she's not real subtle about it, is she?"

"That's what we want, for the lion to know what's coming. Her impulse will be to go *up*. Almost any dog can tree a cougar if it just *seems* threatening enough."

The dog was no longer crossing over in front where she could be seen, she was much farther ahead and had stopped checking back to make sure they were following. As the sound of her breaking through brush grew more distant, the receiver could suddenly be heard again, each blip a little scream, seeming to come faster and more hysterically, but only because the pitch was rising as they drew nearer.

Every step could still be your last before aborting and turning back. Hathaway could go on preparing to receive the cougar, four, five, six days in a row without anything happening, before realizing you won't be showing up. But what would happen INSTEAD? *That's what the target has always been for: when you don't know what'll happen or what you're going to do, put it there in front of you — aim* HERE, *it says, calm down and aim here.*

Then the dog sounded off, a yelp, furious barking that blurred into baying, one dog creating the fanfare noise of a pack. "She's got her!" he shouted, jumping forward into a jog. The single voice cacophony spreading into the dry forest's stillness was being answered by screaming jays and the peevish call of crows flapping from tree to tree. There was no reason for haste, now that the cat was treed. But he ran, the large pack bouncing on his shoulders, as though expecting a similar intuition which would tell *him* when and where to go for refuge. For the next hundred yards, the receiver's piercing signal was echoed by the grunt in his chest as each foot came down, the crash and crackle of dry brush and branches breaking. And Leya's softer crunching footfall staying forebodingly close behind him, like something chasing him, or goading him, or agitating him. Sweat stung in his eyes, the heat shimmered. Each breath was like a fist

pounding his chest, palpitating unevenly, jerking senselessly out of rhythm until he finally stopped, falling forward against a large cracked boulder that had grass,
bushes, even thin trees growing from spreading clefts.
For a second he was alone, let his pack slide off and he
rolled to his back, not quite in a recline, the rock prop-
ping him up. He looked up through the spiraling thin
tops of the parched trees into the extensive bleached sky.
*A biathlete who quits the race because you can't squeeze off a
shot with your oxygen-deprived shuddering muscles, can't even
focus on the target with your fatigued and jittering eyes. One
of those times you wonder if you ever HAVE to move again.
Unless, to prevent complete dehydration, you drink, wet yourself down, unload any unnecessary equipment and retrace your
steps. How far back? Ten years, twenty, twenty-five. Getting
closer to thirty. Five, six, seven nights in a row you would sit
prepared in the bathroom, your impaired feral hormones an-
ticipating their voices next door: one leveling the rebuke and
discourse and instructions, the other whimpering but comply-
ing. Daktari was in trouble. The animals could hear it, but did
they understand? Your mother compelled your sister to par-
ticipate in HER distorted game — ostensibly to cure her child of
her OWN repudiated lesbian leaning, a baldly preposterous excuse for inciting and coercing an affair with her own daughter
— but no one forced YOU to find such primal pleasure in it.
Aren't YOU the one who actually inherited your mother's mutant gene? So why couldn't she have chosen YOU, and let one
aberrant organism destroy the other, or both obliterate each
other? But were your intrinsic responses so jumbled you didn't
know: that you can't shoot a firearm and hold your dick at the
same time? You MISSED. You could've shown everyone else that
there was only one possible individual to accuse, only one left
alive to condemn and penalize — but YOU MISSED.*

The dog's barking had leveled off, indicating the
cat was there but not moving. Leya was standing in front
of him, unusually pale, her sweat-soaked hair dark and
plastered to her skull, her lowest ribs — prominent under her ashen skin — swelling then deflating as she
panted quietly. "I won't miss this time," he muttered.

"That's good. I don't expect you to," she smiled, too brightly, then licked her lips and looked away. "Will we be seeing her soon?"

"Yes."

"Want to rest first, eat something . . . are you okay?"

"I'm fine."

He bent one knee, put the sole of his boot against the rock, and pushed himself to his feet again. With his pack slung on only one shoulder, he pushed through the brush clustered beside the boulder, went around the rock, then climbed a few smaller pieces of granite like stairs to higher ground. From there he could see the dog circling a puny, gnarled tree, half dead, growing out of another granite boulder, this one mostly flush with the earth. The tree was twenty, maybe thirty feet away, the blur of tawny fur about forty feet up, on a horizontal branch that was still alive, prickly with long green needles. Instead of barking, the dog was now uttering softer elongated vocalizations. As Brian crept forward, ten, eleven, twelve steps, he turned off the incessantly beeping receiver, and after the last strident blip sounded, the cat could be heard, hissing its mostly soundless snarl down toward the exhilarated dog. Brian stood still. Leya stepped up beside his right shoulder. The cougar's ears were flattened, pointing sideways, her tail lashing, lips wrinkled to expose her fangs, but in no way did it look anything like a smile, leer, or even a grimace. The cougar screamed silently.

Brian's voice was nearly ceremonial. "*Lord of stealthy murder, facing her doom with a heart both craven and cruel.*"

"Ridiculous, huh?" Leya smirked. Then her tone also became lower and solemn. "By the way, I haven't had a chance to bring this up . . . my friend sent me another clipping. Another cougar was shot in California. It was up a tree looking down at kids on a school playground. In that case . . . what else could they do?" She raised her binoculars to her eyes. "But compared to that, what did *this* cat do that was so awful that we have to chase her and scare her to death, drug her and move her so she doesn't know where she is when she wakes up?"

He was still counting, as though the persistent pitch of the receiver continued, yet the rhythm he heard wasn't like the electronic signal of a cardiac monitor but the uneven thud of a heartbeat. *Whose?* Not his—he was standing motionless, at rest, while this cadence quickened, strengthened, geared-up, intensified. "This one?" he said reverently. "She's not so different from any other deviate: caught where she shouldn't have been, doing what she shouldn't have been doing, holding onto the evidence. The smoking gun . . . so to speak."

"She was?" Leya lowered her binoculars. "You didn't tell me that. What did she do? Kill someone's dog or something?"

"It doesn't matter." His own binoculars went up to his eyes, as though mechanically raised. "Now she has to pay for her transgression. Admit her guilt for the damage she's done, or be removed from normal society."

"You're talking weird, Brian. Cut it out."

He turned his binoculars on her. Her eye, a blurry smear, streaked past the lens.

"Knock it off, Brian. Let's just do our job, if we have to do it."

"Yes ma'am."

The dog had lain down, but not to relax. She had lowered her body like a sphinx, chest barely touching the ground, hind feet flat on the earth underneath her crouching hips — rounded stifle joints like winged fenders protruding above her spine, ready to put her back into action — the line down her back centered and straight, front legs extended and neatly parallel, pointed elbows digging into the dirt. Her head was tilted skyward, tongue flapping back against one cheek, her avid eyes never moving from the treed cougar.

Brian prepared the jabstick, filled the syringe and fixed it in place at the end. The pressurized fast-working tranquilizer would empty into the animal as soon as the skin was pierced.

"I'm sorry I snapped at you," she said from somewhere behind him. "Everyone has their own way of dealing with stress, I guess."

"Are you feeling stressed?"

"No, I meant you. Having to do this. I know you don't want to."

"And what makes you think you know so much about what I want or don't want?"

"Okay, I'm guessing. But I'm right, aren't I?"

He took the binoculars from around his neck, slipped one arm through the rifle's strap, then positioned the rifle diagonally between his shoulder blades. Jabstick in one hand, he approached the tree. The dog got to her feet when he stood beside her. She nuzzled his free hand, and he rested his fingers on her head, looking up into the tree. The cougar spit a snarl down at him. She also was crouched sphinx-like on her branch, surrounded by long needles. His neck still tilted back, looking at her, he began to climb. Ants swarmed on the trunk and the rough, thick bark crumbled away under his boots, his hands blackened with sap. At some point, as long as fifty years ago, the pine had been struck by lightning, splitting it, so it had an uncharacteristic crotch and double trunk starting about fifteen feet up, one branch twisting to the north, one, even more bent, going south. Braced in the crotch, Brian's height giving him six feet, the jabstick adding five more, he still couldn't reach her. The rifle's barrel kept getting caught in branches as he boosted himself, inch by inch, farther up the southern branch, his bare legs scraped raw on the bark. He had to keep his eye on the point of the jabstick, keep it clear, let it lead the way. A warm wind picked up, moving through the branches and past his ears, momentarily melting the pounding thud in his head into a dull roar. The dog was barking again, circling the tree then leaping against the trunk. "Tie her," he ordered, not even looking down to watch Leya do as he said. Ten inches, two feet, another yard. He tested each branch with his boot before using it to pull himself farther up. Some broke away quickly, jarring his whole body. Once he knocked his chin against the trunk as a branch gave way under his foot. Leya down below, "Careful, watch out," a small, far off warning, certainly not related to the long rigid needles reaching to puncture his eyes, the dead branches waiting to disintegrate under his weight, the bark flaying his skin . . . or the cougar hissing above him. She stood, tensing to either climb farther into the tree or make a desperate leap over Leya and the dog. Brian found a sturdy enough branch for each foot, his body propped on the narrowing trunk he'd been following. Only his arms had any mobility. With one hand he slid the rifle's strap around until the rifle was in front of him, then he managed to duck his head out of the strap and tuck the rifle under one arm. With the remaining free arm, he would have to make a clean hit with the syringe at the end of the jabstick. A partial wouldn't inject enough tranquilizer into the animal.

The cougar's hushed snarl broke open into a half-scream when the jabstick, like the strike of a rattlesnake, put the syringe into her flank and recoiled again, and Brian made a hasty retreat down the tree, dropping directly to the ground instead of sliding down the last twenty feet. The dog quieted when he hit the dirt. She was tied close enough to touch Leya's leg with her nose, standing, straining against the short rope. Then she lay down, the rope still taut between her neck and the thin tree where it was knotted.

"How long?" Leya breathed.

"Ten minutes."

"Tell me what she did that's making us do this, Brian."

"I said it doesn't matter."

"But . . .," she bit a nail. "She honed her instinctive skills in one habitat, then was moved to another. Is it really her fault we didn't like the way she coped?"

"*Coped*?" His laugh was a surprising cackle. "Wasn't there a pill, about thirty years ago, called *cope*, sort of a drug for bored housewives? I think my mother took it. She was trying to *cope*."

"Wasn't that valium?"

"Was it? God." He transferred the rifle to his right arm. "So all methods of coping should be considered okay within our original or natural *home* environment. Is that what you're saying?"

"I don't know . . . maybe. It sounds . . . not quite what I meant." She squatted to hug the dog, laying her cheek against one shoulder. "Things that should be clear-cut seem to have become more confusing."

"Like what?"

His careless response allowed her to continue: "Like . . . you. You're kind of like . . . my boss, right? But you're also providing me with this great experience which should either enrich my life or prepare me for a new career, or both. That's something extraordinary you're doing for me. I think it's made me feel . . . I guess closer to you than I . . . maybe should've . . . ." Her voice muffled against the dog, and half hidden by the pounding reverberation in his ears. "Maybe that's why, when you told me about your sister, I thought it meant we were becoming, somehow, more than just . . . . And I'm sorry if I caused you any more pain by opening old wounds. Maybe you already *were* coping the best way you could."

The lioness licked the spot where the needle had punctured her skin, then crouched on her branch, looked at them and hissed.

"Do you hear thunder?" he asked. His heart heaved against his rib cage, a strobe flashing behind his eyes.

"God, I *wish*." With one toe, she drew a half circle in the dirt in front of her stationary foot. "But all I wanted to say, Brian . . . is . . . I don't know, just clichés, that's all I ever have to offer." Her voice became higher, airier, took on a light chanting tenor. "Just that suicide is selfish, she ended whatever pain she had, but left behind a lifetime of it for someone who loved her."

He had his eyes squeezed shut. The hot wind rolled through the tops of the trees like surf, but the air barely moved down near the ground. There was so much sap on his skin, he could've opened his hand and the rifle would've stayed in place, his finger glued to the trigger.

She sighed. "I'm not being sarcastic. But it's really a . . . typical scenario, and people like you do need to learn to . . . get on with their *own* lives."

"People like me . . . ." His voice was eerily hoarse and died away.

"I know, what a terrible thing to say." She snorted a short laugh. "And people like me are royal pains in the butt."

"People like me." This time a raw whisper. Between his ears the distinct, outlined palpitation of a beating heart. As though he could see it. As though he'd ever seen, or even considered seeing, a live beating heart. Or a heart still beating but no longer alive. "I hate it," he muttered, "when other people's radios are so loud you can hear the bass, you can feel it, but you don't know what song it is, and you can't escape, you keep feeling and hearing it until *they* decide to turn it off." It came through the soles of his feet. Tapped against him from every side. Like a fetus jammed up against its mother's organs. *Wasn't there always a radio playing?*

"What brought that up?"

"It's a pain in the butt."

"Like me?" she said. He still had his eyes shut, but could hear the smile in her voice. "It's okay, Brian, you don't have to beat around the bush. I know I've been like a busybody pest, but . . . do you want to know why?"

"No. It's almost time."

"You may think you've been trying to shut me out, but you haven't been doing a very good job. Things have happened between us, Brian." Her boots scraped on the ground. "I'm sorry you're so distressed by it, but that doesn't give you the right to treat me like a piece of meat."

"Excuse me?" He opened his eyes, focusing through water on the cat, still awake in the tree. "A piece of meat? Considering the bait we've been using . . . what a grisly and . . . unoriginal image. And . . . what are you talking about?"

"One minute you kiss me, then the next . . . ."

"I already told you to forget about that."

"I can't. I'm sorry, but . . . despite your . . . reluctance . . . I guess I must be ready for rejection again, because . . . I'm ready to admit — though god knows why — I'm attracted to you, and— Are you okay? Let me help you, come on, over to the shade—"

"*Shut up!*" As her hand touched the small of his back, his arm abruptly flew up, knocking her under the chin with the rifle's stock.

She held her jaw and backed away.

In its last moments of consciousness, the cougar dropped out of the tree on its feet, then collapsed sideways. He stared at the gaunt gut slowly rising and falling under clearly defined ribs. The cat breathed quietly. The dog watched but wasn't panting. Leya remained motionless. And except for the whisper in the tops of the trees, there was no sound at all, a space slashed open by his sudden outcry. *The kind of silence that makes you continue to hear yourself screaming, even if you never opened your mouth. It was your sister shrieking.* SHUT UP . . . SHUT UP . . . SHUT UP . . . *but the radio continued to play. Soft middle-of-the-night country ballads. Paul Simon's sweet childlike voice. Dylan tunelessly wailing. Pet Clark, Patsy Cline, Nancy Sinatra's boots . . . a tiny, 4-inch transistor radio. Your hoarse voice singing breathlessly, tunelessly, just the words in time with your hand. Where would the thumping bass come from except your heart, pumping blood to your dick, gasping* MORE, MORE, MORE. *While she bawled. But your mother always had the radio playing, as though to drown out the noise of her propagandizing and demands, her moans, her animal sounds, and your sister's familiar muffled sobs. Until her watery voice rose to that final raw, fierce, penetrating pitch . . . the sound of stark, absolute fear . . . pushing you higher . . . and didn't the gunshot orgasm blow you directly through the wall, into that room, to take the gun from her flaccid fingers, still holding your dick . . .* DID YOU EVER LET GO OF YOUR DICK? *. . . your mother's body a writhing tornado under the sheet . . .* NO, BRIAN, NO, NO *. . . kneeling in blood, the hot, sweet smell of it, metallic, almost like gunpowder . . . . They never even tested your hands for gunpowder residue. Only Diane's. The report still says she made both shots. They never even knew which shot came first.* GOD NO, PLEASE, BRIAN, HELP! *. . . but your sister's fear already silenced, already draining out of her, too late to take back the first shot, hers —* SO MAKE YOURS COUNT! *But you didn't. You* MISSED. *A mere wound in your mother's fleshy thigh, but the hysterical woman in the bed who was still alive screamed and bellowed enough for all three of you . . . the dead girl with half a head . . . and the moribund but potentially dangerous boy holding the gun, covered with his sister's blood . . . .*

Leya was kneeling beside the downed cougar. Her hand looked like a child's passing over the animal's body. Every detail on her knuckles was in sharp focus, every tiny white scratch, the dirt under her nails, the ragged cuticles torn by her own teeth. While she continued her rhythmic caress, the pads of her fingers probed bumps in the cat's hide. His eyes followed. Stayed on her hand. The movement of the rifle's barrel barely discernible. The cross hair never quivered. He was watching through the sights.

"Shouldn't we remove these ticks?" She turned, one hand still on the cougar, and saw the rifle.

"No. Remove your clothes."

"What?" Her hand went vaguely to her collar. "What's wrong with you?"

"You're the one who knows everything about me. People like me."

"Okay, you're right, I'm sorry. Now cut it out. You shouldn't aim that thing at anyone, even to make a point."

"How do you know I'm aiming at *you*?"

"You're not gonna kill *her* are you? You *are* crazy. I won't let you!"

He let her voice scatter into the dry trees and thin warm air without an answer. The dog barked two, three, four times, ended with a short howl and was quiet. Leya was kneeling, facing him, the lioness stretched on the ground in front of her, both her hands down flat on the animal's lean body. A thready rank odor crept slowly around him. A shooter knows he's in the zone: when even the betraying crash of a panicky heart isn't evident in the rock-steady cross hairs that become the center of your universe, where you begin to exist.

"Take off your clothes. I mean it."

"Why . . .?"

"If you wanted to be so close to me, why wouldn't you even undress when I was in your bed?"

"You bastard." She began to sob.

"Stop that. Be quiet!"

Her mouth remained cracked half open, but she cried silently, tears making smeared streaks in dust on her face, her fingers fumbling with each button. She doubled over, her face down close to the cougar, working her arms out of her shirt. Then her bare back hovered under the cross hair, an unnaturally fragile, unmarred thing in the harsh extreme climate and coarse terrain on the periphery of the badlands. The smooth nubs of her spine clearly evident, seven, eight, nine, ten, he could count them. Then, with a fresh spasm of weeping, her muscles clenched, her shoulder blades jutted out like wings, and her spine melted into her skin.

A shooter in the zone: you make the chaos of any surroundings into the precision of focused concentration, controlled muscles, regulated breathing, unwavering eye, a fixed, narrow consciousness, and if you speak at all, your robotic voice originates from within the sights of your rifle.

"I won't miss again."

"Brian . . . ." It just seemed a shattered and watery sound coming from behind her hands which covered her face which was still bent down to her knees.

"Shorts too."

"No. Please . . . ."

"You wanted to know what happened."

Crying audibly again, she stood, turned away from him, pulled her shorts down, stepped out of them gingerly, and stood holding them, wearing only underwear and boots. Her thin freckled thighs were shockingly white.

"The blood *spatters*. You'll see. It sprays all over you."

"You're not going to kill her, Brian." Almost choking while she sputtered the words. "I don't believe it. I won't let you."

"You wanted to know, *you wanted to know*."

"I wanted to help you," she screamed.

"You can't — *this* is what happened, *this is who I am*."

"No! I don't believe you!" Her shriek only momentarily ripped through and interrupted the pulsating thud.

As though a chopper was circling, but when his eye left the sights for a second to check the sky, there was nothing but a gliding crow, its head cocked earthward, an orange eye visible in detailed, magnified clarity. When Brian's eye returned to the sights, Leya had already flung herself over the cougar, the animal's head at her breast, protecting the cat's other vital targets with her own. Her legs were bent under herself, knees on the ground but hugging the cat's lower body between them. Her arms curled inward, a nearly fetal position that simultaneously embraced both the animal and her own body. Seven, eight, nine darker freckles made a small lopsided circle, a galaxy on her lower back. Her underwear had no flowers nor stripes, no pictures of baby animals nor slogans, just bleached white cotton. A small dark stain on the elastic in the crotch. The end of the rifle shivered minutely. "You're bleeding already — you're bleeding. *You're bleeding.*" The strange screaming voice was somehow familiar, "*Did I do it?*"

"No, it's from my period—"

"*Didn't I do it? Didn't I? DIDN'T I?*"

The dog bayed, jays broke screaming from the trees where the wind was once again buffeting the uppermost branches. Then another gash of silence.

"Brian, listen to me," her words deadened by hitting the earth before coming through the rifle to reach where he was. "I don't know what you're asking. I don't have an answer. I'm sorry your sister's dead, I'm sorry for *you* she's dead, but . . . it wasn't your fault."

Other than the quickening and crescendo of his pulse, the pressure of his cheek against the stock, the taut composure of his hands steadying the barrel and resting on the trigger, the remainder of his body seemed as barren and lifeless as a badlands monolith.

"How do you know that? I'm a classic case study," he said woodenly, "a sexual psychopath. A sexual predator."

"No, *no, no,*" the sudden resumption and acceleration of her coarse weeping was close to retching, "you told me she killed her*self.*"

In a long span of hot silence, while she continued quiet but violent crying, Leya's quaking body seemed to shrink even more around the sleeping cougar. Her pale skin was clinging tighter to her ribs and shoulder blades, and getting pink from either the direct sun or hysterical exertion. A sheen of sweat covered her, but the dark stain in her underwear had not gotten bigger. She was not bleeding to death. But she was miles from anywhere, as exposed and unprotected and powerless as she could be . . . holding a drugged lioness who wouldn't stay down long . . . and she needed the Daktari to pull her to safety. But the Daktari had already lost *her* battle. The queasy knot suddenly flaring in his gut was not pleasurable. Then his voice — not surprising in its bizarre monotone, but astonishing to be uttering such an unanticipated and lucid . . . *fact* . . . .

"Yes, she did. She shot her own head off. I should've killed my mother, and didn't. But . . . even if there was nothing I could've done, did I have to be beating-off in the bathroom?" His voice going lower.

An uninflected growl. "That's worse than doing nothing. Could only think about my own orgasm while she— It's perverse. *You* should've been afraid of me all along."

She raised her head and looked at him. The cross hairs moved to her forehead, between her eyes. Once again tears streamed down her face, her reddened, swollen eyes barely opened a crack. "Okay, I'm afraid now. Is that what you want?"

He swallowed a dry mouthful. Shivered like breaking a fever. His mechanical inflection started to waiver and crack, "I don't know." The queasiness growing heavy, swelling, sinking. His brain thudding like a heart. But not one single clearly understood impulse urging him toward any act. *Like a drugged animal, a poisoned animal . . . but not one, aberrant or otherwise, in rut.*

The cross hairs began vibrating, blurring. A film fogged the sights. Sweat built up between his skin and the rifle, as if he wasn't actually holding it any longer. *There is no zone. No such thing. You're not a shooter . . .* EITHER.

Did you hear that? A shooter is also not what you are. Is why you missed. You're not—

"I'm not . . . No, it *doesn't* give me any— I don't like this. I guess I could be wrong about— I guess I *am* wrong about— What I want, and . . . what I *am*." As though he had been braced in position by a thin wire of adrenaline strung between his ears, and it suddenly snapped, every muscle gave in, broke from rigid control, and the pulse became an aching throb, starting small then thundering through him like a train approaching, passing, and growing more distant again. *You won't, you won't, you won't, you* CAN'T. *It's all over.*

She had one hand in her mouth, biting down, silently sobbing, then her forehead fell against the sleeping cat, the vibration of sobs continued in her fragile skeleton showing beneath her skin. *All over . . . but look what you've done!* The rifle twirled like a baton, as though he'd learned it in a military drill corps: his thumb slipping into and replacing his finger in the trigger mechanism while his arm flew up and out to his side. His other hand caught the barrel and held the muzzle rigidly perpendicular, directed toward his own temple. She was sitting up. Her arms, no longer covering her breasts, outstretched, white and thin. He couldn't hear what she screamed, if anything, as the dog once again bayed, as though the high-pitched howl came from Leya's open mouth, the sound like a shriek of wind ripping branches from trees.

His arms hung at his sides. The rifle dangled from his fingers. Then he bent and placed it on the ground. Looked up and met her solemn stare. She slowly lowered herself until she was once again huddled over the cougar, her knees and elbows tucked back in against her delicate body, her boots like large wooden feet at the ends of dainty-looking ankles, one of the cat's ears just grazing under her chin. She was motionless except for one hand, moving only from the wrist, fingertips stroking the rank cream-colored fur on the cougar's throat.

Some kind of physical endurance quietly returned to him, made him able to move forward, pick up her shirt and drape it carefully over her back. Then as she sat up and turned away — her head bent to watch her fingers at the buttons, the white back of her neck like a weak green branch bent to the ground under dripping leaves — he said, "The worst part didn't start until Diane was about seventeen. But that doesn't explain why I never thought that someone should stop it, that the someone could be *me* . . . until it was too late . . . and even then, I missed my target." He flinched as the ridgeback whined. "But *she* let Diane take the blame for both shots. It was to justify Diane's . . . death. An attempted murder-suicide — allows less pity for the dead one. Makes her deserve what she did to herself." He was suddenly facing the sky, his head tipped back, tears oozing sideways across his temples. "I never corrected my mother's version. And I've been afraid . . . that some part of me . . . not only *agreed* . . . but . . . like a confused carnivore . . . was aroused not by hunger, but . . . by fear . . . and the sensation of the kill . . . . Half a lifetime with the wrong . . . hypothesis." Turning, it took just one motion to pick up the rifle by the barrel, cock his arm across his body then swing it forward and up, a back-handed stroke, releasing the rifle, imagining he heard the *whump whump whump whump* of chopper blades as the rifle spiraled over the ravine and out of view, sun glinting off the blue steel like a beacon, on and off. Then said, "But believe me, I don't expect you to care about that. I just had to . . . say it."

He wiped the sides of his face, one on each shoulder, then took Leya by the arm and helped her to her feet. She felt boneless and flaccid in his hand. While he continued to steady her, she put each clumsy boot through a leg-hole of her shorts. The cougar began to move, the tail flicked, the yellow eyes opened. Brian led Leya over to where the dog was tied, loosened the knot and put the rope into her hand. Although Leya was the one with the scent of the cougar on her, the dog put her front feet against Brian, feverishly sniffing his sweat-drenched body. He guided Leya to where they'd left the packs, got a knife from his equipment, let go of her arm and went back toward the cougar.

The lioness had her head up, swaying unsteadily, but she was able to lift her lips and fabricate a hiss as he got nearer. He bent over her, held onto the radio collar, slipped the knife between the collar and her throat, and in one swift movement cut through the collar and jumped back as the cat made a wobbly attempt to swing at him with one paw.

Still grasping the knife in one fist, he held the collar out toward Leya. "I can scrape up a shell that doesn't fit my rifle, then tell Gallway this is all we found of her. It could've happened." The knife clicked shut in his other hand. "So she's out of the study now, on her own."

He put the collar and his knife into his gear, then took off the hunting vest and hung it from a broken branch. The loops for holding shells were empty.

With slow, underwater motions, Leya raised her arms to brush strands of hair back from her face, passed each limp hand once over each eye, one at a time. She picked up her pack and stood holding it, as though unable to remember how to put it on.

He said, "We can go directly to Casper to send you home, it's closer from here. But if you want to go back to Rawlins for your things, we'll do that then continue on to Cheyenne and get there some time tonight. You can leave from there tomorrow." Then he took hold of a strap dangling from her pack and she let go, looking up at him, bewildered or beleaguered, tearful. He averted his eyes for a moment, then turned and looked at her. "I know I keep apologizing too many times and it won't help . . . ." Leya's eyes shifted to the dog, so Brian also turned to follow the dog's stare behind them toward the cougar, sitting up on her haunches, her back to them, delicately sniffing a new riffle of breeze that reached her first before bathing his face, although it was too gentle to lift the wet matted hair from his brow. "Maybe someday . . . . No . . . I know you and I . . . can only have . . . separate somedays."

Then he turned and with one hand on Leya's narrow back, began to steer her toward the direction they'd come from. "You'll go home," he said blandly, but his heart suddenly lurched, as though it had stopped a while back and just remembered to begin again. "I can claim, take with me what I should've always known. But I also know I won't see you again. I wish it was different, but I don't deserve anything more."

His fingers could sense how her spine was flexible and gracefully absorbed the jolt of each footstep, even when the ground was uneven or rocky. The smooth rounded bones, a supple column under her skin, felt nothing like a scar. She hiked sturdily, both their boots crunching softly in the pine needles. And she turned once to glance back at him, very likely the same look Diane would've given him if he'd burst into the bedroom seconds earlier, before she fired her shot.

## 9

PROTECTED BY NOTHING

She eventually stood up and stretched, reaching out with her front feet, lowering her chest to the ground, her claws extended. But she was still wobbly, lightheaded. Instead of rising and walking out of the stretch, her rear end sank and she resumed a sphinx position. Her eyelids half closed, she blinked slowly. Her nostrils twitched and tensed, picking through airborne scents. Her ears swiveled, flicked, homing beneath the howl of wind in branches far above to intercept and comprehend every tiny rustle of a lizard, sparrow, or field mouse.

In the 180-degree fan of territory facing her — a half-circle thirty miles deep, starting due north and swinging northwest, west, southwest, down to due south — there weren't probably more than fifty humans, but thousands of deer and pronghorn, hundreds of elk,

some bighorn sheep, plus uncountable coyote, porcupine, jackrabbit, raccoons, weasels and ferrets, all
mostly in the west to northwestern quadrant of the
half circle of terrain. For her there was little competition and virtually no predators superior to her on the
food scale. To the south and southwest, possibly close
to a hundred wild mustangs lived on their feet under
the sky, virtually impossible to stalk on the flat, treeless expanse of the Great Divide Basin where little else
chose to stay very long, except snakes, lizards and the
insects they ate. Hard-packed and mostly dry, except
the Chain Lakes which are never more than eight
inches deep — horses could run straight across the
water. Mile after mile of nothing to break the mustangs'
stride, and a cougar could only keep up for less than a
hundred yards.

Yet the still partially-dazed cougar waited less than
an hour. She rose, defecated and scratched weakly, half
covering the meager scat, then silently, in her fluid walk,
headed south along the easternmost ridge of the Green
Mountains.

By nightfall she'd covered ten miles, only stopping
occasionally when alerted by aural or olfactory senses,
or to rise up against a tree and sharpen her claws. The
dry bark crumbled away under her efforts. No trees she
passed were already similarly marked. The trail she left
zigzagged slightly, always southward, as though guided
by maps and compasses, until the trees gave way to sage
and scrub, barren bluffs overlooking the Chain Lakes
Flat, and she remained there 24 hours, sleeping in a shallow hollow against an arid bank, her body blending into
the dry brush and sparse tall brown grass.

Below her, to the south, the Great Divide Basin
stretched 50 miles, surrounded by the ridge of the Continental Divide, but protected by nothing from wind, bliz-
zards, or searing sunlight. Heavily used Interstate 80 runs
through the southern portion of the basin, through a
hundred miles of primarily uninhabited attempts at
settlements and train stops, until it reaches Rawlins and

the landscape begins to change slightly, becoming rolling rangeland decorated with brush-dotted hogback ridges.

The cougar slept through the heat of the day, shaded by a screen of tiny sage leaves clinging to thin, brittle branches. The end of her tail twitched. Awakened by thirst or hunger periodically, she remained patiently languid until dusk.

An impulse turned her eastward, and through the long dusk she traveled steadily, descending from the hills into a stretch of flat grassland, spotted sporadically with old crusty bovine droppings, ant hills, or gopher burrows. She began to move more stealthily, crouching to keep her back and shoulders below the shrubs and grasses.

On a low swell, beside a lone gnarled tree and a dry well, marking a ranch site long abandoned, the cougar sat upright in the extended shadows. A last meadowlark call, then silence settled briefly before the first cricket began. A hare stood on its hind feet, motionless, until a slight shift of wind announced the cougar's presence. But the cougar didn't flinch as the rabbit, with only a slight swish of grasses, dashed toward its burrow. She could see the sunset glinting from tin roofs in the shallow valley stretching below her. A dull rattle of machinery droned. Her nose lifted, searching for and locating a familiar equine scent.